Tea & Crumples

a novel

Summer Kinard

🕯 Light Messages

Copyright © 2015, by Summer Kinard

Tea and Crumples
Summer Kinard
skinard.lightmessages.com
skinard@lightmessages.com

Published 2015, by Light Messages
www.lightmessages.com
Durham, NC 27713 USA

Paperback ISBN: 978-1-61153-123-7
Ebook ISBN: 978-1-61153-124-4

ALL RIGHTS RESERVED
No part of this publication may be reproduced, stored in a retrieval system, or transmitted in any form or by any means, electronic, mechanical, photocopying, recording, scanning, or otherwise, except as permitted under Section 107 or 108 of the 1976 International Copyright Act, without the prior written permission of the publisher except in brief quotations embodied in critical articles and reviews.

for Seraphim

A woman is like a tea bag—you never know how strong she is until she gets in hot water.
~ Eleanor Roosevelt

"But I have prayed for you that your faith may not fail; and when you have turned again, strengthen your brethren."
~ Luke 22:32

Chapter One

On the morning that was to be the second worst day in Sienna's life, the scones did not turn out well. She glared into the trash can in the over-warm kitchen of Tea and Crumples. It was half filled with rejected scones—too soft, too grainy, too crumbly or bitter. The batch in the oven smelled better, at least. It was her third that day and would be on the menu. Hopefully. Maybe. She had come in early to bake before the lingering summer heat filled the shop too much. She left Peter to sort out the dogs for the day.

Peter did not usually take the dogs to the vet. It did not matter that Sienna had told him three times that morning to make sure that he took the dogs through the orange door with the dog silhouette. He was overwhelmed by the movement, the fur, and when the moment arrived, he went into the purple door. Pogo and Jonquil raced flat out towards two different cats on two sides of the room, and Peter fell over a chair.

"It's probably not broken, but they are taking me in for X-rays since I can't stand on it." Peter swallowed and breathed as though he had winced. A rush of small snaps came over the line as the EMT fastened a brace around his leg. "The dogs are staying at the day care next door till we can get them."

"God, Peter." Sienna sucked in a breath and leaned against the cool steel counter. Peter's tendency to minimize ailments had amplified over the summer. If he admitted such severe pain, he might be seriously injured. A wash of panic bleached out the air around her. She needed to get to him. "I, um, I'll meet you there. Wait. Which hospital?"

"University."

"Okay. I have to get these pans out of the oven in five minutes, then I'm heading out."

"What are you baking?"

"Gluten free stuff. Brownies, cookies, another attempt at the scones." Sienna smiled tightly. Peter was trying to take his mind off the pain. She could hear it in his voice. "I'll bring you a brownie."

"That would be great." Peter's throat closed over a moan as the ambulance door shut, jiggling him. "Listen, Sienna, I have to hang up now. I love you."

"I love you, too." Sienna listened to the silence as the cell signal ended.

Something was wrong, something more than Peter's fall. She cast her eyes around the small commercial kitchen, looking for any sign of trouble. Every tool was in place. The floor and counters were clean, and the dishes were stored away. Had she remembered to lock the door behind her when she came in through the front earlier? The butter had been melting, and she had to get it inside quickly. A bell sounded from the storefront.

Sienna walked into the teashop and stood behind the counter. It did not take long for her to see the dark-clad man standing in broken sunlight in front of a display of journals.

Tea & Crumples

He was taller than she by a few inches, even though she was wearing boots.

"Excuse me, sir," Sienna called authoritatively. "We're not open. I just forgot to lock the door."

The man turned toward her and stood very still. He looked towards her without breaking the stillness so that she wondered if he had heard her. "Hmm?" he asked. Her shoulders dropped a fraction. She stared at him, confused at her sudden desire to trust him. "Oh, sorry. I saw that you sell stationery, and I tried the door." He smiled slightly, and his gray eyes assessed her. "When will you open?" He tilted his head slightly, and she tilted hers in response. A white square at his neckline caught her eye. He wore a clerical collar. He was a priest, then. That must have been what she had noticed.

"Our soft opening is tomorrow morning." Sienna felt an odd tug in her chest and put it down to the desire to unload one's burdens on someone strong. She swallowed hard to keep herself from blurting the news about Peter. A timer dinged in the kitchen, drawing her out of the spell. "Listen, I'm sorry for the confusion. I appreciate you dropping in. Wait right here, and I'll give you a free sample of my soon-to-be world famous scones."

"Is it okay if I browse while I wait?" He smiled again, this time with the charismatic grin Sienna associated with great actors and politicians.

"Is that a real collar? Are you sure you can be trusted?" Sienna found herself returning the man's smile.

"It is a real collar. I'm a priest." He cocked an eyebrow rather than answering her second question.

"I'll be right back."

Sienna turned and rushed into the kitchen. An apron covered her front, but she felt conscious of her tank top and shorts as she walked away from him. Was she worried that the priest might check her out? It was her habit to expect respect from all men, especially men of the cloth. Something else must be off. She glanced down at her hand and noticed the absence of her wedding ring. Of course. She had left it by the sink while she kneaded dough.

Sienna pulled the trays of warm cookies and scones from the oven and placed them on wire racks. There was no time for removing the baked goods off the pans if she was going to catch Peter in triage. She scrambled for a small paper sack and placed a piping hot scone into it. This batch looked much better than the last attempt, but she did not have time to taste it. She hoped that it was good for the priest's sake.

She turned to go back into the storefront, then remembered the ring. Sienna pushed the plaited gold band over the wonky knuckle on her left ring finger. That should clear up any ambiguity with the priest. She picked up the scone bag and returned to the front.

The priest was writing on a small tablet when she arrived at the counter.

"Your scone. Father?" Sienna held the bag toward the priest with her left hand so that he could not miss the ring.

"Oh." He seemed startled, whether by her presence or the ring, she could not tell. "Greg. Only a few old school parishioners call me Father these days." He smiled at her again, the light in his eyes confusing her. "Thank you for the free sample."

"You're welcome. If you like it, come back tomorrow when we open. There will be a wider variety available then as well." Sienna fiddled with the knot in the front of her apron, eager to get away. She wanted to speed up her departure by removing the apron, but she liked having the extra layer of cloth between her tank top and the minister.

"Here's my number." Greg slid a thick ivory note toward her over the counter. "I see that you carry my favorite brand of journals but not the ruled standard size. Could you perhaps make a special order for me? I promise to be a faithful eater of your scones." His eyes danced again with an impish smile so that Sienna suspected him of flirting.

"Um, sure," she said. "I'll put in an order first thing tomorrow. But for now, I really must close up here. I have an urgent appointment."

"Of course," Greg said, running his eyes over her again. For a fleeting moment, his brow creased with concern. Then the twinkle was back. "And I imagine you'll have to get out of that apron first."

"Right." Sienna smiled tightly and nodded to the door.

Greg got to the threshold with surprising speed. He nodded a goodbye, then turned out the door with another enigmatic smile.

Sienna locked the door behind him.

When she arrived at the hospital, Peter was already through triage.

"Mrs. Bannock?" A kind-eyed male nurse asked her. "Come this way, please."

Sienna followed nervously. Hospitals made her uncomfortable. It was the smells that got to her. She had been a cook and a baker for too long not to smell the sickness and wounds that the disinfectants masked for most people.

"Here we are," the nurse said, stopping in front of a glass-walled treatment area in the emergency room. "Your husband's compound fracture got him expedited. We've just given him a little morphine for the pain, but he should still be able to talk a little. At least, he'll know you're here. If you have any questions, ask for me. I'm Rob, and I'll be looking after your husband until he's moved to surgery."

"Thank you, Rob," Sienna said sincerely. She watched him out the door, then turned toward the bed where Peter lay, pale and grimacing, a temporary cast around his right leg.

"Sienna?" He tried to lift his hand toward her, but the medication had taken too strong a hold.

"Yes, Peter. I'm here." Sienna squeezed his hand, surprised to find it chilly. Peter's hands were always warm. Hers ran to cold. It had been one of her first excuses for touching him, in the beginning, the Southern version of borrowing a jacket in a chill. Since she could not warm his hand, she kissed it. "How are you, Love?"

"Mmm," he mumbled. "Hurts." He opened his eyes with obvious effort. "Good see you." He attempted a smile.

Sienna smiled back, fighting through the tension building in her jaw and forehead. She could do this. She could smile for Peter. But his hands were so cold. And the hospital smelled dangerous, like loss.

"Don't worry," Peter comforted. He knew her so well. She could not hide her fear from him. "Just clumsy."

Sienna stroked Peter's forehead. His brown eyes fluttered under her touch, and he relaxed, dozing under the affect of the pain meds.

When she was sure he was asleep, Sienna pulled out her mobile phone and pressed the top name on the speed dial.

"Marnie? It's Sienna. Peter's in the hospital. Any way you can come over to see us here?"

"Lord have mercy!" Marnie said, startled. She sounded discomfortingly far away, causing Sienna's heart to sink. "Oh, SiSi, you know I would come right this instant, if I weren't in

Tea & Crumples

Wales."

"Wales?" Sienna knit her brows. Marnie went on pilgrimages a couple of times a year. Sienna sometimes lost track of her friend's schedule. "Oh," she sighed, deflated.

"I'll pray from here, of course. What is it? A broken leg?"

Sienna nodded, used to Marnie's uncanny ability to know what was wrong or right with people. "Yes. His right leg. Compound fracture, but I don't know more."

"Mrs. Bannock?" An athletic blond woman in a long white coat called from the door.

"Listen, Marnie, the doctor is here. I've got to go. Pray."

"You've got it."

Sienna turned off her phone and turned to greet the doctor.

"Mrs. Bannock?" the doctor repeated.

"Yes. Please call me Sienna."

"Sienna. I'm Dr. Murphy, the resident orthopedist. I understand that your husband has a broken right leg."

"Yes," Sienna said, tension narrowing her eyes. The sense of unease was growing, and she could not seem to push it aside.

"We'd like to take your husband in for X-rays. Does he have any pins or plates that you know of?"

"Um, no." Sienna squinted. "No plates or pins. He says he's clumsy, but he's actually never broken a bone before." They were going to take her husband to look at him through machines, and she suddenly felt the need to talk about him. "I think his only surgery was wisdom tooth removal." She tried to smile.

"Good," Dr. Murphy answered. Her voice was low for a woman's, reassuring, like Sienna's grandmother's voice had been. The doctor watched Sienna for a moment, her eyes lingering on the tightness in Sienna's face and shoulders. "Is there anything else you would like us to know before we take him to the back?"

"I don't know. Nothing I can pinpoint. Something just seems off. Do you bake?" She frowned when the doctor shook her head. "Well, sometimes you can smell that an ingredient is off, before you taste it, even if it looks okay." She sighed. "Peter's not supposed to have cold hands," she said, hoping she sounded less wild than she felt.

Dr. Murphy nodded and tilted her head. "How about this? I'll have Nurse Rob bring in some heated blankets, and you can stay with Peter while we move him." She quirked her lips, as if determining whether to speak. "And, this is just a hunch, but I would like to run Peter through an MRI as well, if that's okay with you. Your insurance may charge you an extra fee, but the test can tell us a lot more about what is going on with your husband."

"Yes, do the test," Sienna choked out. Her head started to throb, and her hands were now colder than Peter's.

Waiting seemed to take several hours. Sienna tried to pray, to plan, but she could not think at all. Her only goal was to be near Peter. She held his hand every moment she could without being in the way of his treatment.

In reality, Peter had been lucky to have injured himself on a midweek morning. The hospital was at top efficiency, and Sienna only had to wait until dinner time before the doctor returned, holding files and accompanied with a small entourage of strangers. Peter had been sedated to keep him from injuring his leg and for his comfort.

"Mrs. Bannock—Sienna?" Dr. Murphy asked, moving into the room to allow a few other white-clad persons entrance. "These are my colleagues, Dr. Jameson and Dr. Avery." She nodded to a youngish, dark-haired man and an older woman with bifocals. Three younger persons in scrubs stood attentively

Tea & Crumples

back, obvious medical students. "And these are our interns, Drs. Patel, Chen, and Darcy." The students nodded politely as they were named. "We'd like to talk with you about Peter. Would you mind coming with us to the conference room?"

"Actually," Sienna squeezed Peter's relaxed hand. "I'd rather stay here, if that's okay with you."

"Of course." Dr. Murphy nodded to the others. The interns disappeared for a moment, reappearing with rolling chairs sufficient for the three senior physicians. The students sat on a bench behind them. When they were settled, Dr. Murphy continued. "Sienna, when we had a look at Peter's leg, we found more than just a compound fracture. I'm sorry to tell you, Peter has cancer."

"Cancer?" Sienna gasped. Shock and recognition fought for control of her mind as she ran through what in hindsight were obvious symptoms: his recent lethargy, clumsiness around furniture, and the unusual inconsistencies in the bedroom. Her heart raced, and she choked out her next question. "What kind of cancer?"

"Dr. Avery," the older doctor reminded kindly. "I'm an oncologist. Peter appears to have a very advanced form of prostate cancer, stage three or four. It's unusual for men Peter's age to have prostate cancer, but this form is the most common for those who do."

"Will he live?" Sienna's mouth was almost too dry for speech. Dr. Avery noticed and nodded to one of the students, who brought Sienna a glass of water before the conversation continued.

"His chances of survival are fairly good, and he will most likely be able to enjoy a full life in remission."

Sienna connected a few dots, then looked at the third doctor. "Dr. Jameson?" she asked. "A urologist, perhaps?"

9

"That's right," Dr. Jameson nodded. "We have to wait on a few test results, but we will likely have to do surgery tonight to remove the large tumor."

"Given his weakened state, we prefer to put him under anesthesia only once," Dr. Murphy interjected. "I will repair Peter's leg, and Dr. Avery and her team will take out the tumor."

"I'll be there to make sure we keep Peter's systems as intact as possible," Dr. Jameson finished.

The doctors went on, explaining about radiation and hormone therapies, the different prognoses if biopsies showed that Peter's bone had been weakened by cancer or if the cancer was still fairly contained. By the time they finished, Sienna was numb. They would know more after the surgery to repair the bone, which was the first priority. If the bone was cancer-free, Peter would likely live. Sienna focused all of her energy on willing it to be so. She imagined his ragged bone and hoped that it was only broken.

Marnie called back after the doctors had left Sienna alone with Peter for a few minutes before the surgery.

"Sienna, I have been trying to call you for hours." Marnie's words rushed out as fast as her drawl would allow. "I found the only spot in this valley that has a signal, and it's pouring rain. I have to make it quick. I just called to say, Peter is going to make it. It's going to be hard, but you two are going to be okay."

The signal cut out before Sienna could respond. She hoped her friend was speaking a prophetic truth, but Marnie had been wrong before.

NOTES FROM SIENNA'S TEA FILES

Peter Bannock, architect, wonderful husband, 33: Assam with honey and cream. Golden, malty.

Sienna Bannock, tea master, stationer, shop owner, 32: Keemun with half and half and 1 teaspoon turbinado sugar. High aroma best; floral.

Greg Tippett, priest, musical theater tenor, 38: Moroccan mint tea in a glass cup, so sweet it's cloying. Mint sprig in cup. Pour tea from height.

Chapter Two

Eyes burning, Sienna unlocked the back door to the teashop and pushed it open wearily. Lights were already on in the office and stationery section.

"Tovah?" she called.

Tovah popped her head around a corner, assessed Sienna's bedraggled face, and rushed forward. "Before you tell me what happened, let's get you a cuppa. You need some serious caffeine. Yerba mate?"

Sienna nodded and allowed Tovah to guide her around the tea bar service area in the shop to a round pink barstool.

"Sit," Tovah ordered. She busied herself making tea. Sienna watched detachedly from her haze of fatigue. A doorbell rang at the back, and Tovah scurried to answer it. She returned, beaming, pushing a large baker's rack covered in rich, nutty pastries and croissants. "Perfect timing. I was going to make you eat one of your experimental scones, but the Hearth delivery saved you that trial."

"One of the benefits of being a Christian," Sienna teased,

perking up a bit as the smell of the pastries mingled with the chocolaty cloud of steeping tea. "Save us from the time of trial and all that."

"Drink," Tovah commanded, setting a huge bone china mug in front of her business partner. She laid a napkin on the counter next to the tea and plopped a raspberry pastry on it. "Our second order of plates didn't come in, I see, so you have to be a little less formal." She poured herself a mug of tea, added honey and coconut milk, and leaned forward, waiting.

Sienna swallowed three hot sips before she looked up. "Peter has cancer. They cut a tumor out of him last night that was bigger than they suspected based on the scans. We don't know how bad it is till the tests get in later today. But it's probably stage three."

"Oy, vey," Tovah said, grasping Sienna's forearm softly. "And you found this out last night?"

"Yes, and I have to be here today." She sniffed back the tingle in her throat that preceded tears. "It's opening day."

"Tell you what. Lettye will be here in an hour, and Jessie is coming in at 9:30. I'll call Nina right now and see if she can get here this morning. You stay through lunch, maybe, but let us handle the rest of the day. You should be with Peter."

Sienna nodded. There was no use in arguing with Tovah when she was right. "I'll do what you say, but while I'm here, I'm here."

"Okay. Good. Then finish your tea and pastry, and come help me rearrange the sample books in the stationery section."

"Anything else?"

"Are you still determined that the front cubby has to be computer free?"

"Yes."

"Then, no. We're good. But we should test that the outlets

behind the booths actually work. I'm not going to fight a bunch of angry graduate students on our first day in business." Tovah threw up her hands in the air as though exasperated from doing just that, then walked rapidly around the counter. She surprised Sienna with a firm hug as she walked past.

"Thanks," Sienna said, her voice strained with suppressed tears.

"Eat!" Tovah called, already across the room.

Tea and Crumples had been Sienna's dream business since she first took up tea drinking in college. When she and Tovah met in a midrash class six years before, Sienna was impressed with the woman's rapid mind and exquisite taste in stationery. They had only been in class together a month before the tea and stationery shop was a shared vision. For four years, they tinkered with business plans and casual location scouting. After Tovah survived meningitis with the birth of her third child, the dream congealed. They began preparations in earnest, raising capital, planning inventory and menus, attending conferences, and developing a brand. For six months, they renovated the old downtown office space, working alongside contractors and volunteers.

At last, on the first Thursday of September, they were opening to the public. Even if Sienna had not quite worked out the kinks in the gluten-free scones—they were too grainy for her taste—she felt that they were ready for the big day. Her staff could all pour tasting teas, arrange frou-frou tea trays for the nostalgic afternoon tea crowd, brew a stout, dark tea for the hardy types who drank from thick mugs, steer adventurous students toward pu-erh, and make a perfect Darjeeling without oversteeping.

Then there were the special gifts each employee brought

to the shop. Lettye's effortless poise put people at ease, and her competence and hospitality made her an ideal manager. Jessie, a musician who looked like no one so much as a young female Willie Nelson who favored dark pink dresses to go with her cowgirl boots, was great with children. When Sienna had hired Jessie, it was with fond ideas that Jessie might lead toddler tea groups including Sienna's own future children. Jessie was exactly the kind of tea hostess to convince you that your life was filled with serendipity while she moved dancelike around you; she made sipping into song. Then there was their youngest staff member Nina, hardworking and bright, eager to learn, and possessed of a genuine philanthropic spirit that made everyone feel respected and honored when they were in her presence. Together, they would bring grace beyond what any could put forth alone. Their camaraderie reminded Sienna of recipes, the way so many ingredients were better together.

Sienna went to the cold case and arranged a few trays of sandwiches on bread from Hearth, a bakery that was their near neighbor in downtown Durham. After much back and forth, she and Lettye, the floor manager, had decided not to order in the tiny tea sandwiches they would use for trays. Instead, they bought pounds of dark yellow butter and tangy goat cheese from local vendors, slathered them on freshly sliced bread, and paired them with local greens, fruit, and meat.

Sorting out sandwiches distracted Sienna from her anxiety over Peter, for a little while, at least. She felt the tightness rear up in her chest again as she straightened the last row of country ham biscuits in the refrigerated counter case. The biscuits were Peter's favorites. She pulled her hand back as if burned and stared emptily at the rows of teacups on the wall where customers were allowed to pick their own cups. Her eyes focused on a narrow white mug adorned with a small red heart. The improbability of red in the emptiness was just like hope. She moved her feet to chase it around the shop.

The tables were in place, all except the chess table, which had come in late the day before. Sienna wanted it set up before the door opened at 10:00.

"Nina, could you help me?"

The knobby young woman had rushed in directly after Tovah's call, eager for the extra work hours.

"Sure, Miss." Nina carefully finished prepping the last coffee press pot, set the laden tray into its spot, and walked to Sienna eagerly. "Are we putting that in the front window?" She pointed at the gleaming table.

"Yes. I think we will. Adds a bit more community to the game, don't you think?" Sienna noted the girl's good instinct for flow. Nina would be as valuable for floor service as behind the tea bar.

They set up the table in the larger of the two front windows, to the right of the door looking out. It was specially made for café crowds, with wide empty space to the sides of the inlaid board so that players could have their beverages nearby. The smaller window nook held the head of the manuscript table—a long, wooden, communal table reserved for people watchers and those who write by hand instead of computer. The manuscript table had been Sienna's dream child, the one place in the dining area that most wed the two sides of the business, stationery and tea.

"Do you have the pieces, Miss?" Nina asked, closing the built in-drawer where one might have expected the chess pieces to reside.

"Um, no." Sienna knit her brows and stared hard at the windowsill as if doing so would cause the chessmen to materialize. Gradually, she became aware of a man standing on

Tea & Crumples

the other side of the glass. He was tall, with a warm brown complexion and a dignified carriage. She looked up, returned his friendly expression, and went to the door when he nodded at it.

"Hello. We're just about to open. Would you like to come in?" Sienna asked.

"Hi, there. My name's Cleotis Reed. I'm seventy-four years old. I speak my mind." The man nodded and grinned widely, putting Sienna at ease despite his abrupt introduction.

"Sienna Bannock, proprietor. Thirty-two years old. I make tea." She offered her hand, and he shook it warmly.

"I think you have something missing here," Cleotis said drily. His clear dark eyes were sharp and bright, giving the impression that he could see straight into every corner of her heart and mind.

Sienna was caught off guard. Could he know about Peter? About the baby they had lost? She swallowed and recalled herself from such ridiculous assumptions. The man was a stranger. He must mean something in the shop. She looked around, wondering if they had overlooked the obvious.

"Your chess board is empty," Cleotis supplied, at last. "Do you offer senior citizen discounts?" His rapid change of subject had landed on a topic that Sienna had rehearsed to herself.

"Are you retired?" she asked easily, thinking of the phone app Peter had programmed for her.

"Retired in 2007."

"Alright. Then I'll give you prices from 2007. How's that sound?" It felt good that Peter's app allowed her to answer with such confidence. She had the chance to remember him as strong and supportive instead of drugged and weak in the hospital bed.

Cleotis Reed nodded once without breaking his penetrating

17

gaze. "Sounds fair. I'll be right back."

Sienna plunked a blue mug full of rollerball pens on the manuscript table, triple checked that the hot water reservoirs were filled, and flipped the door sign to "Open." She prayed the only prayer that her weary mind could muster, "Lord Jesus Christ, Son of God, have mercy on us," and turned to walk toward the stationery alcove. Before she got far from the front of the shop, while the words of her repeated prayer were yet on her lips, the light bell on the door tinkled. She turned to find Cleotis Reed backing into the room, an open cardboard box filled with substantial chessmen in his arms.

"Tell you what," he said, walking to the board and arranging the pieces with startling speed, "I'll let you keep this set here. On loan, understand? And in exchange, I hope you don't mind if I have a few friends by here for a game now and again."

"Not at all. Thank you." Sienna smiled. The pieces gave the board, and the room, elegance. She did not want to appear gauche by examining the chessmen for their value, but she suspected that they were worth more than the hardwood and rosewood inlaid table on which they rested. "Seeing as you're our first customer, how about I get you something hot to drink. On the house."

"I'll have a pot of lapsang souchang with half and half and lump sugar, if you have it." Cleotis Reed made himself at home at the chess table, in the chair farthest from the door.

"Right away," Sienna said and began to assemble the tea. A low, mellow soundtrack started as she laid a spoon on a napkin next to a small bowl of brown and white sugar lumps. By the time she returned with the tray, Cleotis Reed had company.

"Thank you much," he said, nodding graciously. "Sienna Bannock, allow me to introduce my *oldest* friend," he smiled at his own pun, "A.C. Whitmer. A.C. here is a coffee man, God bless him."

A.C. stood for the introduction. "How do you do?" he asked, his thick Eastern North Carolina drawl at odds with his friend's lilting clip. He shook Sienna's hand and sat back down.

Sienna smiled and nodded, unable to bring herself to say she was well. "Thank you, Mr. Whitmer. Would you like a mug of coffee, or a pot?"

"Well," he considered, "I think I'd like a pot, if it's an insulated one. I like my coffee scalding hot. Keeps my mouth closed and me out of trouble." He was quiet for a long moment but held Sienna's gaze, clearly not finished speaking. "And please, call me A.C. I still think of my granddaddy as Mr. Whitmer, and he's been dead fifty years."

Sienna agreed and offered that the men should call her by her first name as well, though she already knew that Cleotis Reed was one of the Southern personalities who would always be addressed by his full name, even in thought. When she returned with a mug and a carafe of dark coffee, the men had already captured several pieces from one another. She set down the mug, as unobtrusively as possible, and Cleotis Reed said, "Checkmate" in the sort of low, strong tone that indicates long habit.

"Come on, now, Cleotis. I haven't even had my coffee yet," A.C. joked. He turned to Sienna. "Cleotis here has been whooping me at chess since 1964."

"Here. Don't you let on to everybody about my age," Cleotis said gruffly, resetting the board.

"You tell everyone you meet how old you are, and you know it," A.C. rejoined. "Bark's worse than his bite, this one," A.C. said to Sienna, with a nod toward his friend. "Unless you're playing him. Then it's the other way around. My advice," he dropped his voice low and leaned toward

Sienna conspiratorially, "is not to lay money on the other guy. Meaning me."

"Come on, now. I don't always win." Cleotis doctored a fresh cup of tea and sipped it. "Every now and again, you beat me."

"1964, 1971, 1985 and '87, '93, '98, '01, twice in '03, four times in '07 when you had pneumonia, and twice in 2011 when you had the cataract surgery." A.C. seemed happy about his long losing streaks.

"Look here, Ms. Sienna, A.C. is my best friend and too humble to tell you how often he lets me win."

"Not today, old friend. I'm about to add to my list."

The men settled into a gentle rhythm of banter and rapid play. Sienna happily met several new customers as Nina and Lettye bustled about serving them. To her count, Cleotis Reed won every game at the chess table, though the only real indication was A.C.'s laughter whenever he succumbed to another checkmate. The shop was in order and running well. Even the scribe table was being put to good use. She smiled when she saw a thirty-something young man sit down to write a pile of postcards across from a young woman filling page after page in a battered red journal.

Content that she would be leaving the shop in good hands, Sienna went to find Tovah. "I'm heading back to the hospital. Email me if you want to catch me up. Peter should have a room by now, and I will probably be able to use the browser on my phone." Tovah stood from the desk where she had just entered their first custom stationery order, but froze as she hugged her friend.

"May I help you?" Tovah asked tersely as she addressed someone over Sienna's right shoulder.

Sienna did not have to turn to know who it was. Her spine

tensed with the knowledge of being watched. She forced a polite smile onto her face and turned to meet him as casually as possible. His direct gaze disquieted her; it was the expression of someone looking for what they knew you couldn't give. She had the uneasy sense that he wasn't only looking for stationery.

"Well, hello," Greg burred. "I came to see about those scones and journals." A slow smile warmed his handsome face, and he turned with obvious effort to Tovah. "Greg Tippett." He extended his hand. "I happened in on Sienna here yesterday, and she gave me a hot biscuit on her way out."

"Charmed." Tovah was curt in her handshake, clearly not at all charmed. "Tovah Rosen, shop co-owner. May I help you?"

"Well, I'm heading out," Sienna said to Tovah, with a tense smile toward Greg. "Tovah is the one you want to speak with about those journals."

Tovah stepped between Sienna and Greg and gave her friend a big hug. "Take care, honey," she whispered. Then she gave Sienna a little push toward the back exit and planted herself so that Greg could not speak with Sienna again.

Sienna blinked into the late summer sun. She breathed deeply to steady her racing pulse and leaned against the old red brick of the alley. Why had Greg affected her so? *Because he's attractive and he likes you,* she thought. Her breath caught, and she coughed. For a fleeting moment, she tried to convince herself that she was imagining things with Greg. But Tovah's hackles had been raised by his attentions, too. *Maybe he does like me. He came back, just as he said he would.* She pulled her rebellious thoughts back in line. It shouldn't matter to her if he showed up every day; he was just a customer who liked stationery and had an overly easy air with strangers. She took a deep breath and shook the memory of his gaze from her head.

"Peter. I need to go see Peter." Wearily, she pushed away

from the wall and went to her car.

The trip to the hospital was brief, and she drove it automatically. Distantly, she was aware of the grace in going somewhere by rote. She had only driven to Peter at the hospital once, but she could go there without conscious thought because he was there, drawing her. *This must be how geese make it through their migrations*, she thought, weaving through foot traffic and up an elevator to Peter's ward. She was surprised to find her exhaustion-stung gaze focused on a nurse's face. The nurse wanted something. What had she asked?

"May I help you?" the nurse asked again, not unkindly.

Sienna started and gave Peter's name and her own. The woman nodded and spoke to a male nurse behind her in low, coded language.

"Mrs. Bannock?" he asked. "I'm David. I've been looking after your husband today. Come this way, please." He walked down two hallways and pushed open a heavy door.

Then she was there, standing by Peter, and he was still the wrong color. She felt dizzy and plopped onto a hard stool. Nurse David was talking, but his words did not make it through the spinning in her head. Her vision began to darken, and she swayed. Just before she tipped sideways, she felt a firm hand on her shoulder, and she attempted to look up. She failed. A strong arm pushed her head between her knees, and she gradually felt her ears settle. Harsh sobs raked against them. They were hers—she was crying.

"Keep your head down for a few minutes, Mrs. Bannock," Nurse David said calmly. "The faint will pass soon." Gradually, it did.

"Sienna?" Peter whispered.

"Here." She drew a deep breath at last and leaned toward him, grabbing his hand. It was warm, and that was the first

Tea & Crumples

and best good news she'd had, in her whole life, it seemed.

Nurse David explained that the doctor would be around in a few minutes, that Peter could have water if he wanted it, and how to call for assistance. He left them alone.

"Goodness, Peter!" Sienna said, helpless under her husband's anxious gaze. "Next time you need this much attention, let's just go to a spa."

He smiled at her attempt at levity and squeezed her hand. She squeezed back and kissed his knuckles. She watched him quietly as his gaze pulled in and out of focus. Nurse David had said something about a sedative wearing off, hadn't he? It didn't matter. She and Peter were together.

The doctor walked in and shook Sienna's free hand.

"I'll be direct. The news is not as bad as it could have been. Peter has stage three cancer. We're working on treatment options now, but in brief, you'll be considering additional surgery and radiation down the road, and starting soon, chemotherapy. The usual prognosis for this type of cancer is four to six months with no treatment, six years to a normal life with treatment. About two-thirds of patients with these cancers make a full remission."

Numbers swam in the air around them, and Sienna, even with all her business acumen, found that they made no sense at all. Two questions climbed to the surface. She asked the one that seemed polite, but held back her fear. "Can Peter come home while he's on chemo, or will he stay here?"

She listened as the doctor explained the necessity for rapid action, the probable stay of several weeks so that recovery could be closely monitored, and the invitation to bring in items from home if desired. The room would be Peter's own for his stay. When they had gone, she bent to Peter's face. His eyes fluttered a little, but they focused on her. She kissed him and waited until he slept.

Then she got up and started towards home. Peter would want his old afghan and his laptop. And an orchid, and some decent tea, and the iPod he used when he was painting. She closed the front door to their home behind her and let her eyes roam the room, asking the second question as they lit on the couch, the candles, the fireplace, and the stairs leading to their bedroom. Would they be able to have children?

NOTES FROM SIENNA'S TEA FILES

Tovah Rosen, 36, teashop owner, stationer, mother to 3, friend: Black tea blended with cocoa nibs and toasted coconut, hot with coconut milk and honey. Smells like a bakery and a mother's love.

Cleotis Reed, 74, retired mechanic, chess grandmaster: lapsang souchong with lump brown sugar. Do not oversteep. Serve with spicy cheesestraws. Or strongly flavored cookies.

A.C. Whitmer, 88, retired banker, Cleotis Reed's oldest friend: dark roasted pressed coffee, very hot. Serve in carafe to maintain temperature, black and strong.

Chapter Three

Sienna woke to the buzz of her cellphone on her neck. She must have fallen asleep on the bedroom chair covered in Peter's afghan. Wrapped in his favorite blanket, Peter read there every night to overcome insomnia. The chair smelled like him—the heady blend of cedar and mountain mint and the sweet overtones of honey-sweet Assam tea—and she curled into it, missing this healthy fragrance. She yawned a waking breath and answered the phone.

"Hello. Sienna Bannock." She wondered if she sounded as sleepy as she felt.

"Sienna! Oh, I woke you. Sorry." Marnie's voice was clearer than before. "I was just having tea, and I thought of you, and lo! We have cell reception here. How are things?"

"Horrible. No, not all horrible. Peter has stage three. But the shop opened without a hitch. I haven't seen the dogs in a few days. I have hardly slept. And before you ask, I don't know my right hand from my left right now, so no, I haven't really prayed much. Unless, 'please, please, please,' counts."

Tea & Crumples

"It counts," Marnie replied somberly. "I am so sorry about Peter's diagnosis. Don't you worry about the praying. We've got your back here. The blessing and curse of the Church, you know. You're never alone."

"Thanks, Marnie." Sienna sighed. "What do I do? I mean, there's nothing to do. They are going to keep Peter in the hospital for a few weeks because of the effects of surgery and meds and so he doesn't reinjure his leg."

Marnie waited a few beats before answering, to make sure Sienna was finished. Her ability to pay attention was what had drawn Sienna to Marnie at church. They were in the same prayer group for a while, and they stayed friends and prayer partners when the group had run its course.

"Go get the dogs and let them be crazy with you. Eat, drink tea and water, get some sleep, bathe, and go see Peter after you've had a refresh. Is Tovah up to speed?"

"You know Tovah. I could fall off the planet, and the shop would suffer about as much as if I took a restroom break."

"But you will go back to the shop soon?"

"Of course."

"Good. The busy work will help you stay calm. It can be part of your prayer."

"Right." Sienna smiled. "You know, I found a prayer rhythm in the cups—last week, before all this started. I can wash a teacup to the Jesus prayer. I almost worked out a rhythm for the tea prep, but not quite. It works for two reps of the short version, 'Lord Jesus Christ, Son of God, have mercy on us,' but not for one longer one."

"And you said you weren't praying." Marnie's smile came over the line.

"You know what I mean. The Prayer Book I'm not, but I understand from a trusted source that God understands the prayer in clattering dishes." Marnie had told her as much more than once when Sienna showed up for a visit frazzled from the brute quantity of work in setting up a commercial kitchen and dining area.

"If not dishes, then paperwork or laundry. It's not like God leaves us alone until we come up with poetry."

"Amen." Sienna yawned.

"What will you do now?" Marnie was quiet, and Sienna thought she heard a cup settling back into a saucer, the soundtrack of friendship broadcasting to her from somewhere in Wales.

"Well, since you can tell I need a shower from across the ocean, I think I'll start with hygiene. Then I'll go see those crazy dogs. They've been boarding at the doggie day care at the vet since the accident. I can tell Peter how they're doing when I take him his blanket."

"Then the shop?"

"Yes. I'm on afternoon duty today. Tovah insisted." Sienna glanced at the bedside clock. It was 9:30 in the morning. "Wisely, I see."

"Well, I won't keep you, except in my prayers."

"Thank you, Marnie. And listen, if you find a miracle shrine over there in the hills, put in a word for Peter, will you?"

"Of course."

They ended the call, and Sienna uncurled herself from the chair. She would have to rush her shower in order to get in a visit to the dogs before she stopped by to see Peter.

"But first, tea." A gentle smile touched her face at the thought of the ritual. Tea was Peter and her, their honeymoon teapots, the mugs and cups that did not match a thing but their personalities. Putting on the kettle was as good a salve to her weariness as a week of sleep. She pulled a thick red mug from the cabinet and placed it on the counter. Not for the first time, the solidness of a good mug made her think of the Holy Grail.

She looked in the fridge for a loaf of bread. It was a little stale—nothing toasting couldn't cure. The butter was on the counter in a special dish that Marnie had brought back from a shrine gift shop in France. When the tea was poured and the toast buttered, Sienna brought her breakfast to the seat at the table that afforded the best view of the garden.

Improbably, the bee balms had survived the hot summer to flower again in the sheltered nook by the shed. They were her favorite plants, purchased two seasons before to fill out a niche in her herb garden. Her eyes had nearly ached with joy when she saw the bright red and pink blossoms, so flagrant among all the green and subtleties of the rest of the herbs. She had been unable to resist buying a wagon full of the plants when she heard that they were also called wild bergamot.

"Just like you," Peter had laughed. "Refined, but not really domesticated."

"Thanks," she said aloud, alone at the table, repeating her response from that day. It seemed longer ago than spring. Her belly had been swollen then, just a little grapefruit under her waist. Everything was happier when they expected the baby.

A rush of medical terms filled her mind in the wake of sudden grief. "Almost a still birth," was the worst of them. They had lost their daughter at nineteen weeks gestation and buried her in the churchyard near Peter's ancestors. Her name was Susan Rose, and she rested near her namesakes. Sienna's eyes stung at the unused name. In better moments, the name was empty like a row of teapots on the shelf, not less beautiful for being unfilled. But now, with all that had happened, all she could do was ache for the child she wanted to hold. They had planned to take her baby portraits in this garden. She might have liked the bee balm. She might have liked the sun.

Sienna left her plate with the half-finished toast at the table. She hugged the hot mug to her chest and walked out the back door. In the herb garden, she sat and stared until the variety of greens faded to a soft blur. Gradually, the tea cooled, and the scent of lemon and mint overcame her. The day was growing warm. She needed to go bathe and go see the dogs and Peter.

Standing, Sienna tipped the cold tea onto the plant bed and walked back toward the house. Sitting in the garden had made her feel more alive, and she noticed the coolness of thyme on her bare feet before she reached the stone path. She tried at first not to think of tiny toes sinking into the fragrant groundcover, but the thought was too lovely not to wish for. Of all the plants in the garden, only the thyme that made up the lawn would have leaves smaller than a newborn's toenails.

Showered, dressed in a linen big shirt, jeans, and leather sandals, hair down to air dry, lipstick applied, Sienna thought she could pass for pulled together. She patted her pocket to make sure her hair clip had not gone astray. Long hair was easy because of the invention of hair clips. Pick the right one, and it would look as though you had thought about your hair. Sienna glanced in the mirror and tried not to start at the pain in her eyes. She added a pair of gold earrings and took a deep breath.

"You'll be okay," she said to her reflection, and the truth of it hurt.

The dogs were happy to see her. Pogo jumped as high as her head, his midair squirm all joy. Jonquil, whom Peter had named when the yellow fluff of puppy fell over the flowers as it ran to them the first time they met her, rubbed her big golden head under Sienna's palm. Jonquil always knew the right thing

to say.

She knelt and greeted the dogs. Jonquil laid her head on Sienna's shoulder. She was a hugger. Pogo tried to lick Sienna's entire face in three greedy kisses. Then he nearly knocked her over in his excitement, causing Jonquil to bark softly, calling the pup to heel. The dogs sat side by side, the golden retriever dwarfing the black Labrador who was, if one interpreted dog faces correctly, Jonquil's life's cross to bear. Sienna rubbed them both behind their ears, then hugged them tightly. Pogo yapped.

"I know, boy. I missed you, too."

"Ayaragh?" Jonquil questioned, placing a large paw on her arm. Jonquil was Peter's dog, really, and Sienna suspected, rightly, that she wanted to know where her master had gone.

"Peter is at the hospital. You won't be able to see him today," Sienna answered.

Jonquil whimpered and laid her big head on her paws.

"I know, honey. I want him to come home, too."

She played with the dogs for a while in the yard of the doggie day care, then arranged with the keepers for an extended stay. The doggie day care workers were sympathetic. One of them, a large crag of a young man named Jon, looked especially taken with the situation. Sienna was not sure if he was more concerned for Peter or the dogs, and the uncertainty comforted her.

"I'll take real good care of them, Ms. Sienna," Jon said in his quiet, deep voice.

"Thank you. I know you will."

She took the knowledge that the dogs were well looked after with her to the hospital room, where Peter was awake and glad to see her. He smiled and nodded when she told him about Jon.

"Oh, good. He loves them," Peter said. His voice was weary,

but alert. Sienna liked the change from the drugged Peter she had encountered the past couple of days.

"The bee balm is still blooming," Sienna said by way of spinning her morning as positively as she could.

Peter squeezed her hand gently, understanding her feelings without her saying them. "I miss her, too."

Sienna nodded. The lacuna had opened up before them, the lid off the pot. Who would fill it? "Peter, do you think we can—?" she began, but Peter had started talking as well.

"They don't know if I can father children afterwards. It's about fifty-fifty. They just don't know." He rubbed her hand in the silence while they both swallowed back fears. "I am so grateful for Susan's life, even though it was too short. But I want her to have siblings."

Sienna met Peter's eyes, saw the mixture of grief and anticipated pain there. "I know, Beloved. Me, too. I miss her so badly right now. I don't even want to think about the what-ifs, but I can't help it. It's like having leaves caught in my hair. I can't get one of them out without the others rustling."

Peter nodded. "Sienna, we'll get through this. And we will have children—somehow. And we will remember Susan. Those things are all going to happen." His certainty soothed her.

"I wish I could hold you."

"Okay. Let's call the nurse. They aren't going to need to poke and prod me for another hour yet. I bet we can get you in here under these wires."

After some maneuvering and the long-suffering condescension of a nurse with a slow drawl and a twinkle in her eye, Sienna was arranged next to Peter on the narrow bed. She had to hold her hips back against the railing so as not to pressure any of the broken places, but she could tuck her head under his chin. She listened to his heartbeat and let it be her prayer rhythm. When the door opened for the next round of medications and monitoring, Sienna kissed the prickly hollow on Peter's neck.

She stayed by him until he was sedated again to relieve nausea. His afghan tucked as closely as the nurses and tubing would allow, Sienna kissed her husband's forehead. She felt better about Peter than she had in days. Maybe their conversation had helped, or the holding one another, or the reunion of Peter and his proper smells on the blanket. Whatever the reason, Sienna was hopeful when she made her way downtown to the teashop.

Lettye was explaining afternoon tea to a group of middle-aged women in linen and silks. Sienna sighed relief as she watched her manager sail confidently through the encounter. Tovah bustled up alongside her behind the counter and nodded in Lettye's direction.

"She's perfect. Marc deserves a medal for sending her to us." Tovah's husband had redirected Lettye toward them when she had applied for a department administration position. The young woman had a master's degree and a failed marriage to a bigwig pastor, and she needed a place to use her gifts of putting people at ease, hospitality, and organizing crowds.

"I hate her reason for needing this job, but I sure am glad she's here." Sienna turned and smiled at her friend with tired eyes. "I'm glad you're here, too. You have no idea how much it's eased my mind, having y'all taking care of the shop while I looked after Peter."

"You know I have your back," Tovah patted Sienna's shoulder. "Are you up for business talk now? We have a few interesting emails I'd like you to see."

"Sure." Sienna gave the tea bar a once over and nodded.

"Let me just check the cups in back and I'll meet you in the office."

Nina was removing the last of about a dozen cups from the sanitizing sink when Sienna walked in.

"Hey, Miss." Nina smiled and efficiently began to transfer cups onto a tray. "Business is good. I've washed, like, fifty cups already since breakfast, and that's not counting the to-go cups."

"Great," Sienna smiled brightly, glad that the girl answered her question without her having to ask. "Are we keeping up pretty well? Do you think the cup wall works okay?"

"Oh, yeah, Miss. All the little old ladies love picking a cup, and even the guys take their time finding the one that they like. Keeping up with the dishes is no problem. Lettye and Jessie do all the other work, and Tovah keeps making tea faster than anyone else, anyway. That gives me plenty of time to take care of things back here."

"Thank you, Nina. And thanks for coming in so much more than you had originally planned. It's been a lifesaver for me."

"No problem, Miss. I need the hours." Nina placed a container of clean forks and spoons on the tray and walked toward the shop.

Sienna watched her go. She noted the threadbare edges of the girl's clean, neatly pressed chinos and cotton button down, the worn look of the rubber soles on her chunky shoes, the cheap, but tasteful, bow that held back the long, dark hair. Nina reminded Sienna of herself as a teen: hardworking, poor, too bright for her station in life. Sienna hoped that the shop took off. She wanted to be able to give Nina leadership opportunities down the road, raises, and maybe a flexible enough schedule to allow the girl to go to college.

"You coming?" Tovah called from the doorway, two mugs in her hands. "I've poured your favorite."

Tea & Crumples

Sienna followed her business partner to the office behind the stationery area. She closed the door behind her and plopped into a plump leather armchair in front of the desk. The armchair had come from her grandfather's house, one of those relics of masculinity that did not fit well in her home but that gave unwonted comfort to the small office. She and Tovah had both napped in the club chair more than once in the harried weeks before opening.

"Here. Drink up." Tovah slid a bright pink mug in front of Sienna and opened the laptop that was bolted to the heavy wooden desk.

"Thanks," Sienna said into the steam above the tea. She sipped before continuing, "So, what do we have?"

"Mostly requests to book the shop for special events. I already approved three sorority tea parties and a bridal shower. The sororities need extended hours, but the bridal party just needs the manuscript table and champagne. Which," Tovah slid an official-looking piece of paper across the desk, "we can accommodate, since our special license has finally arrived. I included the $5 club member surcharge to the booking."

"Wow. I had no idea we would be popular so soon." Sienna skimmed the computer screen that Tovah had turned toward her. She tapped a square on the event calendar with her pinky finger. "What's this one?"

"That's mainly what I wanted to talk with you about." Tovah clicked through a few windows until an email filled the screen. "Read this. She doesn't want to book right away, but she wants to talk with you in person about booking."

Sienna read the brief email and noted the signature aloud, "Elsie Pinkwater, TEA Party Organizer." She sipped, her brow knit. "Is she one of those independent tea party consultants that takes one tea appreciation class and calls herself a tea master?"

Tovah shrugged.

Sienna sighed. "When did you schedule her to meet?"

"Tuesday at 1:00. I figured that, if nothing else, the midafternoon rush would give you an excuse to end the meeting early if she gets on your nerves."

"I guess that's best. Anything else?" Sienna sat back, the warm mug between her hands.

"I ordered more Moleskines." Tovah looked at Sienna directly. "Hardback, full-sized, lined. They have been rather popular with one of our customers."

Sienna tilted her head, trying to take Tovah's hint. She gave up and shook her head in confusion. "Well, you never know with paper lovers."

"I don't think he's here for the paper." Tovah took a long draw from her mug while her words sank in. "Sienna, I don't like this Greg. I think he's into you."

"Wait. Greg bought enough notebooks for a separate order?" Sienna's voice held her surprise. She thought back to their first meeting. "Well, he did say he wanted a different sort of notebook than we stocked. Let's just be grateful for the business."

"But Si, the way he looks at you—"

"All two times I've met him." Sienna raised her brows. "Come on, Tovah, he may just be a flirt."

"Forgive me for pointing this out, but he did not check out Jessie or Nina or Lettye. Just you, the one wearing a wedding ring. I don't like it."

"Okay." Sienna nodded briefly. "Noted. I will be careful not to encourage him."

"Good. The last thing we need around here is a stalker."

"A stalker?"

Tea & Crumples

"Well, maybe not a stalker, but a creep with boundary issues. Look, Sienna, I don't want to pry, but this guy reminds me of all those skeezy women you hear about who steal husbands away from wives dying of cancer."

"What?" Sienna sat back, stunned.

"There's got to be a reason that so many people fall into that trap. I'm not saying you have any desire to cheat on Peter. I'm saying, you're vulnerable, and even if this guy doesn't know why, I think he sees it. I think he's going to try to exploit that vulnerability."

"But I love Peter. I don't want to be with anyone else. Surely that much is obvious to anyone, much less a pastor."

"And if he uses his perceptiveness to a bad end?" Tovah let the question hang. She looked at her friend with compassion, but her gaze did not waver.

"I think I understand you. I'm not as in control of my grief and fear as I want to be. I guess it's obvious to anyone who works with the hard parts of people's lives." Sienna thought about how her body seemed to respond to Greg's attention, despite her conscious thoughts. There was just that little-too-much desire to be liked by him that must have shown in her body language. "Maybe I'm not as in control of my physical responses as I'd like to be, either." She sighed. "Why do you think that is? Why would a woman totally in love with her husband even feel the slightest twinge for someone else, much less someone unsuitable?"

"We're dust, Sienna. We're weak. Our bodies always crave a backup plan, no matter what our minds say."

"And Greg wants to be my backup plan."

"Looks like it. Just be careful, Sienna. I know you love Peter. You are about the most faithful and loyal person I know. But you've been through a lot, and you are more afraid about Peter than you've admitted. Don't let that fear get misdirected."

Sienna rubbed her forehead. "What was it we talked about in midrash class? That the only one worth fearing is God, and He's the only safe one to fear? Who said that, anyway?"

"I think you said it."

"Me? But it sounds so wise." Sienna smiled.

"So, sometimes God lets heathens in on His secrets," Tovah teased. Her eyes creased in a wry smile that Sienna returned. Sienna knew that her friend spoke from the wisdom she and Marc had forged together when they recovered from Tovah's near death a couple of years back. She had not expected to need it in her own life, though she was glad her friend offered it so openly now that Peter was so unwell.

Sienna nodded and drank her tea in the companionable silence. "Peter starts chemo next week."

"Surgery first?"

"They got out the tumor when he was under for the leg repair. They are letting him heal up a bit before they start busting up his immune system."

"Let me help you. Come to our house for dinner."

"No, thanks, Tovah. I need the quiet."

"I understand. I'll bring you a meal at the hospital. Whenever you need it. Say the word."

Sienna smiled slightly. "Southern people are all the same. Feed a problem, and it will go away."

"Southern, Jewish. If I don't feed you, I'll either go to Sheol or be haunted by my grandmother. Pick your reason. Just let me take care of you."

"Okay, I will. But can you make it take out?"

"Starting today, I will have a boxed supper ready for you."

"Today?"

"I planned ahead." Tovah smiled. "Marc made Korean

Tea & Crumples

barbeque last night. I brought you some."

"Of course you did." Sienna grinned and thanked her friend. She set down her cup and saw the invoice for the chess table on the top of the filing pile. "Hey, did we ever find the chess pieces that came with the table?"

"Nope. But your gentleman friend seems content to extend the loan on the pieces he brought."

"Oh, yes. Mr. Cleotis Reed. Was he here again this morning?"

"He had three pots of tea and made at least four people's days before he left."

"How about that? We have our first regular."

"Oh, he's not the only one. There's a journaling woman and a man who writes about a dozen postcards each day, plus a fluttery woman named after a church, and a couple of ladies who lunch."

"A woman named after a church?"

"You'll meet her. She's sat at the same spot at the counter all three times she's been in. She works downtown at her family's business. I think she steps in to escape office politics."

Sienna's carriage lifted a bit. "This is so exciting! Tovah, we are becoming that place we wanted to be." She smiled wryly. "Well, if two weeks of business is a pattern, anyway."

Tovah nodded. "Look, I'm sorry for worrying you over the notebook guy. Why don't you go out and tend the tea bar, mingle with the customers? You need a chance to see how great things are going."

Sienna agreed. She stood and stretched, breathed deeply, and opened the door.

"Oh! Do you work here?" A polished middle-aged blond woman with an antique brooch pinned to her teal blazer lapel turned toward Sienna with obvious interest.

39

"Yes. Sienna Bannock, proprietor." She shook the woman's hand.

"Dr. Liz Elliot, History Professor. That only matters in this case because I have the dubious honor of hosting the grad student reception off-campus next week, since my colleague took an unexpected paternity leave."

"Unexpected?" Sienna couldn't help but express her curiosity.

"I know. It's not a very attractive story, in terms of Ian's character. He knocked up a former student and only found out when she was in labor with their wee bairn. Which means that the hosting duties fall to me. Listen, Ms. Bannock…"

"Sienna."

"Sienna," Liz continued, conspiratorially, "I don't do housekeeping. I spend my money on travel and clothes and books and keeping up with foolish men. We usually have a tenured faculty member host the reception, which means Ian, me, or old Dr. Casey. Between you and me, Dr. Casey food poisoned everyone the last two times he hosted. Absent minded professor type, you know? So I have to pull this off, for the health of all involved." The woman's features were animated.

"When would you like us to host your group?" Sienna asked in the pause. She suspected that the professor was used to having to explain herself several times, and, lively as they were, Sienna wanted to curtail further illustrative anecdotes before getting down to business.

"Oh, good." Liz sighed relief. "Down to business. I knew this place was right. We have a group of between two and three dozen. They love fatty foods, sweets, and booze, if you have it. Cheap French wine is *de rigueur*. We'll need the place for two and a half hours, next Thursday evening."

"Just let me check the schedule, and then we can get down

to details."

Sienna popped into the office. Tovah silently questioned Sienna's smirk.

"Last minute academic reception. Do we have time on Thursday, 6:00-8:00 or 9:00?"

Tovah typed quickly into the laptop and nodded. "Thursday at 6:00. Group size?"

"Three dozen, probably. Reserve under Liz Elliot." Sienna picked a reservation form from a file folder on the wall.

"Okay. Done." Tovah smiled and mouthed, "I want details," before Sienna ducked back out of the office, pulling the door closed behind her.

"Dr. Elliot?"

"Oh, call me Liz."

"Liz, we can do it. Shall we go over the details at a table?" Sienna gestured toward a café table just on the other side of the stationery display.

"Yes, let's. God, what a relief!"

Liz seated herself, and Sienna laid the papers and a pen on the table in front of a second chair. "Let me get us some tea. What will you have?" She guessed the professor was a Formosa oolong type, but wanted confirmation before she prepared the tea.

"Oh, thanks! I'd love some oolong with honey. I've been trying something your manager recommended. Formica?"

"Formosa." Sienna smiled. "I'll be right back. You can do a mental count on how much food and wine you think you'll need while I get the tea."

Liz waved Sienna off with shiny, manicured fingers. "Will do."

Sienna quickly started the tea for Liz. She selected two cobalt blue floral teacups, solid but pretty, and added them to the tray. On impulse, she added a little plate of raspberry thumbprint cookies. She was just setting the honey pot next to the stacked cups when she felt a warm shiver on her neck.

"I'll have what you're having," a flirtatious male voice spoke quietly.

Sienna turned toward the tea bar. Greg was leaning against the counter, sans clerical collar, clearly admiring her. "Excuse me?" Sienna asked. She felt her heart speed up, but fought to retain her composure. "Would you like some oolong?"

"Oh, heavens, no." His eyes roamed her face. "No, I have a sweet tooth."

"Ah." Sienna said. She cast around for Lettye and motioned her manager over with a head tilt. "On the house," she said to Greg, sliding two cookies across to him on a saucer. "Lettye, could you make this gentleman a pot of Moroccan mint tea, please?" She turned back to Greg to find that he had not moved his eyes from her. She ignored the heat rising in her neck in response to his look. "Am I right?"

"Oh, yes. You've got me."

"Thank you, Lettye," Sienna said, moving past her with the tray. She was glad to have an excuse to get away from Greg. Maybe Tovah was right about him. He certainly seemed to be seeking Sienna out. She tried to push the man's smoldering attention out of her mind. "Right. Graduate student booze." She smiled at Liz.

"Oh?" Liz pointed at the teapot, surprised.

"No!" Sienna smiled. "This is oolong. But we have to calculate the booze intake needs of your department. Any ideas?"

"Hmmm. Somewhere between fish and the British aristocracy."

"So, a bottle per person?"

Tea & Crumples

"That sounds about right." Liz pulled a half-smile. She glanced over Sienna's shoulder, and the smile broadened into an impish grin. "I think you're the dagger in that man's smile."

"Hmm?" Sienna looked up from the form. She resisted turning her head. "Oh, you know, he's just a happy customer."

"Mmm-hmm!" Liz teased.

"Not like that!" Sienna chuckled despite herself, then spoke in a low voice. "I think he likes me, but I hope he'll notice before long that I am obviously and happily married."

Liz nodded, but her expression spoke of dropping a subject rather than agreeing. "Well, about the booze. Make two-thirds of the wine red. We'll need lots of fatty foods to absorb it. Cheese, pastries, quiches, anything like that. There might be a couple of children there, but they can make do with grapes and foods that resemble pizza."

Sienna poured tea for them both and began to fill in the catering form.

"Oh, my word. And add these little cookies, if y'all have them all the time. These are amazing!"

Sienna smiled, glad that her hunch had been accurate. "Of course. We make them on site, so we can have as many as you need."

"Well, then we'll need about six dozen. No, eight dozen. I'm going to put some of these in my purse and sneak them home."

Sienna finished the order form and the pot of tea with Liz and left the professor with a to-go box of cookies to seal the deal. She had just returned to the tea bar when a plump, shortish young woman lifted herself onto a stool with a puff.

"You must be Sienna," the woman said. She smiled pleasantly, and her bright blue eyes receded to twinkles above her round cheeks.

"Yes. Sienna Bannock," she said, extending her hand. The woman grasped it and shook enthusiastically. Her hands were warm and slightly damp.

"I'm Bethel Bailey. I'm already a regular; I hope you don't mind." She giggled.

"Well, that's wonderful. And what will you have today, Ms. Bailey?"

"Oh, call me Bethel. It's what everyone calls me. Grandmother saw to that. I'm named after a church, you know."

"Okay, Bethel," Sienna began cautiously, not wanting to interrupt the woman's story. "What will you have?" The woman's smile encouraged her to humor. "Something with religious overtones?" she added.

"Laws!" Bethel responded on a chuckle. "I'll have to share that with Daddy. 'Religious overtones!'" She laughed again, and her face turned a bright red. "Well, I suppose, now that you mention it, that a good cup of Darjeeling is religious. I'll have a pot of that, with a bowl of sugar, if you please." She smiled when Sienna nodded and began to make the tea. "Aw, heck! Excuse my French. I forgot to pick my cup before I got up here."

Nina appeared next to Sienna behind the counter. "I can bring you a cup, Miss," Nina offered. "Which one is your favorite?"

"That's right sweet of you," Bethel gushed, and proceeded to change her mind three times about her preference. By the time she had settled on a pink lusterware cup with roses inside, Sienna had readied the perfectly brewed pot of tea. "Oh, thank you!" Bethel said to Sienna, and she scooped two tall spoons of sugar into the cup before pouring in tea to the brim. "So, there's something I've been meaning to ask you since yesterday."

"Oh?" Sienna replied, opting for quiet curiosity to balance the young woman's exuberance.

"Why is your name misspelled?"

"Beg pardon?" Sienna wondered.

"Your name, Sienna. It's spelled wrong. I've been to Siena, so I know firsthand that it only has one *n*, is why I ask. I figured there was a story behind it. Like my cousin Micheal, whose name is spelled wrong owing to an ignorant clerk. But maybe your story is nicer?"

Sienna waited for Bethel to sip her tea, then spoke into the brief silence. "It's a short story, really. I'm named after the color, not the place. My mother was an artist."

"I'll be! I've only ever heard of burnt sienna, but I guess I'm no artist. Crayon boxes don't tell all there is about colors, I suppose."

"No," Sienna replied, when she realized the woman had paused for her to respond.

"Well, now, an artist! What must that have been like? Were you allowed to draw on the walls when you were a girl? Because my friend Antonia had an artist father, and he let them all paint and color on any walls they pleased. I would have had my hide tanned, personally, if I had marked up Mama's wallpaper, but there you have it." Bethel slurped noisily and refilled her cup. Somehow, she had managed to drink an entire cup between outbursts.

"I wasn't allowed to write on walls, but it was because we lived in rentals. The landlords didn't even let us put up pictures with nails, much less color the walls."

"Did y'all move around a lot?" Bethel's curiosity was direct and friendly, growing so obviously out of open acceptance of others that Sienna decided to answer.

"Yes. I didn't see a lot of my grandparents growing up. My

parents were at odds with them. Sometimes I think we moved because of lack of money, and sometimes because they wanted to avoid my grandparents."

"Well, what a shame. Grandparents can be such a joy."

"Not mine. My grandmother pinched me on the few occasions I saw her, and my grandfather talked badly about my father when we saw him. Mom tried to keep the family ties, but I think it was probably best that we stayed clear of them, on the whole."

"But you must have had someone older to look up to?" Bethel gaped.

"Mrs. Johnstone," Sienna smiled at the memories, "and Mrs. Hopkins. Neighbors near the rent homes we stayed in longest. Mrs. Johnstone taught me to garden, and Mrs. Hopkins showed me how to crochet. I made a doll dress with her one summer, before we moved again."

"That's good, then." Bethel beamed. She was like a benevolent cherub, blessing Sienna's personal history with her interest. "Whoops. I've got to go finish some accounts before I clock out for the day. Thank you for the tea and chat." The woman drained her cup and set it back on the counter with a gentle thunk.

"You're welcome." Sienna smiled. A question occurred to her as she watched the woman struggle to her feet. "Why Bethel? You said you're named after a church?"

"Oh!" Bethel grinned, clearly glad of the notice. "Grandmother made Mama name me Bethel when the church moved to the other side of town. They settled on 'Second Baptist,' but Granny maintained that they ought to have kept, 'Bethel,' and that was that. She's donated near about all the hymnals in my honor, just to get the real church name in them." Bethel laughed and moved toward the door. "See you tomorrow!" she called.

Sienna smiled into the woman's happy wake and began to clear the place setting where Bethel had sat. More than anything, Bethel's chatter had taken Sienna's mind off her worries. She reflected that perhaps Marnie had been right in more ways than one that work would be good for her. Between Liz and Bethel and the need to make and clear place settings, Sienna was pushed along by the rituals of tea. The flow gave her the freedom to risk being herself, despite the pain of her situation. In that way, tea was the best part of religion. She took to the rhythms it offered, and by day's end, she felt that she had prayed.

NOTES FROM SIENNA'S TEA FILES

Bethel Bailey, 28, accountant, friend, Orthodox, wife to priest in training: Darjeeling with two teaspoons of demerara sugar and sometimes cream. Light and fruity start, substantive finish. Make sure to fill the pot to the top so she gets three full cups from each sitting.

Liz Elliot, 41, American history professor, friend: Formosa Oolong with honey. Moderate, soothing, deep flavor with light finish.

Marc Rosen, 37, philosophy professor, Tovah's husband: Genmaicha, all types. Drinks at all temperatures but will allow when pressed for an opinion that if he had time to be demanding, he prefers good tea at about 185 degrees.

Chapter Four

Peter tried to smile, but the effort made him gag. He leaned over the kidne- shaped pan that Nurse David held out in front of him. Sienna rushed to Peter's other side and rubbed his shoulder.

"Oh, Beloved, I'm so sorry," she soothed. The back of her hand brushed his neck, which was cold and clammy. To Nurse David, she asked, "Has he been like this all morning?"

"Just for about half an hour. It's a common side effect, especially at the beginning." He gently wiped Peter's chin with a warm cloth and supported him as he leaned back.

"Glad to see you," Peter managed weakly, and his eyes smiled at Sienna through his pain.

Down the hall, an alarm sounded with a voice announcing a code. Nurse David stood, moving the pan to the side table. Sienna saw the steam coming out of another pan on the table, where the nurse had placed the clean washcloths. Another bin held the wipes that had been used. Sienna was disconcerted to find that the discarded cloth pile was so tall. How much had

Peter suffered in her absence?

The nurse explained to her the procedure should Peter need assistance again. Then he left, leaving Sienna with the precious double gift of being alone with Peter and having something to do to help him.

Long years of hearing him breathe told her that Peter was awake, though his eyes were closed. The room was quiet but for a piano sonata playing on speakers Sienna had brought over the weekend. It was Peter's favorite, one of the lesser-known movements of a Beethoven sonata. They had driven to Washington, D.C. a few years prior in order to hear Murray Perahia play it. The memory pearled before her, and she touched it in lieu of tears.

"Remember when we heard this together?" she asked. Peter's eyes wrinkled in the closest approximation of a smile that he dared. "That was the night you told me about winning the renovation contracts. We finally had the money to build our house." She reached for his hand and sandwiched it between her own. "On the way home, way too late at night, we debated wall colors."

"Hat rack," Peter added, not attempting to open his eyes.

"Yes! How could I forget? That was when you bought me the hat rack made from deer feet and antlers at that truck stop." Sienna giggled. "And it really does look lovely in the house." Peter squeezed her hand. "Who knew that we would have such a perfect spot for it in the laundry room?" She smiled, letting their old joke settle into the closing chords of the music.

"Tea," Peter mumbled. The word was nearly swallowed in a grimace.

"Oh? Shall I make you some? I brought the things up last night, but I thought, with the chemo, that maybe you wouldn't be up for it." She stopped at the slight shake of Peter's head.

"Shop?" he finished.

"It's going well. Too well, almost. It's almost overwhelming, how blessed that place seems. Tovah and Lettye and Nina are amazing, and even zany Jessie is exceeding expectations. We have this one customer," Sienna began, pushing aside the thought of another customer, a handsome one she did not wish to talk about, "her name is Bethel Bailey. She comes in a few times a day, and even for afternoon tea on Sunday. That woman could talk a brick wall into a yoga class. Yesterday, she told me about how her grandmother gave a Waterford crystal chandelier to the parsonage. Only, it was too big for the room, so that it only cleared the table by eighteen inches. To hear her tell it, her grandmother would put a brass memorial plaque on absolutely anything related to church."

"Missed her calling."

"Probably," Sienna sighed. "So many women of a certain age became busy bodies when they were kept from serious ministries by their churches." She and Peter liked their parish in part because one of their priests was a woman. It set an inclusive tone. "But, hey, Bethel's granny keeps the trophy shop in business, single handed."

"That's something." Peter's voice was a bit stronger. Sienna watched him swallow slowly. Even though she could see how the effort must cost him, she hoped he would be able to talk with her. She missed his burring, beautiful voice. At length, he continued, "How is the manuscript table?"

"It's one of my favorite things at work," she shook his hand in excitement. "There's a morning crowd and an afternoon crowd. We have postcard and letter writers, a couple of journalers, and at least one woman who is definitely writing a book there. She comes in the late afternoon and asks intelligent questions about the teas before ordering strong-brewed

Keemun and almond pasties. And!" she paused to smile as Peter cracked open his eyes a little, "almost no one has stolen a pen from the jar."

"That'll please Tovah."

"Oh, it does," she grinned.

"What else? Favorite?"

"Well, I didn't expect it, but the chess table is probably the best part of the store. These two old men hold court there in the mornings, and they seem to have a small following late in the day. I even heard a woman trying to convince them to have a 'toynament' the other day. I think she was from New Yawk."

The dogs? Home yet?"

"No, I haven't been able to be there enough to make the effort. But I have visited them twice, and they are crazy, as usual."

Nurse David returned then. "How is our patient?" he asked Sienna. To Peter, he said, "Good. Your stomach is settling." Then, to both, "You two make a good team."

Peter squeezed Sienna's hand and smiled a very small smile.

"We're going to try for lunch today, Peter. Broth and Jello first." He paused for Peter to wince. "I know. It's gross. But it's protein. Tomorrow you can eat normally. Which means," he turned toward Sienna, "feel free to bring in requests. Favorite foods usually help. This type of chemo dampens the appetite a bit."

You hear that, Peter? I can bring you my new scones," she teased. Peter had suffered through many revisions of the scone recipe over the previous year. "Or tarts or quiches or pastries."

"Almond croissant?" Peter asked hopefully.

"Almond croissant it is," she replied quietly. A knock came at the door, and an unseen woman announced catering.

"But first, broth!" Nurse David said.

Sienna looked at the clock. It was already 12:30. "Oh, no! I'm late for a meeting. I'll be back this evening." She kissed Peter's forehead and stroked the hair over his temple. "I love you."

"Love you."

Elsie Pinkwater did not seem amused. She glared at the young Latina who served her. "What's this?" she demanded. The girl had set a mug of dark, fragrant tea in front of her, alongside a tiny pitcher of cream and a small bowl of brown sugar crystals and a small spoon. "I asked for plain black tea with sugar."

"Yes, Miss. This is the Keemun, English Breakfast," Nina gestured gracefully to the tall mug, then to the sugar bowl, "and the sugar."

"Well, I don't know how you all drink tea where *you're* from, but I am accustomed to good black tea bags and white sugar."

"I could get you some white lump sugar if you'd like, Miss, but this is the only granulated sugar we have."

"Well, what about Sweet'N Low?"

"We don't carry artificial sweeteners, Miss. I could bring you some stevia extract to try."

Elsie huffed. "No, I guess I'll make do with this," she snapped mistrustfully. "I don't suppose you know when your boss will be here, do you?"

"She called a minute ago to tell us that she might be a little late. Her appointment ran late," Nina said protectively. She didn't want this mean old lady to know that Sienna was hurting.

"Well, why didn't you tell me?" the woman roared.

"May I be of assistance?" Lettye asked, appearing at Nina's side. "That'll be fine, Nina, thank you. Could you see to Mr.

Reed's table, please? He just got a new opponent." Lettye calmly watched as Nina walked out onto the floor, then turned her attention back to Elsie Pinkwater, who was eyeing Lettye with poorly disguised disgust.

"I don't know. Is your boss usually late?" She pointed to a small wristwatch with hours marked in diamond chips. "It's already five till 1:00, and we had a meeting."

"Yes, Ms. Pinkwater. I saw your name on the schedule for Sienna's 1:00 meeting. I'm sure she will be here as soon as possible. In the meantime, may I offer you a pastry? Or lunch?" She watched the woman's eyes widen at the selection in the pastry counter and cooler, then narrow suspiciously. "It's on the house, for the inconvenience of your wait."

"Do you have quiche?"

"Yes, ma'am." Lettye explained the varieties.

Elsie chose a slice of quiche by pointing.

"Please let me know if there's anything else I can do for your comfort," Lettye smiled, setting the heated quiche in front of the old woman.

Elsie fell to, and the plate in front of her was bare but for a few crumbs when Sienna arrived at 1:05. Sienna rushed up to the stool where Elsie sat sipping and scrutinizing the tea in her mug.

"Ms. Pinkwater?" Sienna asked. "Sienna Bannock. I'm so sorry I'm late. I hope you enjoyed the quiche."

"I did, thank you." Elsie perked up. "Your people did their best, but I'm not used to having to wait for meetings." She cast a withering look toward Nina, who was explaining green tea varieties to a blond woman at the manuscript table.

Sienna suspected that the woman's disgruntled attitude might have had to do with the brown skin of the tearoom staff rather than their quality of service. She breathed deeply and

Tea & Crumples

answered simply, "I understand. If you'd like to join me at a table, we can talk about your event ideas."

When they were settled with a fresh pot of tea delivered by Lettye as soon as they sat, Sienna began pleasantly, "So, your email said that you organize tea parties. Would you be interested in having the parties on site, or would you rather discuss catering or tea sources?"

"Tea parties?!" Elsie drew herself up and looked at Sienna with disdain. "No, I'm a TEA party organizer."

Sienna stared blankly.

"You know? T-E-A, the sorority? We have a fair number of members and alumnae in the area. I chair the committee for our fundraising events, and I schedule parties locally."

"Oh," Sienna said simply. Her mind whirred to switch directions with the new information. "Then, would you want to plan for an after-hours event here?"

"Well, no, actually. I was hoping to have you all donate tea and things for our Fall Charity Ball. It benefits University Hospital's Cancer Center."

Sienna reeled at the mention of the hospital where Peter was being treated. She tried to think straight. "I'm sorry, Ms. Pinkwater. We just opened a few weeks ago, so we aren't yet in a position to donate substantially." Sienna wanted to continue, to offer an alternative way that the shop could help, but her feelings prevented it. She looked down at the teapot while guilt and longing and confusion grappled for her attention. "Would you like another cup?" she asked at length, lifting the pot toward Elsie's cup.

"I guess not." Elsie said, glaring around at the shop. Sienna could hear Nina offering a free sample to a couple at a nearby table, while Lettye's warm, "on the house!" carried from the grad student booths where she was distributing samples of cookies. Sienna felt her face go warm at the contrast between their generosity and her words to Elsie.

Just then, Tovah came out of the office. She walked toward the table. "Hello. Tovah Rosen, co-proprietor. Ms. Pinkwater, right? Have you decided to have an event here? We do great quiches!"

"No, your associate here has just informed me that you aren't in a position to make substantial donations this autumn." Elsie eyed the tea tray and glanced toward the bar where she had eaten lunch, her face drawn in conclusion.

Before Tovah could correct her on either score, Sienna jumped in, "Ms. Pinkwater represents the TEA sorority fundraising committee. She organizes parties."

"Oh, well, I'm sorry we couldn't help you at this time," Tovah said. "But I hope you'll stop by personally, for lunch or tea."

"I did like the quiche," Elsie conceded.

"How about I get you another piece to go, for your troubles?" Tovah asked. "Which kind did you have?"

"Cream cheese and Brussels sprouts," Elsie answered confidently.

Tovah and Sienna exchanged confused glances. After a moment, Tovah's brow cleared. "Oh! The artichoke and chèvre quiche."

"No. It was definitely Brussels sprouts and cream cheese. I ate it. I should know."

"Yes, ma'am," Sienna interjected, "But we don't make that variety here. The artichoke chèvre would look similar."

"If you say so." Elsie drew herself up. Lettye arrived with the quiche in a to-go box at that moment. Elsie picked it up, nodded at the three women, and made her way toward the door.

Tea & Crumples

"Thank you for coming in!" Sienna called to her retreating back.

"Lord, have mercy!" Lettye breathed.

"I second that," Tovah agreed. "What? She walked into a shop owned by a Jew and an Episcopalian, saw our black and Latina staff, and thought we were pulling one over on her?"

"To be fair, she mentioned the Cancer Center, and I froze up. I'm sure she could tell something was wrong, and we clearly are generous here. She must have thought we had something against her sorority, to not want to support its event," Sienna reasoned. "We may have just invited her into a situation that made her uncomfortable. I doubt she's used to anyone refusing to donate to her causes."

"That's no reason for her not to have even paid for her tea. She got here fifteen minutes early and started in on how you were late," Nina added.

Sienna started, not realizing the girl was there. She would have to nip the gossiping in the bud. The last thing she wanted in a business was a bitter wait staff. "Well, let's forgive her that debt. I'm sure she was doing the best she knew how, and we did invite her to the meeting, even if we were going on a misunderstanding. Best to look at all of our customers in the best light possible. That way we can treat them the way they ought to be treated."

"Amen," Lettye said.

"Besides, maybe she was just hungry." Tovah added. "And now we've fixed that, so perhaps she'll be nicer to everyone all day."

Nina nodded and walked behind the counter. Sienna joined her, carrying the tea tray from the truncated meeting.

"That was for me, huh, Miss?" Nina asked, taking the tray and unloading it.

"What was for you, Nina?" Sienna answered, looking into the girl's dark, intelligent eyes. Nina raised an eyebrow in challenge, and Sienna relented. "Yes, Nina, that was for you. But for the rest of us, too. We all need grace, and dispensing it is part of the vision for this shop. I don't want any of us to get upset over little things. Ms. Pinkwater was in a difficult situation, maybe outside her comfort zone."

"I get it, Miss. She won't get nicer if we make her feel bad about the misunderstanding. I'm sorry for talking about her not paying. I just—" Nina sighed and looked down for a moment, "I just felt bad, the way she was looking at me like I was a cockroach or something. I get that a lot, and I didn't want it here."

Sienna followed Nina to the kitchen, where the girl began to wash a tray of cups. "Nina." She waited until the girl looked up. "I do not ever want you to feel that way. Not here, not anywhere. You are a good person, made in the image of God, and no one should look at you that way. But if someone does, you have to know now that it's about them, not you."

"That doesn't make it better, though, does it? If that old lady has a shriveled-up heart, that doesn't make me happy."

"It would be easier if she saw you as you really are, Nina, as a child of God. A gifted, hospitable, bright young woman who was extending kindness. You don't have to be a roach, and she doesn't have to be mean. We can pray that God will open her eyes to see properly. And ours as well." Sienna walked to the sink and rinsed the dishes that Nina handed her. "Okay?"

Nina nodded but did not speak. Sienna heard a small sniffle and decided to let her youngest staff member have a few minutes alone to sort herself.

"I'm going to go check out Cleotis Reed's crowd," Sienna said, setting her cup in the rinse tub. "When you finish here,

Tea & Crumples

could you make sure the wine glasses are all dusted? We'll need them for Thursday's event." She thanked Nina and left.

Out by the chess table, Cleotis was soundly beating a young woman with long, curly hair. The woman smiled as her pieces were dispatched.

"Checkmate," Cleotis Reed announced. He lifted his cup and sipped his smoky tea.

"Awesome!" the woman laughed. "Thank you for letting me try." She offered her hand, and Cleotis stood to shake it.

"May I?" A man with a quiet demeanor rose from a chair that had been pulled over to watch the match. He had a long beard, which he wore over a black cassock and a pectoral cross. Sienna saw immediately that he was an Orthodox priest.

Cleotis assessed the man and smiled. "Please," he gestured to the seat the young woman had vacated. He offered his hand. "Cleotis Reed. I'm seventy-four years old, and I speak my mind."

"Max. I'm fighty-eight years on this earth, and I'm glad to hear it."

The men quickly reset the board, but they did not begin to play at once. Instead, the priest noticed Sienna's attention and looked up.

"Father, may I bring you some tea?" she asked.

"Have you Russian Caravan tea?"

"I have. We sweeten it with pineapple juice. Will that do?"

"Yes, please. Thank you."

When Sienna returned, the men were engrossed in a game. Though they both moved rapidly, there was no accumulation of captured pieces. Smiling, Sienna wondered if Cleotis Reed had met his match. She decided it was time to freshen his tea, one way or another.

Cleotis Reed said, "Check," just as Sienna set down a piping hot pot of tea at his elbow. It took her a moment to realize he was absorbed in the game, not asking to pay. She leaned against the windowsill along with the other rapt spectators.

"Check," Father Max echoed after moving a piece.

They volleyed checks for another few moves, until, at last, Cleotis announced, "Checkmate."

Father Max shook Cleotis' hand and took up his teacup. The men eyed one another respectfully and agreed to a rematch the next afternoon, before they were inundated with questions from the enthusiastic onlookers. Sienna cleared empty pots and made sure that everyone had all they needed, then returned to the back of the shop.

After dropping the laden tray off in the kitchen to a recovered Nina, Sienna decided to talk with Tovah. She found her in the office.

"Something amazing just happened," she announced, sliding into the chair.

"A graduate student bought a second pot of tea to make up for hogging a booth?" Tovah smiled. In truth, she was glad to have the students there, but the two had teased each other about the phenomenon of booth hogging when they were putting the shop together. They had settled on a long section of half booths along one wall with outlets so that the students might be accommodated without impeding other customers.

"Cleotis Reed almost lost a match."

"Ah. Well, one can hope." Tovah smiled at her friend, then scrutinized the tired line of her shoulders. "How was Peter?"

"Sick to his stomach. But we got to talk a little. I told him about the shop and about Bethel and the dogs."

"Well, that's something, yes?"

"Yes." Sienna rubbed her forehead against the tightness around her eyes. "Marnie says it's good that I have work right now, to have something to do. As much as I hate being away from Peter, I know she's right." She dropped her hand and smiled a tired smile at Tovah. "Especially with you doing all the heavy lifting. I can never thank you enough for carrying the show while I pop in and out."

"Listen, Sienna, you may not always notice, but you're human. You have to eat, to rest, to work, and to spend time with your husband. I know you skipped church on Sunday. You shouldn't. Don't let this cancer get between you and the things that make you strong."

"My spiritual advisor, the Jew," Sienna smirked.

"Exactly. And if you would listen to me, you would be better off." Tovah pointed at Sienna with a pen as her friend rose to leave. "That's in the Bible. Look it up!"

Smiling, Sienna walked into the stationery section of the store. There was a particular type of creamy smooth, pink cotton paper that always soothed her. She walked to the wall of open paper stock, removed a sheet from the tray, and ran her fingers along it. When she wasn't frazzled with fear, Sienna loved to write long letters to her old school friends and Mrs. Hopkins. The thought of watching wet ink absorb into the page steadied her. What could be written could be tamed, or at least sanctified. At least, she hoped it could be.

"You should try that with a fountain pen," said a musical voice behind her. Sienna did not have to turn to know it was Greg. He had a habit of catching her unawares.

"Ah, Greg," she said simply, turning to face him. He wore a charcoal grey sweater that set off his eyes. Her heart skipped a bit; he was so gorgeous. Sienna noted the warm flush this man inspired and knew she would have to overcome it. Nodding to herself, she decided to approach the problem head-on. No more sneaking up on her if she could help it.

"You like fountain pens, then?" he misinterpreted her nod. "I have one here you could try." He held out an ornate silver and lapis pen in his open palm, where its beauty drew her eyes against her will.

Examining a strange man's pen felt somehow untoward, and Sienna pulled her eyes away. To change the terms of the encounter, she looked Greg directly in the eye, catching him unawares. Unfortunately, his open surprise and vulnerability caught her unawares as well, and she almost reached out to touch his face the way one comforts a child. She fought herself to finish what she had started, to look him in the eye and invent pleasantries. "Oh, no, thank you. I prefer rollerballs." Her voice gave away her nervousness. She composed herself by returning the paper to its slot. "But, why don't you join me at the manuscript table, and we'll have tea?" She reasoned that the formality of tea in the informality of a public table would allow her to figure out the man's appeal without committing to any of the ideas that arose. Then she would overcome them easier.

"That would be," he smiled, "perfect."

Sienna prepared the tea tray and brought it to the table. She sat opposite Greg with her back against the wall and poured for them.

"Morrocan mint for you," she handed him a piping hot cup of greenish, sweet-smelling tea. "Keemun for me." She pulled her cup near, scooped in sugar, and poured in cream. "Now, I understand that you love notebooks."

"Yes." He sipped his tea, his eyes following Sienna's movements as she stirred and raised her cup.

"Are you a writer?"

"An artist."

"Oh," Sienna sounded disappointed.

Tea & Crumples

"What's wrong with being an artist?"

"Nothing. It's just, we ordered ruled notebooks for you. Did we get it wrong?"

"Oh, no. I like ruled notebooks. It's part of my style, coloring outside the lines." He spoke into his cup, so that Sienna wondered if she only imagined the flirty lift of the corner of his mouth.

"Altered books?"

"Something like that. But I also write in them."

"Oh?" Sienna had not intended to ask a question. "Oh," she corrected neutrally, not wishing to pry or to invite sharing.

"Mostly just my secrets, and what I feel comfortable noting about the secrets of others."

"I thought priests couldn't tell secrets."

"Not from the confessional, no. But there are other ways to come by knowledge. Sometimes it's forced on one."

"Like Elinor Dashwood."

"Yes," Greg smiled, "and no." He sipped again.

"How so?" Sienna wanted not to be curious about this man, but she was a sucker for conversations about Jane Austen characters.

"Elinor Dashwood was given an embroidered handkerchief," he began, and Sienna realized he had only seen the movie, not read the book, "and I have been given embroidered alibis."

Sienna nodded. Jane Austen reader or no, Greg was obviously deeply wounded by the alibi giver. She searched for a way to take the conversation back to casual footing. "Well, I hope our notebooks offer you a small source of consolation." Pretending interest in her teacup, she fiddled unconsciously with a pen someone had left on the table.

"You really should try a fountain pen sometime," Greg said, watching her. "Here." He slid a notebook across to her and opened it, then laid his fountain pen on the blank page. "Write your number. Give it a try."

"Um," Sienna's brows knit. "You have the store number already." She glanced up, saw his unhurried interest. She was just about to say, "No, thank you," when a deep, kind voice called out to her.

"Sienna," Father Max intoned, "I wanted to compliment you on the tea. It's the best preparation I have found." His eyes were quick in his calm face. Sienna suspected he had seen her discomfort and had come to the rescue.

"Thank you, Father." She rose and came around the table. "Shall I freshen up your pot? We were done here." From the corner of her eye, she saw Greg flinch at her dismissal. She thought it was for the best.

"No, thank you, but if you could sell me a packet?" He began to walk toward the tea counter. Sienna was drawn into his direction and kept apace, grateful to have a reason to go where she felt at ease.

"Of course." Sienna went behind the counter and lifted down the large tin. "How much?"

"Four ounces."

She weighed the tea, added an extra scoop, and handed it across to the priest. He paid in cash and picked up the small paper bag, plump with tea. He paused for a moment, his eyes making her feel as though he saw more than the surface of things. She thought he might have been praying for her, and she worried that her exhaustion and fear were so obvious. Her smile tightened as he turned to go. To avoid crying, she busied herself with wiping tea leaves from the back of the counter.

When the bell over the door announced Father Max's exit, she turned around to find Greg approaching her. He wore a contrite expression that was not entirely convincing.

Tea & Crumples

"I didn't mean to offend you."

"Listen, Father Greg," Sienna began, using the priestly title to distance herself, "I'm married. I don't think I've been subtle about that fact, but you don't seem to have gotten the message."

"Greg," he corrected. "Just Greg, and I noticed."

"Well," she searched for words. If he did not admit to flirting with her, what could she say? She thought of Peter, lying sick in the hospital. "I'm going through a lot right now. My husband is in the hospital. And I don't need any ambiguity."

"Of course," Greg said, tilting his head slightly. He looked as though he cared for her suffering, but Sienna was not sure. Compassion might be just another line he would cross.

"I hope you will still feel free to come here for tea and, well, crumples," she gestured toward the stationery section, "but please, no more trying to get my personal number." She set her hand on the counter in front of her, making her words final.

"If you need a friend," Greg laid his warm hand on top of hers, "let me know." He held still for a beat longer than was casual, then walked back to the manuscript table.

Sienna watched him go, his strong back evident under the cashmere sweater. She rubbed the hand he had warmed with her chilly one. It had been too long since someone had warmed her, and she felt a little tug toward Greg for the simple expedient of contact. After losing the baby, she had craved Peter's touch. It was her only consolation when the grief overwhelmed her, the heat of his hands on her shoulders, her face and back. She breathed deeply to calm her heart rate and made herself look away from Greg. It would not do to allow herself to be attracted to him, not when she had so many other battles to wage.

Cleotis Reed waved and smiled. Sienna had been looking

toward him, unseeing. She smiled back at him and walked over.

"How is my best customer?" she asked.

Cleotis looked around and behind him. "Well, I don't know. Do you want me to ask when I see him?"

"Aw, come on, Mr. Reed, you know I meant you."

"I'm having a right fine day." He cut his eyes toward the manuscript table, and the door. "I found another worthy opponent. And how about you?" He lifted his teacup, his hand steady with the sort of grace that only comes of self-command.

"I have a feeling you won't believe me if I say I'm doing well, but I am pleased with how the shop is going." She looked over the group of chess enthusiasts at neighboring tables, several of whom were pretending not to listen. "Very pleased. Not least because of you, Cleotis Reed."

Cleotis nodded. "You have a good place here. I'm glad to be a part of it." Again, he looked toward the manuscript table. "Chess tells you a lot about a person, how he thinks, what he's after. I don't suppose everyone is so forthright about why they're here."

Sienna resisted the urge to turn, but she suspected that Greg was watching her. "No," she agreed, "I don't suppose they are." She was spared further comment by a lanky young man who cleared his throat by way of approaching Cleotis for conversation.

"Excuse me, ma'am," he said, his voice wavering with the bravery of youth. "Sir." He nodded. "I was wondering, Mr. Reed, if I might have a game with you?"

Sienna smiled and excused herself. She checked on the corduroy and scarf-clad line of laptop users along the far wall. Two of them beamed their thanks when she offered to refill their hot water, but the others did not look up, isolated by their earbuds and the obscurity of their fields of study. When she had tended all of the other customers, she retreated behind the tea counter and allowed herself a glance at the manuscript table.

Greg was still there, sipping tea from a clear tea glass, writing languidly in a journal. He was left-handed. Sienna watched his careful progress across the page. A sudden shaft of reflected afternoon sun poured through the window, catching on a thin gold band on his ring finger. Her breath caught in surprise. For all her emphasis on her own marriage status, she had not noticed his. Greg looked up, lifted the thick fountain pen from the paper, let a slow smile linger between them, then returned to writing.

Sienna decided that she liked Greg too much. She would have to make herself remember all the reasons why she could not like him. She always thought best with busy hands. Turning to Lettye, Sienna made a decision.

"Lettye, let me know if we get too busy this afternoon. I'm going to bake."

"No problem, Sienna." Lettye smiled graciously, and Sienna rejoiced again at the woman's gift of putting others at ease. "Nina and I have it covered."

Sienna went to the back room, pulled out almond and white rice flours, hazelnuts, dates, bananas, and honey. She carried a tub of coconut oil to the counter after putting on a bright, ruffled apron, one of many they had purchased from a local seamstress who specialized in creative reuse sewing. After several failed attempts at gluten free scones, she was determined to find a recipe that worked.

She added dates and bananas to the bowl of a large food processor, measured in generous heaps of almond flour, a smaller mound of rice flour, and pulsed the ingredients into a thick paste. She felt the texture, smelled, and tasted it. In went a scoop of coconut oil. She pulsed, tasted. Almost there. A dollop of honey, a coarse pulse of hazelnuts, and the dough was ready. She plopped the scones onto a lined pan by handfuls and placed them in the oven.

A reassuring smell of the good earth and fruit met her while she waited for the scones to bake, her gaze unfocused. Gradually, the almond scent came forward. She recalled the massage oil that Peter had used to relax her over the long, exhausting summer. It was only slightly sweet, like the memory of a baby one could not hold. Her eyes swam. The timer dinged.

The scones were perfectly golden brown and firm. Sienna was sure, in the same inexplicable way that she knew which tea was right for each person, that she had finally lighted on the perfect recipe. As if drawn by excellence, Nina appeared at her elbow.

"Miss? Are those what smell so good?" She gestured to the smooth pastries.

"Yes. Would you like to try the first one?"

"Oh, yes, please." She picked the edge off a piping hot scone and blew on it, then popped it into her mouth. "Mmm!" She nodded. "This is it, Miss! You did it."

Sienna smiled and followed suit, a smile washing over her features as she chewed. "I did it! Great. I'll go get some paper and write this down before I forget."

"Oh, Miss, I almost forgot. There's a lady here, Liz something, says she wants you to meet her friend." Nina looked down sheepishly. "I was supposed to come tell you, but I guess I got distracted by the scones."

"Tell you what," Sienna said, removing her apron, "Why don't you plate a couple of these for Liz and company and bring them out? That'll make up for your moment of distraction." She smiled, clearly not upset at the lapse.

"You got it."

Liz was sitting at the table where they had met before, animated in conversation with a woman with sleek red hair. "I mean, if you asked, 'Who's afraid of Virginia Woolf?,' she'd raise her hand!" She laughed. The redhead shook in silent laughter. "Oh, Deborah," Liz exclaimed when she spotted Sienna, "look who's here!" Liz stood and looped her hand through Sienna's arm. Sienna felt a little sheepish at the enthusiastic welcome, but she smiled politely. "This is Sienna Bannock, the woman who saved my life! She even has wine, so no one will have to talk to one another unlubricated."

Deborah raised an eyebrow at her friend's description, but smiled warmly at Sienna. "Deborah Lundquist. Good to meet you." She shook Sienna's hand and somehow managed to extricate her from Liz's grip at the same time. "I hear you're feasting the history department on Thursday. Brave woman!" She offered Sienna a seat with a gesture that brooked no refusal.

"Oh, come on! You know your department is worse," Liz teased.

"I don't deny it," Deborah smirked. "But at least my people can hold their drink."

"Don't listen to her unless she agrees with me," Liz said, squeezing Sienna's upper arm. "Anyway," she pursed her lips at Deborah, "I brought you here to meet someone who knows more about tea than you." She beamed proudly at Sienna and nodded toward Deborah. "That's rare for this Miss. Well, this *professor*, 'scuse me."

"Don't let my friend here give you a false impression about my formality," Deborah said with a good-humored smile. "She just likes to tease me in retaliation." She sipped her tea and raised her eyebrows. "This is amazing tea."

"Let me guess." Sienna closed her eyes and feigned concentration. "Victorian bridal green blend?"

"Yes! How did you know?" Deborah seemed genuinely surprised.

"I blend that one here with orange peel, a delicate green tea, myrtle oil, a touch of white rose petals, and…" A lump rose in her throat as she recalled the last ingredient. She swallowed and smiled an apology. "Wild bergamot. The usual bridal bouquet, plus a little something Southern to make it special."

"Well," Deborah began slowly, searching Sienna's face for further distress, "it just so happens that I am a bride. Two months until the big day."

"I wish you all the best. Will you have the wedding locally?"

"Yes. Brad and I will be married at the church where I serve as deacon."

"Well, if you need any tea, I hope you'll keep us in mind."

"Hold that thought, Sienna, because I'm going to do a shower for them here, or for her, at least," Liz interjected. "But first, what do you mean, 'in retaliation'?! What have I forgotten that I'm retaliating for?"

"Let me see, I believe it was a disagreement about soy. I said soymilk isn't good for anyone, and you cited a commercial as evidence that it was an ancient beverage."

"Oh, that. I wasn't offended at you calling me on that malarkey. I was upset because you took five minutes telling me which soy foods were and were not actually ancient food sources and GMO's and paleos and what not."

"Me?" Deborah raised her eyebrows in mock surprise. "No, I'm sure I never lecture."

Sienna watched the friends stare at one another for a long moment. Then they laughed.

70

Tea & Crumples

"Anyhow, Sienna here agrees with you. It's right on the menu: coconut milk, rice milk, dairy, but no soy."

"I'm to blame for that," Sienna explained. "Soy allergy."

"No! How do you eat?" Deborah asked. "It's in everything."

"Not here, it's not," Sienna explained. "Are you allergic, too? So few people realize that soy is in so many foods."

"Deborah here is used to scrutinizing labels on food."

"Oh?"

"I'm a part-time wild foods activist. That is, I still buy things that past muster, but I forage for a lot of my food. My sister put me up to it at first, and once I found out how much stuff grows on the side of the road, I kept it up."

Sienna nodded, trying to make sense of the polished professor before her next to her mental image of foragers as wizened, wide-eyed, and shabby hippies. She shook her head slightly at the incongruity.

"I know." Deborah smiled and sipped her tea. "My parents look at me the same way."

"So, you'll understand why I'll want to feed her up good when I bring her in for a bridal shower," Liz said to Sienna, adding an affectionate squeeze to Deborah's arm. "Which is the other reason I brought Deborah to meet you. She may dig up clumps of flowers on the side of the highway, but she's a total tea snob. I didn't want to have to wrassle her in here if she had doubts as to your standards."

"Will it be a large coed bridal shower?" Sienna asked. "You may want to plan for an after-hours event so you can use the whole space."

"Oh, no. I'm just in charge of Deborah's shower. Brad's coworkers are doing his. His bachelor party, I mean. He's an OB who specializes in low intervention childbirths. The matrons of honor have little babies, so they abdicated the showers to a bunch of professors and midwives, which is to say—can you *imagine* how bawdy it's going to get?"

"Are midwives bawdy?" Sienna asked. She tried to push away the thought of her midwife, the long silence they shared when there was no heartbeat.

"*Professors*, Sienna!" Liz's scandalized tone jerked Sienna from her remembrance, unintentionally rescuing her from a fresh wave of pain. "Well, you'll see tomorrow night."

"It's true, I'm afraid." Deborah set down her teacup with an air of resigned authority. "One can't talk about all manner of human behavior and body parts with scholarly distance without squeezing one's baser humor into after-hours exhibitionism." Her tone was dry, but her eyes twinkled mischievously.

"Oh, go on, Deborah. Just say it. We get tired of behaving ourselves all the time. When we let our hair down, we *really* let our hair down." Liz tugged one of her flyaway blond locks, then sat back, looking from Deborah to Sienna. "Which, with you two, both with your perfect hair, should be fantastic. Look at her hair, Deborah. That doesn't come in a bottle."

"My hair?" Sienna touched her temple above an elaborate golden comb that Marnie had brought her from Israel. "Thanks."

"I'm not the only one who noticed," Liz whispered, leaning forward. Deborah darted her eyes around, pausing in the direction of the manuscript table. "Am I right, Deborah?"

"I think you have an admirer," Deborah said directly. "One who paints while staring at your neck." She was quiet, clearly observing Sienna's reaction.

Sienna sighed and tried to diffuse the situation with a smile. "Ah." She did not turn to look. "Yes, I think I know who you mean. Let's not encourage him."

"Agreed," Deborah said and became very interested in Liz's

teacup. "But I want to know how you can tell so easily which teas we like. Is it the fragrance?"

"No," Sienna said, relaxing. "You said you're a deacon. Are you familiar with spiritual gifts?"

"Yes." Deborah nodded. "You, Liz?"

"Well, don't spread it around, but I happen to know that my spiritual gift is for teaching. My eleventh grade Sunday school teacher wasn't too sure, owing to my being a female, but I think God and a few fine universities will agree with me."

Sienna nodded. "Yours is teaching. Mine is tea."

"God tells you which tea I like?" Liz asked, incredulous.

"More like, I see the good in people, and I have a sense of what they might like, just right away. Like, I saw you the other day, Liz, and I knew immediately that you have a gift for teaching and encouragement and healing through storytelling. And it just popped into my mind, like that," she snapped her fingers, "that you would prefer Formosa oolong."

"Oh! Do Deborah, too," Liz said excitedly.

"With Deborah…" she looked over Deborah's face and paused at the rich red hair. "Well, I noticed your hair first." Sienna chuckled, a warm sound that drew the other women in. "But I also saw a glow—of joy and healing through listening and pastoring. You know those old Christian paintings of bishops and such with long staffs in their hands? That's you. Sacred, old school, guiding. I just knew that you would like the Victorian bridal blend."

"But is it like a feeling, or an image, or a smell?" Liz asked.

"Maybe all of those," Sienna said, considering. "Have you heard of the gift of knowledge? When I studied in school, I would pray about what to look over, and I would always study the right things for the exam. I would ask God to tell me what I needed to know for a paper, and outlines would just line up in my head. I got in the habit a long time ago of asking God about people. He would show me good things about them, so that I just knew what I needed to know to love them in that moment. And tea is how I love people here."

"That's beautiful," Deborah said quietly.

"It really is," Liz agreed, tender-eyed. She reached out and squeezed Sienna's hand.

Deborah sat straighter suddenly. "I enjoyed meeting you, Sienna, but I think now might be a good time for you to go check on something in the back."

"What?" Sienna sputtered. She smelled a waft of minty air. "Oh. Yes. Thank you, Deborah," she whispered. Aloud, she continued, "Well, I hope you like the scones. I had better go start the next batch and start on those cookies you like, Liz." She winked at Liz, smiled at the women, and walked quickly toward the kitchen.

She almost made it before Greg's musical voice crossed the space between them. "Please. I'd like to show you the use I'm making of the notebooks."

Sienna turned and eyed Greg warily. He kept his distance on the far side of the counter, a colorful drawing extended before him. From where she stood, she could make out a bright pink blossom in dark hair, an impossible ornament poised above a golden neck. Her breath caught, and she stepped closer, her voice ragged. "How did you know?" She touched the paper, tracing the irregular petals with her forefinger. It was *her* flower, her and Peter's flower, wild bergamot.

"It's the flower I think of when I look at you," he answered, looking at her as she touched his painting.

"But you can't know that," Sienna said, incredulity strengthening her voice.

"And you can't know I like real Moroccan mint tea. I

Tea & Crumples

haven't drunk it since my honeymoon, not the real stuff like you make."

"I guess we've both been paying attention to God." She thought of their wedding rings, of his intense attention, and her brows knit in concern. "At least…"

"Sienna, I see you. I'm the real deal. I don't want to hurt you." Greg laid the notebook down and slid it closer to Sienna. For the first time, she noticed that the shoulders were bare under the thick dark waves of hair and the bright ornament of wild bergamot. "I just want to get to know you better."

"Greg," Sienna looked directly at the priest, "I believe that you are the real deal. You have spiritual gifts, and I know you see me. But I don't think it's a very good idea, us getting to know one another better."

"Why?" His voice was quiet, seductive in its simplicity and the music in the one word.

"Because we may be blinded by one another's haloes. You see what God shows you, and I see what God shows me. Let's leave it at that, or we might be dazzled enough to think we're in… we have more going on than we do."

"So you think I have a halo?" Greg looked at her as though he certainly did not.

"Yes. And I'm not going to be the one to tarnish it." Sienna backed away. "Excuse me, Greg." She went into the kitchen and walked into the cooler, pulling the door closed behind her. Her hands shook, and she put them on her cheeks, which were flushed and hot. The cold fingers made her think of pressing ridges into piecrusts and cookies. She felt pliable, unset.

For years, she had not noticed any man other than Peter. He was her soulmate, her beloved. Now she realized that he had made her solid. Without him near her, with the fear of losing him, she was softening like wax in the sun. She was melting, sliding down the slope that Greg's attraction was creating.

"What is going on, God?" She thought of the wild bergamot, of her desire for children, of Peter, maybe unable to father again, and Greg, waiting. Unbidden, the thought of kissing Greg, of making babies with Greg, rushed into her mind. "No. I want Peter," she whispered. But she understood, now, the effect Greg had on her. His body was whole, unbroken, and he was offering her a way out of her worst fears. Her heart pounded, her senses raced, and Sienna tried to calm herself with deep breaths of cold air.

"Show me," she prayed, focusing on the memory of Greg standing in the tearoom to keep her mind from illicit images. If he was attractive, there must be some holy quality that was drawing her. There must be some good characteristic that the enemy was trying to pervert, to catch her off guard while she was vulnerable. Gradually, a window cleared in her mind.

Greg was cooking, painting, laughing, a curvy woman with auburn hair laughing at his side. She had a leather purse. No, it was a briefcase, sturdy and expensive. The woman smelled like chocolatey boutique lipsticks, citrusy perfume, and leather. But also scotch whisky, and Greg was grimacing when he smelled it. Another man was kissing the woman, and Greg stopped laughing. The scene went dark.

"Embroidered alibis." Sienna nodded. She crossed herself, her hands warm with the vision. She would need to call Marnie to help pray for this one. But for the moment, she breathed out, "Lord, have mercy."

NOTES FROM SIENNA'S TEA FILES

Elsie Pinkwater, bitter old crow: Lipton tea from bag. Or an astringent breakfast blend. Serve with white sugar. Puts teeth on edge but can be tolerated.

Father Maximos (Max), 58, Orthodox Priest, Monk, Author, Chess Enthusiast: Russian Caravan tea sweetened with pineapple juice or blueberry jam; sometimes a dark Keemun or Lapsang Souchang when hospitality demands it.

Deborah Lundquist, 32, Christian ethics professor, Episcopalian, deacon: Victorian bridal blend green tea— my blend (delicate China green, chunky orange peel, myrtle oil, white rose petals, wild bergamot). Subtle but surprisingly insightful blend.

Chapter Five

Marnie did not answer her phone. Sienna made an entire baker's rack of raspberry thumbprint cookies, enough for the history department and the chess crowd. Baking steadied her erratic emotions, but her soul was still troubled. She stepped into the quiet alley behind the shop and called again. This time, a quiet, sleepy voice returned her greeting.

"Oh, Marnie! Thank God. I need to talk with you about a man."

"Sienna, honey, I was out cold. We walked at least twelve miles today." Marnie sighed, and Sienna heard the bed creak on the other side of the ocean. "Okay. I'm up." The sound of swallowing and the clink of a glass came over the line. "I'm ready to pray. Be brief, though."

"There's a priest named Greg who wants me to love him, and he's married to a beautiful woman who cheated on him. I am 100% married, but my heart is in shreds over Peter and… and Susan, and I keep feeling attracted to Greg even though

I don't want to. I am not giving into the attraction, but I'm afraid, Marnie. You know that makes it harder. What if Peter dies, or he can't have children, and I'm alone or forced to be the strong one when you know I'm not?"

"Whoa, Sienna. Slow down. Take a deep breath." Marnie took her own advice. A whoosh of air crackled the line. "First, your feelings are normal. The body survives by means of a backup plan. But you don't have to believe those feelings."

"Agreed, but they still bother me. I thought they would go away if I just told myself how inappropriate they are."

Marnie chuckled.

"I know. That's not how feelings work."

"Why do you think he's attractive?"

"He's very handsome." Sienna sounded unconvinced. Greg was handsome, but that's not why she felt attracted to him. She had been around plenty of good-looking men without developing even an eye twinkle of desire.

"And?"

"He's convenient," Sienna swallowed a lump in her throat. "It feels base to say that, but he's made it clear that he's available to me."

"Is he, really?"

"Of course not. Even if, God forbid, we were both free from our marriage vows, he would not really be for me. He's trying to use me to get back at his wife."

"And you feel tempted to use him as well?"

"For physical comfort. And there's more. He has an aesthetic approach that I find pleasing. He likes paper and pens and cashmere, and he moves beautifully."

"What does that tell you about why you're attracted to him?"

"Isn't it obvious? I want babies."

"Ugly, uncultivated men can make babies just as well as beautiful ones."

"Hmm." Sienna leaned against the alley wall and worried her hair comb. She felt a warm rush of longing for life before her loss. "Oh." She swallowed back tears. "I miss it, all the beauty we used to share." She continued slowly, entranced by the vision of remembered happiness. "Peter and I would turn on opera and open the windows to the patio. We would sit in the evening breeze with a pot of tea and simple food. Peter would sketch impossible shapes on brown paper, and I would write longhand until the light faded and the soprano died." She laughed when she realized that she was quoting Peter. "He said that, you know, the last night before the cramping. 'Come away with me, beloved, and sit in our paradise until the light fades and the soprano dies.' I want that back." Sienna sobbed, and Marnie listened for a few minutes, the soft flutters of her spiritual prayers the only words she offered in return for Sienna's grief. Gradually, Sienna quieted. Marnie picked up right where Sienna had stopped speaking.

"SiSi, honey, I know you do. You've been coming back to us all summer long, you and Peter, both."

Sienna cleared her throat. "But I can't pull myself back into the light by the hand of another woman's husband."

"No, you can't."

"I guess I'm just sad. I mean, I'm also afraid, but it's the sadness that's making me feel crazy."

"What will you do if you see this man again?"

"I don't know. Be polite? It's just so hard to stay distant." She remembered the drawing. "Oh! I forgot to tell you about the drawing. He drew me with wild bergamot in my hair."

"Lord, have mercy!" Marnie said, sucking air through her teeth. "This is worse than I thought. He's misusing his gifts."

Tea & Crumples

"And I think he knows it."

"You have to pray for wisdom." Marnie yawned. "And be careful. Don't be alone with him. He's a priest, so he has charism that could really confuse you if he turns it inside out."

"Thanks, Marnie, for waking up to talk with me. I'll let you get back to sleep. I'll do what you say. Just promise to pray for me?"

"Always."

Sienna put her phone in her pocket and pressed her hands against the rough red wall. The bricks had absorbed the day's heat, and they relieved her cold hands. She had hidden in the kitchen all afternoon. Surely Greg would have left by now. One way or another, she had to go through the shop to speak with Tovah about the final preparations for the next evening's history department bash.

A swift breeze fluttered the weeds clinging to the sides of the alley just as she turned to go inside. Her ears roared with it, and the wind rushed up her nose. She breathed in carefully but deeply, the way she took in incense on holy days at church. The very action was the highest prayer, the prayer of acceptance and welcome, of gratitude. For the first time in days, Sienna did not feel alone.

When she walked into the front of the store, Bethel Bailey caught her elbow.

"Sienna! Look at you, with flour all over your nice red top! Come and sit with me, will you? Or is that what you're supposed to say? Oh, well, I would love your company, one way or another."

"You know, Bethel," Sienna smiled, "I could use a cuppa." She walked back behind the counter and prepared a pot of her favorite brew. While it steeped, she popped in to the kitchen and returned with a plate of the thumbprint cookies. She set the lot on a tray and brought it to where Bethel sat at a central table.

"So, did you hear the latest?" Bethel began, diving right into conversation and the plate of cookies. Sienna knew that Bethel required no response, so she only smiled. Bethel paused to eat a cookie before she continued, "These are great, by the way."

"Thank you."

"I want the recipe. But back to my news. Granny is moving to Durham. She's given up being queen bee back at Second, a.k.a. Bethel Baptist, and she's moving in with Mama and Daddy and me. Can you believe it? I guess she ran out of things to put a plaque on after all."

"Wow. That's some turn of events," Sienna mustered, trying to find an appropriate response to events in the lives of persons she did not know. "Are they happy?"

Bethel scoffed. "Are you kidding me? Mama has been hectoring Granny to get her hide down here for the past four years. She has no business trying to navigate down a country road with her head barely peeping over the wheel and her walker in the front seat, not now that the dog died." Sienna was taken aback by the emphasis in the tale, which was on the fact of the dead dog.

"Well," she began, "was the dog very important to your granny?"

"You ask me, Granny only had one equal in temper in her whole life, and that was Rufus. It was owing to him that she drove to the cemetery every day. Leastways, at first it was. But now, what with the heat and no Rufus to get help if she turns a spell, it makes Mama nervous."

"Does your granny like Durham?"

Bethel chewed her lips in uncharacteristic silence for a moment. "Well enough, I suppose. She doesn't approve, you

Tea & Crumples

know." Bethel ate a cookie, keeping Sienna in suspense as to what Granny did not approve.

Sienna sipped her tea a few times and waited, but Bethel did not explain. At length, she attempted a way forward. "I hope her disapproval won't lead to family discord."

"Oh, it won't come to much so long as she's at home. But I fret my nerves thinking of how we'll take her out to eat every Wednesday and Sunday." Bethel cast her eyes around nervously, leaned forward, and whispered, "It's the liquor. Granny can't abide it. She's lived in a dry county all these years and accounts her happiness in marriage and widowhood to that fact."

Sienna nodded and considered staying silent, but her conscience twinged. "Bethel, you know that we sell alcohol here, don't you? Not for everyday, but at events."

"Oh, that!" Bethel toshed. "Now, don't you pay that any mind. I'm not Granny, and what she doesn't know about this place won't hurt her." She emptied her teacup and refilled it. Sienna watched the golden liquid pour into the cup, a slight music ringing in the porcelain as it splashed. She smiled. Bethel looked up suddenly and caught Sienna's eye. "Now, what have you been up to? You look like my old preacher man after he came out of a prayer meeting."

"As a matter of fact, you're not far off. I just got off the phone with my best friend and prayer partner, Marnie. She's on pilgrimage in Wales."

"Oh, tell me about her. What does she look like? I want to picture her." Bethel closed her eyes in an exaggerated manner and leaned back so she could peek from under her lashes.

Sienna laughed. "Hold on." She pulled out her phone and scrolled through a few screens, then held it up for Bethel's inspection. "Here's a photo. That's us in the spring at the Plant Delights sale."

Bethel dropped the pretense of peeking and grabbed the phone. "Oh, she's pretty! I love the curly hair. And those bracelets! Where does she get them?" She held out the phone and tapped the image over one of Marnie's wrists. Both of her arms were adorned with thick golden bangles formed with elaborate Celtic patterns.

"Some of them she picked up overseas, some of them she made in a jewelry class at the community college. She must have a dozen pairs."

"Does she wear them all the time?"

"As far as I know. I've known Marnie for twelve years, and she's never been without them. I joke that they are her Wonder Woman bracelets."

"Well, they're beautiful. She's beautiful. And y'all pray together even when you have to pay overseas roaming?"

"I hadn't really thought of that." Sienna frowned slightly. "But yes. We help each other through our trials." She looked down into her tea and held the mug with both hands. Bethel reached out and touched her wrist with a soft, warm hand.

"Listen, Sienna, I'm not going to pry into your trials. Don't be surprised!" she added when Sienna looked up sharply. "But you and Tovah and the ladies have made a glorious place here, and I see God all up in you." She moved her hand back to her side of the table and resumed her tea and cookies. "That's my two cents, leastways, and I hope you know you're worth whatever troubles your friends take for you, and more!" She bit into a cookie with finality.

Sienna sat with Bethel while the latter regaled her with stories of yarn bombing around downtown and Duke campus. A rash of decorated statues started in February when the camel statue on West Campus turned up with a crocheted masectomy bra, and they had gotten more flamboyant in the ensuing months.

"Isn't that something?" Bethel concluded. "Before long, they'll be yarn bombing cars!"

"I don't know about cars," Sienna concluded, setting down her mug after draining the last of her tea, "but I wouldn't mind having a lamppost or a bike rack covered in crochet flowers."

"Well, I'd better let you get on with your work. Thank you for stopping to chat."

"Thank you for inviting me. I needed a little chat."

They exchanged pleasantries, and Sienna stood to clear her dishes. On the walk back through the shop, she noticed the animated conversations in the chess corner as men and women of various ages discussed strategies and moves. The soft rustle of pens and papers came from an active manuscript table, where four adults and a little boy made words on pages. Rhythmic clicks filtered from the graduate student wall, and a low hum of laughter and gentle conversation filled in the spaces between the quiet jazz. She smiled as she made her way to the office.

"We have made a lovely place here, Tovah."

"I'm glad you noticed."

"Have I been that distracted recently?"

Tovah tightened her lips over her first response and looked at her friend with compassion. "For good reasons." She nodded slightly. "Did you just stop in to congratulate us on the place, or...?"

"I just wanted to make sure everything is on par for the history department bash tomorrow night."

"It is. The wine came in while you were baking."

"Did it? I didn't notice."

"Good. Then you probably did good work."

"We have enough thumbprint cookies for the party and the weekend chess crowd. I can set some aside for the sorority party as well, if you think they'd like them."

"About that," Tovah began, worry edging her voice, "we no longer have to concern ourselves with the likes of those particular Greeks."

"What do you mean?"

"They canceled. Said this place was not right for them after all, and that we could keep the deposit, as they would not be rebooking."

"What?!" Sienna plopped into the club chair and sank forward. "That sounds sort of hostile, no?"

"Very hostile. I imagined that the girl who called to cancel had venom seeping out around her smile."

"I wonder what they could mean by it," Sienna sounded perplexed, even to her own ears.

"Well, let's not concern ourselves with them any more, as I said. This history department gig will give us an in with university sorts, and that's a good thing."

"Right." Sienna held her breath for a moment. "Do you think it's because I haven't been here much when we advertised a resident tea master? Or is the store missing something?"

"Honestly, I think the sorority has its own hidden agenda. Look, Sienna, you know I always miss you when you're gone, but you've done well here. Our staff is trained, and everything has gone well when you have been out." She eyed her friend's gray face. "Which you should be now. Why don't you head home now—go see Peter. Take him a cookie or one of those chocolate cookies from Hearth that have made me gain two pounds."

"You're right." Sienna patted at the flour that still clung to her shirt where the apron had not protected it. "I'll go now while it's daylight. I haven't been outside except for phone calls and walking into the hospital. I want to get in the garden. Or maybe hug the dogs. I'm just not sure what to do first, with Peter sick."

"Go hug the dogs, then weed your favorite flower bed, then shower, and then go see Peter. He'll like the look of you better if you're happier."

"Thanks, Tovah. You always say the right thing."

"It's a gift." Tovah held her hands out and shrugged. "What else can I do?"

The dogs were very loud about her entrance into the visiting pen. Pogo barked as he leapt to kiss her, and Jonquil lectured her in dog speak rich with pathos. Sienna rubbed Jonquil's head and knelt to get in a good ear scratch.

"I hear you, girl," she spoke into the dog's large brown eyes. Pogo squirmed and wagged eagerly next to her, pressing himself to her side as if to keep her there. "I am chastised. I should have visited more frequently." She transferred one hand to Pogo's ears and gave both dogs a good petting. "Your daddy is not feeling well. I haven't been able to get out much."

Jonquil answered in dog, her sad eyes indicating that she understood.

"Thank you, honey. I had hoped you would understand." She stood up and pulled two balls out of her pockets. "Now, who wants to fetch?" She threw them to the far end of the yard and watched as the dogs dropped their sadness and became the very sight of joy.

When her arms were tired and the dogs had mellowed, Sienna hugged them both goodbye. "I'll be back as soon as I can." She knelt and let them lick her face, then left them in the capable care of Jonathan, who was clearly their favorite keeper.

On the way home, the dog spit stiffened on Sienna's face in the breeze from the car's air conditioner. The feeling reminded her of summer, when sweat and dog kisses made up what she jokingly called a free facial mask. She would have to rinse before she weeded or her canine beauty treatment would make her itchy.

At the house, she paused in the entry hall to inhale the rich layers of cedar, beeswax, tea, and paint that made up their life. She thought of Marnie's words, that she had been coming back all summer, and she understood with sudden clarity that her life was filled with joy. Hot tears washed over her cheeks as she made her way to the kitchen. She put the kettle on and watched it begin to boil through bleary eyes. Tea meant Peter and home.

When the fisheye bubbles clung to one another and the low roar of excited water filled her ears, Sienna came to herself. She turned on the tap and rinsed her face in the sink, the tepid water cooling her hot skin. For her tea, she chose the special egg blue porcelain pot that made her think of her wedding night, added tea, and filled it.

Marnie had given them the pot as the "something blue" for their wedding. When they were leaving for the honeymoon, Sienna had noticed Peter holding a velum bag in his left hand. Their friends threw chamomile flowers or blew bubbles as they walked the path to the waiting car, hand in hand. She had been so happy that it had not mattered that chamomile stuck in her mouth, her hair, and bodice. At the hotel, Peter had surprised her by making tea while she changed into her night things. He had said there was no knowing how the night might develop, and it was best to start things out on a civilized note. He poured them each a cup, but most of the tea grew cold before they remembered it in the wee hours.

More than any other lovely object, Sienna thought of the egg blue teapot as their wedding china. She retrieved a thin green and pink cup and saucer set from a high cabinet and set it next to the teapot. The colors meant healing and life. She poured tea and turned the colors and memories into a prayer.

Instead of weeding the garden, Sienna sat on the back porch and sipped. At length, a sweet apple smell caught her attention.

"Chamomile," she spoke aloud. The late sun must have reached the sheltered patch and warmed it until the fragrance spread. Its sharp sweetness was like the warmth that kept one in bed on a winter morning. Sienna could not resist its draw. She gathered a large handful of the longest stems and blossoms.

"Peter will like these." She carried their bright smell into the house.

When she came downstairs after her shower, the air was lighter, richer, more complete. She smiled as she picked up the little vase that held the chamomile.

In the hospital room, Peter smiled before he opened his eyes. "Mmm. I know that scent." He found Sienna's face, and his eyes twinkled. "It's my bride."

"Hello, Beloved," Sienna said quietly. She set the vase of chamomile on Peter's bed table and leaned in to kiss him. "Did I really smell so herbal on our wedding night?"

"I'm in no condition to describe it accurately." He spoke into her ear, "I'm too weak to act on the impulses that would call forth."

"You're so gallant."

"I am."

"But are you glad I brought it?"

"Oh, yes." Peter leaned forward slightly and kissed Sienna again.

In the hall, a doctor was paged. Sienna stood up straighter, but held Peter's hand.

"How are you feeling tonight?"

"Am I allowed to say, even if it's not gallant?"

"Yes."

Peter cussed.

"So, better than yesterday?"

"Much better. They're running tests right now, but they'll poison me again soon. If you want to have your way with me, this is your window of opportunity."

"You know how I like a man in a gown."

"Oh, tell me more." Peter pulled Sienna's hand so that she was leaning over him again.

"Excuse me," a voice interrupted from the doorway. "I knocked, but…"

Sienna straightened and turned, the smile not quite leaving her eyes. "Of course. Please, come in, Doctor?"

"Doctor Who?" Peter whispered, and Sienna swallowed a chuckle.

"Doctor Vager. I'm not here to prod or poke, just to say that Mr. Bannock here is responding well to treatment."

"Which means you'll do more treatment tomorrow?" Peter asked.

"Yes, exactly." Dr. Vager smiled. "I just came on shift, so I can come back later if you would rather."

"Thank you, Dr. Vager. I would, rather," Peter said.

The doctor waved and departed.

"You are saucy tonight!" Sienna mock chided.

"I have not slept with my wife in over a week. Of course I'm saucy. A man has needs." He pulled her back down and kissed her.

When she came up for air, Sienna was flushed. "I had tea from our wedding china tonight."

"Ah. That's why the chamomile."

"No, the chamomile was because it smelled so strongly

when I walked outside. It was like it was speaking to me, making all that scent right at that moment."

"Hmm." Peter was conspicuously quiet.

"What is it?"

"Only, the chamomile has smelled that strongly ever since it started blooming in March…" He paused.

"And I didn't notice it." Sienna finished the thought. She squeezed his hand and bent to kiss him again, gently. "Well, I noticed it tonight."

"I'm so glad," Peter managed between an onslaught of kisses. "So glad you remembered."

NOTES FROM SIENNA'S TEA FILES

Marnie, 35, Homeschooling mother, pilgrim, prayer partner. Meditates on the Crucifixion. Pu-ehr poured from seasoned clay pot, drunk from a clay cup or Chinese style porcelain teacup. Rich, strong, full bodied tea taken in smaller doses. Keep back pu-ehr balls for repeat steepings to draw out fullest flavor range.

Jonathan (Jon) Casey, 24, dog caretaker and groomer: Iced green tea with cucumber slices. Drunk from a stainless steel bottle is best. (Thank you gift sent: stainless bottle in pale green enamel. Included good citrusy green tea in pouches.)

Chapter Six

In her dream, Sienna felt the baby kick. She woke up laughing and reached to Peter's side of the bed to grab his hand so he could feel it, too. Her palm ran over the cold expanse of mattress once, twice, before she opened her eyes and remembered. Susan would have been full term that morning, had she lived. The thought made Sienna's throat close over a swift rush of grief.

She breathed through the pain slowly, until she had enough air to move without a pounding head. Then she got up and padded to the nursery. It was painted a soft garden green. Hugging herself, Sienna walked to the empty space by the window where they were going to put a crib. It had a view of an oak tree that was perfect for a tree house. A bright cardinal sang on the nearest branch. By and by, its song broke through Sienna's reverie, calling her back to the present. She tilted her head and listened until the chirping made her smile despite herself.

A tear fell on her long sleeve, and she looked down at the

darker green patch it made on the pale shirt. The tear stain almost matched the wall. Somehow, having the portable connection of tears made it easier for her to leave the room and face the day. She sniffled, wiped her face on her thumbs, and walked to the bathroom. The toilet roll was out, so she dug under the sink for more. With all of the work of opening the shop, plus Peter's illness, Sienna had forgotten to buy many household items. She found half a roll that had been splashed and subsequently dried in wrinkles at the back of the space, next to an opened mega pack of pregnancy tests.

She thought bitterly that she might never need them again, if Peter did not recover. All those months before he was sick, when they had to wait for her to heal, and now that she was about to be cleared as recovered enough to try for another pregnancy, her husband was gravely ill. She picked up the box and threw it hard against the tile. Little foil-wrapped tests clattered into the bathtub. She glared at the random pattern they made and remembered old stories of ornithomancy. The tests were frail as bird bones and made less sense. She kicked them viciously as she got into the shower, not caring if they might be damaged. It was fair payment for the pain they'd caused her. She cussed them soundly when they washed down to her end of the tub to scratch against her ankles.

The phone rang while she was drying her hair with a towel. What if Peter was worse? Panic quickened her, and she answered on the second ring.

"Sienna," Marnie's voice soothed, "I am calling to tell you that I love you, that you are a good person, that none of these bad things that have happened to you are your fault, and to remind you that it's going to be okay. And also, that you are having PMS again."

"And how would you know that?" Sienna yelled.

"Ahem," Marnie cleared her throat softly.

Sienna breathed out deeply and rubbed her forehead. "God, you're right, Marnie. I have been having just a horrible morning. I dreamed about the baby, and then I got very sad, and I ran across my pregnancy tests. I have basically been pitching a fit for the past half hour."

"Sienna, if you needed pity, you know you would have it. But what you need is rest and someone to take care of you."

"Tovah's doing her level best."

"I mean soul care. What are you going to do to get yourself some spiritual rest?"

"I don't know." Sienna sighed. "I don't feel like going to church today. I mean, I want to pray, but I'm tired of having everyone talk to me as though my career or my life circumstances define me more than my prayer life. That's just not refreshing at a time like this, you know?"

"Okay. Let's stop and pray." Marnie left a broad quiet space on the line, with only a hint of fluttery prayer. At length, she spoke again. "What do you see, Sienna?"

"Jesus."

"You mean, a vision?"

"No, a painting. On a ceiling."

"Hmm. Do you know an Orthodox parish nearby?"

"Well…" Sienna thought of Father Max. "I know an Orthodox priest. He drinks the Russian caravan tea at the shop."

"Good. Talk to him."

"Just go up to a priest and say, 'Hey, you don't know me, but I lost my baby, and I'm frightened I'm going to lose my husband, and frankly I find the whole situation infuriating'?"

"Yes."

"And that without Peter, I feel as though my faith is just a series of good memories, and all I want to do is cry, and I feel like I'm whining at God?"

"Yes."

"And that I know God never leaves me, but I'm just too tired of having to fight to feel connected, when it seems as though everyone around me wants something from me that I can't give?" Sienna began to cry again.

"Yes."

"And that I'm starving for," she sobbed, sniffed, swallowed, then finished, "the beauty of holiness?"

"Yes, exactly."

"That's what it is, Marnie. I'm sad, yes, but more than that, I'm craving holy beauty. Before the baby died, Peter and I were flirting with the idea of Orthodoxy. We visited a few churches, on vacation, you know?"

"I remember you saying so."

"The icons and the services were just so beautiful. Even though we couldn't take communion, we went away each time feeling fed."

Marnie was quiet, but a gust of wind fuzzed the connection for a moment.

"Where are you, anyway?" Sienna asked when the wind died down.

"Outside an abbey. I was praying at some relics when I had a laundry list revelation and got up to call you."

"A laundry list?"

"You know, a word from the Lord. 'Speak a word in season with her who is weary,' sort of thing. It just came to me that you were beaten down and weary and feeling broken and hormonal and needed someone to reach out right away."

"Is that really how it works for you?"

"Sometimes, yes. I've seen you pray that way, too."

Tea & Crumples

"My teas!" Sienna half-smiled. "I guess that's sort of the same thing; only I don't always know why I'm making a particular tea for someone."

"If we had to understand mercy before showing it, what would become of us?"

"Thanks, Marnie." Sienna sighed. "I had worked myself into a state."

"Go and talk to Father Max. Find out where his church is, and pray there. Don't worry about your parish or whether you're doing anything right or whether I'll still be your prayer partner."

"Will you?"

"Of course."

"Then I'll go."

"Were you really worried about that?"

"I was. I thought that if I went to an Orthodox church to pray, God would rope me in somehow, and then I would lose all of my friends and be left alone with just some icons and strangers."

"I didn't know you could be alone with icons."

"You sound like Peter."

"Good. Go pray. And next time you throw a holy hissy fit, call someone. Me, Tovah, your midwife, this Father, anyone."

"Okay."

"Now, I'm going to eat some good lamb stew. God bless you, SiSi. Mwah!"

"Mwah! You, too." Sienna ended the call on her cellphone then rubbed the glass against her terry-cloth robe. Her wet hair had wrapped around the phone while she talked, leaving droplets in the camera crevice as well. She busied herself for a few moments, drying carefully.

When the device was dried to her satisfaction, she flicked

the screen on. The camera had reminded her of the photos stored on the phone, and her heart raced in anticipation of seeing a picture of Peter before, of Peter whole. His off-color in the hospital made her ache. She scrolled through a dozen photos of the teashop that she had texted to Mrs. Hopkins. Next came a long section of flowers from a brief trip she and Peter had taken to Virginia the month before. There should have been a couple of awkward shots of the two of them, skootched together so Peter could click the photo with his outstretched arm. Before the flowers, there were only shots of the dogs running in fields and by a river. She sighed and navigated to the main photo menu. Then she remembered that Peter had had his phone on the trip as well. Perhaps...

Sienna clicked on the photo stream that they shared and scrolled down. There they were, she and Peter, smiling in front of an ornamental tree covered with ridiculously orange blossoms. A strand of her hair had blown across her chin, and they both laughed with smiling eyes. She drew a sharp intake of breath when she saw the paleness around Peter's mouth and nose. He had been sick even then, and she had not noticed. But how could she have missed the wan complexion?

Idly, she scrolled through the remainder of Peter's photos. He had photographed her bending to touch clover, her dark hair falling over her far shoulder to make a red-gold sheen where the sun broke through. The way he had framed it, her fingers brushing over the clover seemed transcendent. She smiled slightly, feeling loved. Next came a series of screenshots: a grocery list, a new floral tea blend, and a gift certificate for a couple's massage. She pretended not to see the last one. He must have been planning to surprise her. Before the accident, he had teased that he was going to see to it that she relaxed after the store opening. She scrolled swiftly through the next few screenshots, not wanting to spoil any other surprises, but the logo on the pages caught her eye.

She had visited the medical site often, after she lost the baby and after Peter's diagnosis. The print was tiny, so she enlarged the final image in the series. She slumped hard against the bathroom sink. He had known, or at least suspected. Urgently, she checked the other pictures. Yes. Peter had saved his symptom searches. He had known he might have cancer.

The knowledge hit her like a wrecking ball to her middle. What must she have been like to live with, if Peter had not felt comfortable sharing his suspicions with her? The grief had hurt, had throbbed through her so loudly. She had not expected remorse to hurt as well. She had thought she was holding herself together. In a wave of new perspective, she saw how Peter must have seen her: a workaholic, a busy shell pretending that activity could fill the hollow place inside her. There had been moments of restfulness and peace and connection, but on the whole, she had felt alone, had left Peter alone.

At first, her body had ached with the gone child. It had hurt to be touched, hurt to not be able to touch when her need for connection had come on strongly before her body was healed enough for lovemaking. For weeks, her breasts ached. It had been hellish, needing to hold Peter but wincing when she did. Every pain was a reminder of what they had lost. One day she had been pregnant, and the next day she was not. The normal course of healing was perverse without a baby to hold. Why should healing function so well, go on so steadily and predictably, when her child was taken from her?

She saw that Peter had known how she felt, had given her the space inside his arms to reel from the juxtaposition of pain and providence that had taken over her body. She wished she could do the same. Perhaps she should go straight to the hospital, spend all morning there, and postpone her trip to pray under an icon of Jesus. A voice that was Marnie's and more than Marnie's echoed in her mind: *Go to the church.* She would heed it. Maybe then she would be able to offer back to Peter some of the solace he had offered her. She dressed quickly and headed to the teashop in search of Father Max.

When she walked in, she had to stop short. A couple of cashmere and pearl studded sorority sisters with glowing brown skin had crossed their arms and were glaring at Nina, who looked calm, if out of her element.

"Yes, Miss. I'll get her right away." Nina started to walk toward Lettye, but she did not have to go far.

"Geniece? Sharonda? My word, I am glad to see you!" Lettye beamed, embracing the younger women in turn.

"Hey, First Lady! We wondered where you went. All the trustees told us was that you had chosen to leave Raleigh but remained in the area."

"It's just Lettye now, ladies. But it really is so good to see you all off at college," she gestured to their Greek-lettered tees under their posh sweaters, "and right here where I can get you a cup of tea. What'll you have?" She smiled warmly, and the young women relaxed.

"Oh, do you work here?" Sharonda asked.

"Actually, I'm the manager here. Come on and let me get you a table." She nodded to Nina, who busied herself bringing a tray of complimentary cookies and an ornate water pitcher to the table Lettye indicated. Sienna leaned against the wall by the chess players to watch her manager put the women at ease. Not for the first time, she thought, "full of grace and truth," when she saw Lettye in action.

"Thank you, Nina," Lettye said as she sat with the sorority sisters. "Could you bring us a pot of orange-spiced tea and one

Tea & Crumples

of maple lapsang, please?" She smiled again as she turned to the women. "Now, did I hear you asking to see the manager when you came in? How can I help you?"

"Well, the thing is, First Lady," Geniece began. She bit her lip and glanced toward Sharonda, who busied herself looking at the cookies on the table and avoiding eye contact.

"Go on, Geniece. I want to hear what you have to say," Lettye encouraged.

"Well, we came in here to cancel our brunch this weekend."

"Cancel?" Lettye raised one eyebrow rather than her voice, but the girls straightened up a bit when she spoke.

"It's the reviews. We looked you all up to double check the location and parking, and there were all these bad reviews."

"How interesting. Do you mind telling me what they said?"

"They were mostly about how bad and condescending the service was, and how they disrespected sorority members and made them wait and argued with customers." Sharonda rushed through the words, then ate a cookie, as though she did not want to have to say anything else unpleasant.

"Given what you've told me, I have no wonder that you wanted to cancel. But, ladies, I hope you know that I would never allow you or any other person to be treated rudely on my watch. And neither would the other staff. I hope you'll reconsider."

"You know what, First Lady?" Sharonda began, at the same time as Geniece said, "Of course we'll reconsider."

"Go ahead, Sharonda," Geniece said. She helped Nina arrange the tea and cups on the table and smiled at the delicious fragrances that wafted up from the teapots.

"Well, I was just thinking," Sharonda tilted her head and looked right at Lettye, "I bet that was one of those scammy business practices where some mean person gets a bunch of people to write bad reviews online to make their business look better. There is no way they could have been talking about this place. I was not exactly polite to the server who met us at the door, and butter wouldn't melt in her mouth."

"Hmm. Maybe. I'll have to look into it." Lettye looked thoughtful for a moment, then smiled contagiously, "But in the meantime, can I expect to see you two and your sorority in here on Saturday?"

The girls beamed their assent. "Yes, ma'am," they said at the same time.

Sienna smiled along with them until she felt someone watching her. She turned her head to see Cleotis' eyes twinkling. He was soundly winning a match against yet another young challenger, who was taking his time deciding his next move.

"Good morning, Cleotis," *Reed*, she continued in her mind, "I hope you're enjoying your tea today."

"Oh, yes," he said, almost smiling. "I'm also enjoying the show. You have a right fine manager."

"I agree wholeheartedly." Sienna smiled, proud of Lettye and grateful she was part of the team. Cleotis' opponent made his move, so Sienna held quiet for a moment.

"Check," the old man said, then he returned his attention to Sienna. "You look to me as though you want to ask me something."

"Yes, I do. You wouldn't happen to know the name of Father Max's church, would you?"

He gave her the name and general location. "He told me yesterday that he would be back for a game or two after mid-morning prayers." Cleotis consulted a well-made pocket watch. "Service starts in forty minutes. You can get there in time if you leave now." Sienna held her breath in wonder at

Tea & Crumples

Cleotis' perception of her needs. She thought of mentioning his keen insight, but noticing the chess crowd hanging on their conversation, decided that it was not the best time to do so.

"Thank you, Mr. Reed," Sienna said instead. After waving goodbye to Lettye, who smiled confidently from the table with the sorority sisters, Sienna walked back out to her car.

While she waited to turn onto the road that would take her to the highway, Sienna noticed a dark-clad man walking with hunched shoulders down the sidewalk toward the shop. His body language was so sad that she did not notice it was Greg until the light changed and he was a blur in her mirror as she turned.

Father Max's church was not hard to find. The ornate roofline set it off from the surrounding trees. Sienna walked into the narthex just in time to see three giggling children grab beeswax candles from a wooden box. She stood still while they held the offerings up in baby-soft hands, helped each other open the heavy door to the nave, and rushed down the aisle to a votive area under an icon. She smiled at their joy in lighting the candles and pressing them into sand.

"Welcome," a kind voice said beside her. A woman with a long braid and a big smile stood near a table piled with service books. "Is this your first time?"

"Um, yes," Sienna managed. She felt immediately at ease with the woman and had to stop herself from blurting her reason for coming that day. It would be strange enough to pray with new people without telling them she had come by way of a vision and the divine intervention of a transatlantic phone call.

"I'm so glad you're here. This is the service book for third hour prayers. Everything's in English."

"Oh. Thank you."

"Come," the woman said, holding the door open. She walked with Sienna up the aisle and stopped under a dome in the center of the space. "My children are here." She gestured to the row of chairs on her right. "You are welcome to sit with us, but we may be distracting. Or you can pick any place where you feel comfortable."

"Thanks," Sienna said again, making herself maintain eye contact enough to be polite. She had a strong urge to gaze at the icon of the Savior looking down at her and to study the gentle faces staring out from a field of gold on the iconostasis at the front of the room. She smiled at the woman and slipped into a chair opposite the woman's family. Directly, the woman and children went up to venerate the icons on the stands at the front of the space. Sienna watched, distracted, as they made the sign of the cross over themselves, knelt and kissed the icons, and bowed. The smallest child was one of the ones who had delighted so much in lighting a candle.

Her attention was caught by a sweet fragrance and the light tinkling of bells. The incense reminded her of the happiness in her dream, and she allowed her sadness and hope to rise up with the sweetness into the broad space above where the Savior silently blessed. A man in a richly-colored garment came forward from a side door in the wall of icons, a cloud of incense floating around him as he smiled at those gathered. It took Sienna a moment to recognize Father Max, so transformed was he in his element as priest. When she did recognize him, it was with the startling knowledge that he would favor blueberry jam in his tea rather than pineapple juice. She almost smiled at the way their gifts worked, both brought out to their fullest in worship.

Father Max smiled at her with kind eyes then beamed a smile at the couple of dozen women and two men gathered

Tea & Crumples

and began the service. Soon the prayers were taken up by the women readers at a stand to one side. The chants were ancient and revolved around a central theme of praise. Sienna felt natural rather than awkward joining in on the responses with the others. She sang, "Lord, have mercy" and crossed herself at every glory be. By the end of the short service, one thought stuck with her from all the prayers, the phrase, "For thou art gracious and lovest mankind."

It was that thought that drew her attention again to the dome where the Savior looked down at her from his glory. She was startled when she looked at the painting, because Jesus seemed to be looking back at her. His eyes, which before had seemed a light golden brown, had deepened into a rich chocolate. Perhaps it was a wisp of lingering incense, or perhaps there was a cobweb in the dome, but she thought she saw a thin line of tears by his left eye. A thought raced through her, that Jesus had heard her desperate prayer of pain and longing, and her heart raced in its wake. She closed her eyes and breathed deeply to calm herself, but she had to stop mid-breath. A sweetness unlike any she had experienced filled her nose and mouth, seemed to fill her whole person. The scent got inside her pain, moved it through her acutely, and left ecstatic joy in its wake. She coughed and opened her eyes, to see Father Max waiting quietly before her.

"Are you well, Sienna?" he repeated.

"Father Max!" she jumped a little at his sudden appearance. "I didn't see you there. Sorry. I, um," Sienna glanced up at the icon, which had returned to its usual format, tearless and with gold-brown eyes. She looked at Father Max, confused, and tried to think of something to say. What she said surprised her. "Do you know, Father, how hospitals try to cover the smell of sickness with antiseptics? There is another way. There is a fragrance that actually heals and restores. It's very like myrrh, I think." She had reached out to him without thinking, and she looked down to see that he held her hands quietly in his. It was the gesture of one who understood that the confessions that counted most in the Christian life were those of gratitude. Sienna felt a lightness throughout, and she smiled at the priest.

"For God is great and loves mankind," he said quietly.

"Yes!" she smiled, and released his hands. The kind woman with her children waited nearby.

"Oh, I see you know Father." She smiled and reached out to shake Sienna's hand. "I'm Maria. A group of us are going to coffee now, if you would like to join us."

"Sienna," she introduced herself, shaking the offered hand. "Thank you, Maria. I'm afraid I won't be able to make it today, unless you plan to trek to Durham to my teashop."

"You own a teashop? Wait. Are you the one supplying Father with good tea?"

"That's me. My shop is called Tea and Crumples." She turned and smiled at Father Max. "But I think Father is drawn there for the chess rather than the tea."

"Both," he admitted. "And I will be there later. Maria, I'm afraid I have to miss the gathering today, but I hope you all have good conversation." He made a gesture between a wave and a blessing and walked toward a door in a corner of the church.

"I love tea!" Maria said, patting the head of a child who hugged her enthusiastically around her middle.

"Here." Sienna fished a business card out of her pocket. "Come in next time you're in the downtown area, and I'll set you up with your favorite tea."

"I'm looking forward to it," Maria said, and smiled. A child at her knees drew her attention for a moment, but she looked up to Sienna once more to say, "It was so good to meet you, Sienna. I hope to see you again when we can talk more."

"Thanks. You, too," she smiled. As the woman worked her way by degrees down the aisle with the several children, Sienna looked one more time at the dome icon. Jesus was quiet and still, as he had always been. His stillness and sameness stuck in her like a sharp seed. If he was always the same, then the sweetness and the tear were always there, too. *And maybe*, she thought as she pulled away, *maybe the joy*.

NOTES FROM SIENNA'S TEA FILES

Maria Nicholas, 31, Orthodox Christian, mother, classical guitarist, art teacher. Drinks tea from a glass stein so it stays hot. Strong, malty Assam drunk straight or with a little honey. Would prefer it with English golden syrup (treacle), if she knew it existed. Introduce her to it next time she's in.

Chapter Seven

Sienna's visit to the hospital was curtailed by Peter's unconsciousness. The nurse on duty explained that he had been given an anti-nausea drug that made him extremely drowsy. Sienna sat by his side for a few minutes to look at him and pray. She held his hand, kissing his knuckles. Usually, Peter's palms were smudged with drafting ink or graphite. The cleanliness was strange on his skin, and she rested her cheek against the places that were usually smudgy, to remind Peter's hands of whose they were.

"I know you're asleep, Beloved," she said quietly, "but I wanted to tell you something. I know you've been bearing so much alone recently, but I'm here now. I'm back." A ripple of sadness glanced through her. "I'm coming back to you." She kissed his hand again. "I love you so much. And here's a little secret I learned today." She paused, trying to put into words the compassion and sweetness and joy she had experienced at prayers that morning. "Well, I'll have to work on telling you what the secret is, but—" Again she stopped, lost for words.

Finally, she stood up and kissed him on the forehead, letting her lips linger there while she thought of the sweetness, of the fragrance that healed. She hoped that the action and intention would transfer the healing joy into Peter's body, would anoint him with the myrrh that fell from Jesus' eye. "Surely, Peter, surely you know already. God is great and loves us. And I love you so much."

Back at the teashop, Sienna found Lettye double-checking the supplies for that evening's history department party.

"Is everything set?" Sienna asked, running her eyes over the neatly arranged bottles, glasses, and lists.

"Yes. The white wines are chilled, the food is cooked or ready to be cooked, and we even got in a fresh load of pressed linen napkins." Lettye smiled at the last item on the list, knowing how Sienna and Tovah loved linen napkins. "Cocktail size and luncheon," she answered before Sienna could ask.

"You're a miracle worker, Lettye!"

"Maybe I am."

"Speaking of miracles, I saw how you calmed down the sorority sisters earlier. What was that about?"

"It seems that someone has been spreading vitriol about us online—and getting her cronies to do so, too."

"Who would do that?"

"Does cream cheese and Brussels sprouts ring a bell?"

"Elsie? Why would Elsie spread vitriol about us? Surely she didn't take it personally that we couldn't sponsor her sorority event."

"I couldn't say. But she could. Here. Read this." Lettye pulled a paper from the bottom of the stack on the clipboard she carried and handed the sheet to Sienna.

"Oh, my," Sienna said. "Sounds as though maybe some of

Tea & Crumples

the younger members of the sorority took exception to Elsie's news that we couldn't sponsor them." She drew a steadying breath as she read through four nasty reviews, each more offended in tone and less factual than the next. The final one listed several spurious character defects as the reason none of the staff could ever have joined the exalted sorority they were shunning. "Well, when you put it like that, who needs four letter words?"

"Mmm-hmm."

"Any ideas? I mean, is there anything we can do about these?"

"Tovah reported the reviews to the web admin as offensive and malicious, but they may not be able to do anything since the reviewers all used different email accounts. My friends Sharonda and Deniece said that they would ask their sisters to post good reviews after the event on Saturday, and they will write up their good experience from this morning. Other than that, we could just ask that other folks go on with positives and hope for the best."

Sienna sighed. "I don't feel right asking customers to post reviews in general. How about we mention it to our regulars if it comes up? Liz and Bethel and maybe some of Cleotis' crowd, you think?"

"And maybe the postcard man," Lettye added. "But I agree, nothing in general. I'll ask Jessie and Nina to refer anyone to me or you if they ask about the reviews. Till then, we do our best and hope that it bears good fruit and the shop prospers."

"Agreed." Sienna sighed, relieved. She smiled at Lettye, who had quietly and confidently returned to her checklist. "Thank you, Lettye. I really don't know what we would have done without you."

When she returned to the front of the shop, Bethel was

struggling up onto a pink barstool.

"Sienna! Just the lady I wanted to see!" Bethel arranged herself and smiled at Nina, who had already started Bethel's usual tea to steep. "Thank you, Nina." She turned the smile on Sienna. "I hear that you were at my husband's parish this morning."

"Um, sorry?" Sienna said, eyebrows raised. She had not imagined Bethel as Orthodox, especially given the provenance of her name. If she were honest, Sienna also had not imagined bubbly Bethel as married. "I thought you were Baptist." She hoped Bethel did not guess the reasons for her astonishment.

"Oh, I was. I sort of still am. My husband is in seminary to be an Orthodox priest now, and even though I've converted officially, well," she leaned toward Sienna and whispered, "I still sing the hymns."

"Do hymns count?"

"Depends on who you ask. But since my husband is a subdeacon now, I have started secreting away my Baptist hymns."

Sienna laughed at the incongruity of Bethel sneaking hymns like some women hid shoes and handbags. "And what does your granny think of that?"

"Well, she encourages it, of course," Bethel grinned. "Every time I'm at the house, she goes on about how it would do her soul good to hear me play and sing a hymn or two."

"What do you play?"

"Standing bass," Bethel deadpanned.

"Really?" Sienna stifled a laugh.

"No. Piano." She smiled as Sienna lost her battle with the laugh. "But I made you laugh. Could you imagine? Well, now that's not right fair of me! I did know a little bitty lady who played bass once, but it was quarter sized."

Tea & Crumples

"I suppose if your talent is bigger than your body, it's good to have modifications."

"Isn't that so?"

"So your husband is in seminary? Is he at a local one?"

"No. He's away on a three-week run of classes. Does it show? I get so lonely when he's away. Daddy says I haven't talked so much since I was nine, and if I carry on so while Ben is home, I'll worry him into another religion." She paused to pour tea, then lifted her cup to her lips before continuing, "Daddy believes women generally drive menfolk to all sorts of extremes. He holds me accountable for Ben's conversion. Mama says that she doesn't regard one change or another, as long as, one, we're Christian, and two, she gets grandbabies."

"So, no pressure."

"Well, there's one place where Mama is kinder than you might think. She's ready to bide her time on the grandbabies." Bethel looked into her cup. "Especially after we lost the first one."

"Oh, I'm so sorry, Bethel." Sienna reached out and held Bethel's hand, struck with sharp compassion. "It's such a horrible thing to go through. I had no idea, or I would not have pressed."

"You weren't to know. It happened when we were newlyweds, almost two years ago now." Bethel looked into Sienna's eyes, which had filled with tears. "You lost one, too." It was not a question.

"In the spring. Nineteen weeks. Her name was Susan Rose."

"*Is* Susan Rose," Bethel squeezed her hand. "May her memory be eternal."

Sienna swallowed back her sadness and nodded. "Thank you."

"What have you done to remember her?" Bethel asked,

uncharacteristically quiet.

"There was a funeral, and she has a stone in the churchyard."

"And her life? Have you found a way to mark her time with you?"

"How do you mean?" Sienna asked, thinking of the garden where she had wanted Susan's portraits.

"Well, this may not work for you, but when we lost ours, little Gabriel, we called him, that's when I knew that Ben was going to be a good pastor as well as a priest—I was beat, Sienna, just beat—I couldn't think of what to do with myself. So Ben took me out one night to our favorite restaurant, and after the waiter took our order, he set a little card on the table with three words on it." She paused for tea.

"I love you?" Sienna guessed.

Bethel smiled. "Sort of. Gabriel was here." She waited for a moment while Sienna went through several expressions. "Ben took me to different places that weekend, and at each one, he brought out that little card. Gabriel was here. We made a little scrapbook of me and Ben holding that card at all the places that seemed special while I had been pregnant. It helped me remember our baby's life instead of just his death."

Sienna caught her breath and stared at Bethel, not sure whether to sob or smile at the wave of hope and recognition that Bethel's story produced. For the first time in months, she had a way forward in her grief. "That's beautiful," she choked out, tears welling up again. "Sorry," she amended, dabbing her face with a paper napkin from the tea bar.

"Listen, Sienna, what are you doing right now?" Bethel asked, looking at her with concern.

"Um, well, I'm probably mostly just taking up space." She chuckled darkly. "I have to be here tonight, but right now, I think I'm just a blubbering mess."

Tea & Crumples

"How about I take you to lunch?"

"Um, well," Sienna flustered. She was not sure she should take advantage of a customer's compassion.

"We'll go Dutch, but I'll drive."

"Um, okay," Sienna relented. "But where?"

"Did you have a favorite restaurant when you were pregnant? Any place you craved?"

"Yes, as a matter of fact. Savitri's café Love and Lentils. I could not get enough of her uttapams with Susan. Peter had to take me at least twice a week."

"Savitri's it is. Give me ten minutes to go get my camera and my car and tell Daddy I'm taking a long lunch, and I'll be back to pick you up."

"Thank you." Sienna sniffled. "I'll be ready."

Bethel scooted off the stool with more good humor than grace and set out. Sienna made a carafe of Bethel's favorite tea to take along. She was stashing the carafe along with a couple of paper to-go cups in a canvas tote when Tovah approached.

"What's up with you?" Tovah assessed her swiftly. "You look happy."

"It's Bethel. She's taking me to lunch. We're going to remember Susan."

Tovah raised her eyebrows in surprise, then shrugged. "You pray for healing, you get lunch with a little Baptist lady. God's mysterious ways."

"Only, she's not Baptist anymore."

"To be honest, Sienna, I can't tell most of you Christians apart. But I'm glad she's helping you. If she wants a lifetime of free tea, that's worth it to see the light in your face again."

"Thanks, Tovah." She hugged her friend, then noticed a little bright green VW bug pull up in front of the store. "I'd better get out there before Bethel stops traffic. See you tomorrow for the run-down of the history bash."

"See you then."

On the way to the restaurant, Bethel told Sienna about her baby book, the highlight of which was a glorious panorama from the top of Hanging Rock, with a perfectly focused shot of Ben and Bethel holding a banner with the healing words.

"Are you a photographer, then?" Sienna asked.

"Me? Not professionally. We're in property management in my family. But I have a pretty nice camera, and I like to click a bit. Ben, now, he has a gift. No time to develop it," she snorted at her pun, "but he has an artist's touch with a camera."

"Peter is the artist in our family. I can do gardens and rooms and cooking, but Peter can draw. Well, of course, he's an architect, so he draws for a living, in a way, but he can also capture the feel of a place or a person with a few lines."

"You sound worried about him," Bethel observed, turning onto the street to the restaurant.

"He's in the hospital with cancer. It's been less than two weeks since we've known, but he is already really sick."

"I'm sorry. Do you have family in town to help you?"

"No, we don't have much family. No one close, Sienna said.

"Well, I'm sure they would make a long trip under the circumstances!"

"Actually, I meant they aren't close emotionally. Peter's parents had him when they were older, and they both passed a few years ago. My dad died the summer I graduated high school, and my mother hasn't spoken to me since."

"Wait a minute!" Bethel yelled, "Your own mama hasn't spoken to you in years? Bless her heart! Why would she do such a thing?"

"I was with my dad when he died. We were in an accident, and he asked me to stay with him while he died rather than

116

Tea & Crumples

running for help. Mom never forgave me for staying with him. She convinced herself that if I had run for help, he would have lived. But, of course, he was already dying when he asked me to stay."

"That is so sad. And now you are bearing all this alone. Did she at least come to the funeral for Susan?" Bethel glanced at Sienna, saw her wince in pain, and turned back to watch the road. "I'm sorry. My big mouth. You don't have to answer that."

"She didn't come," Sienna said quietly. She swallowed and looked out the window.

"I have a mind to share a few choice words with that woman, with all due respect," Bethel said through tightened lips.

"She wouldn't answer." Sienna smiled sadly. "I've written her at least once a month since Dad's funeral. You have her to thank for my love of stationery, in fact."

"How's that?"

"At first, I thought if I found the perfect card, she would be convinced that I loved her and forgive me. Then, I tried to appeal to her artistic sensitivity. I found the most beautiful papers I could, wherever I went. I even made my own paper a few times in college. But after awhile, I started to look at the letters differently. I started writing them for me as much as for her. I find a beautiful sheet of paper and say things that help me feel good about my life."

"It's the way you've found to keep your dignity in the situation," Bethel nodded.

"Yes. I'd prefer happiness, but dignity will have to do."

"So you and your Peter have had to go through a lot by yourselves."

"Not entirely. You know Tovah, and you've heard about

117

Marnie, and now there's you, helping me right now."

"I'm glad to be here with you, Sienna. I only wish there was a way for me and Ben to help Peter as well." She nodded to herself. "We'll pray about it, and when Ben gets back in town, we are going to get together with you two. Try to put a smile back on both of your faces."

"Thank you, Bethel." Sienna did not often allow herself to be on someone's project list, but she thought she might make an exception for Bethel's goodwill. "When I see him in the morning, I can show him the beginnings of this project, and that will make him smile. I have a feeling he has been waiting to see me heal for a long time."

Bethel parked, then reached across and patted Sienna's shoulder, "come on, let's get your healing started."

They met Savitri on their way into the restaurant. The courtyard was full of diners taking advantage of the perfect autumn day that had followed brief morning showers, and Savitri bustled with hospitable energy. She stopped and set down a water pitcher when she saw the women.

"Sienna! I haven't seen you in months." She hugged Sienna to her warmly. While they embraced, she said, "I heard about the baby. I'm so sorry to hear about your loss. I have been praying for you."

"Thank you, Savitri. That's why we're here, actually. My friend Bethel," she gestured to the woman beside her, "told me about a way to honor the baby's life. We're going to take photos of me at the places where I went while I was pregnant, to celebrate and remember Susan's life."

"That's beautiful," Savitri said, her warm brown eyes deep with compassion. "Come," she gestured for them to follow and set off at a quick pace into the restaurant. When they were seated in front of a richly-colored rug, Savitri sat two mugs of steaming chai in front of them. "What would you like for lunch? I would like to cook for you."

They ordered uttapams, chole, and a curried goat dish. Bethel got out her camera and leaned over to Sienna. "Now, I wanted to surprise you." She slid a thick card across the table and grinned. "Mama's a calligrapher. She whipped this up for you when I told her why I would be taking a long lunch."

The card read simply, *Susan was here.*

"It's perfect." Sienna brushed the words with her fingertip, feeling the brief indent of the name inked there.

Savitri returned sooner than Sienna would have guessed was possible, laden with a tray of delicious foods, lovingly prepared. The familiar smells wafted up, of spices and laughter and hope, and Sienna allowed herself to feel nourished by the kindness of her hostess. She suddenly knew the best way to start her project of remembering.

"Savitri, would you pose with me?"

That evening, just before she finished loading silver trays with cookies, Sienna felt her phone buzz. It was a text from Marnie. She had quoted a folk tune, as prescient as ever.

When Jesus wept, a falling tear in mercy flowed beyond all bounds.

When Jesus groaned, a trembling fear seized all the guilty world around.

Bless you, SiSi.

So Marnie knew about the weeping Jesus. It did not surprise Sienna. She did not always feel close to God, especially in the darkest moments of grief, but she had never felt abandoned by him. There were too many people around her who refused to let her go; she was never quite able to believe that God was done with her. Still, her friend's choice of words disturbed her.

Why quote the entire verse, when the first line seemed most relevant? She slid her phone back into her pocket and went back to preparing trays.

Liz called out to her as she set cookies and mini pizzas out on the manuscript table.

"Sienna!" Liz bustled up and squeezed her upper arm affectionately. "If I were the type to declare, I would. Oh, heck. I declare!" she smiled. "This is amazing. Sippy cups for the little ones and everything. And good thing, too, because a few of our graduate students have large families."

"I'm glad you like it. Let me know if you need anything special. I'll be coming in and out of the kitchen to keep an eye on things."

"Well, there is one thing." Liz let go of Sienna's arm and turned to dig in a huge lime green leather bag slung over her shoulder. "Can you play this as the soundtrack tonight?"

Sienna raised her eyebrows and smiled. "Big bands? I'd love to." She looked over the CD insert and laughed at the names of a few of the songs. "This is a Durham band? I've never heard of them. I have got to get out more, I guess."

"They are so much fun, too. Next time they play the armory I'll take you. Oh, but you have to promise to wear that red lipstick! It's so retro."

"I think I can manage." Sienna smiled, showing her usual red lips to their best effect. "It's a date."

"Good. I'm going to go find the wine before my research partner arrives and tries to talk to me about nylons and war rations." She rolled her eyes and puffed her cheeks in mock exasperation, then finger waved as she spotted the wine at the tea bar. "See ya."

Sienna returned to the task of laying out food. She had several additional trays of mini pizzas lined up to be heated for the grown-up guests, but she suspected the children would rather have their food a bit cooler. Peter had always said she had a quiet thoughtfulness toward children; it would make her a good mother.

Soon the first wave of students arrived, a passel of children in tow as predicted. The children exclaimed when they saw the table laden with pizzas and cookies and the crayons and brown paper set out to help them pass the mealtime pleasantly. Jessie greeted them, and soon they whirled around her happily, the pizzicatos of their voices answering her invitations. She helped each of them settle into the ease of the shared table, then touched the side of her nose and retreated to the kitchen. Sienna smiled at the children and greeted the parents warmly when they looked up from their earnest discussions of cloth diapers and racquetball. She supplied the children with sippy cups of lightly sweetened decaf iced tea and returned to the kitchen.

Jessie was there, humming something familiar but unexpected enough so as not to be recognizable. Sienna tried to sort out the tune while she heated pizzas and helped Jessie transfer mini quiches onto trays. It was when Jessie loaded her arms with trays and slipped out the door to the crescendo of the chorus that Sienna remembered the hymn. "Come, ye disconsolate." It had a catchy beat and spoke of mercy in such a cheery way that one almost forgot the suffering that made the healing so vital. *Rather like Bethel*, Sienna thought, and smiled.

For the next hour, Sienna stayed in the kitchen, timing food and loading trays that Jessie and Nina quickly replaced with empty ones. She peeked out at the tearoom and saw Lettye holding her own with a red-nosed older professor and a waifish young student. Lettye listened, added to the conversation, and poured steady glasses of wine for students and professors who approached the bar. There seemed to be about a dozen more people than Liz had told her to expect, and the crowd, punctuated with an occasional child's squeal, was noisy. She decided to make a turn around the room to check on things. Jessie and Nina could handle the next round of food, now that the eating was slowing down a bit.

"Are you the owner?" a young mother wearing a pixy cut, trendy glasses, and a baby asked. Sienna almost stumbled on her when she stepped from behind the bar.

"Yes." Sienna extended her hand, which the young woman shook awkwardly with her left hand. The other hand held a glass of iced tea and two gummed cookies sticking from a linen cocktail napkin. "Sienna Bannock. Lovely to have you here."

"Well, I was coming to find you to say it's lovely to be here." The woman raised her voice to be heard above the crowd. "So few places are hospitable to babies, but my partner says you have a fully stocked changing table in the men's room. I was just going to check out the one in the ladies'. Thank you so much for welcoming our littlest ones!"

Sienna smiled and bid her welcome. She tried to keep the conversation short. It was jarring to be thanked in shouts, and the subject matter made it hard to keep up her happy façade. The changing tables were supposed to be for her benefit as well, and for Susan's. She was glad when the woman's baby cried, expediting the trip to the restroom, where Sienna expected the woman would avail herself of the nursing corner as well.

A group of older children had surrounded the chessboard and seemed to be setting up for a game. Sienna hoped they would be kind to the expensive chessmen. She decided just to check in on them since the pieces were on loan. Halfway across the room, someone grabbed her elbow.

"Sienna! Just the person I was looking for." It was Liz,

and she was none too sober. "Great party! I was just telling Harold here about how you can guess which tea people like. Do Harold!" she shouted jovially. Sloshing her wine a bit, she pushed a thirty-something man in corduroy forward.

"Um…" Sienna was uncomfortable at the phrasing and at the request. She was distracted by the crowd and her duties. Straight away, she could only tell that he liked matcha, nothing more specific. It would be too awkward to tell a stranger, "So, you like matcha?" as though she were assessing the sports fandom of someone wearing a team jersey. She smiled tightly and was about to excuse herself when Liz interrupted.

"Come on. Ask God which kind of tea he likes. That's how it works, isn't it? You can tell what people like through prayer?" Liz seemed louder than ever, but Sienna guessed she only seemed so because Liz was exposing herself. People saying things that embarrassed her always seemed to shout.

Harold reddened and tried to pull Liz back toward a table. He mouthed an apology to Sienna and leaned forward to ask Liz an inconsequential question. Too drunk, Liz forgot the previous topic and laughed. Sienna heard her say, "Nylons!" before she was out of earshot.

The children were playing politely with the chess pieces. A young African-American girl in braids was playing a tousled hair blonde boy of about the same age. They moved slowly and stood up to look the table over before each decision was made. Though it was early yet in the game, Sienna thought the little girl was winning. She asked the surrounding children if they needed anything then left them to their game and the attentions of Jessie.

In the middle of the crowd, amongst the animated chatter, some academic, some related to family and home, Sienna stopped to breathe deeply. The air smelled of electricity and tea, of wine and cheese and beeswax crayons. What it lacked was chocolate. She decided to remedy that, and she headed to the kitchen to make hot chocolate.

When she had distributed small cups to the chess children—the girl had won and was laying into her next opponent—and the eye-rubbing younger ones at the crayon table, she had only one cup left. She decided to offer it to the nursing mother who liked the changing tables. Sienna found her at a table near the stationery, leaning in to speak to an older woman in a long batik skirt. She smiled brightly when Sienna offered her the cocoa.

"Thank you!" Relieved of her baby duties, the woman stood and hugged Sienna. She sat back down, and the older woman smiled warmly at Sienna. It was too loud for conversation between standers and sitters, but the woman made a telephone gesture and handed Sienna a business card. Sienna nodded, smiled, and slipped the card into her pocket.

Back in the kitchen, Jessie washed dishes. Sienna could tell that she was singing under her breath, but the tune was again unclear. Whatever it was, the tune reminded her of a hope so beautiful that she forgot it had died with Susan. Sienna had wanted Susan to learn music with Jessie, whose pick up group music lessons at local libraries and gardens had caught Sienna's attention a few years before. Sienna had liked Jessie and admired her talents ever since the first time Jessie taught her to play a chord. But it was the thought of her daughter that inspired Sienna to bring Jessie on board at the shop. She had rubbed her belly and mused that the tiny kicking girl in her belly would take up ukulele or standing bass one day alongside the pink song that was Jessie. She touched the cold steel prep table and suddenly remembered that Susan could not sing. She busied herself for a few minutes setting plates and glasses

Tea & Crumples

into the washtub while Jessie worked her way across the line, rinsing and sterilizing and stacking, all the while humming the tune that tugged Sienna's hope into the open.

Sienna dunked a cup into the water and watched it fill. Wasn't heaven meant to be full of song? Perhaps Susan was singing, too. She held her breath to hear it, but she had to stop and breathe when she swayed into the tub. It was Tovah who called the sink a tub. The thought made Sienna smile. Tovah had a gift for making the shop feel hospitable. She tucked the edges around the staff by calling the wide front window a cubby and the sink a tub. No wonder Jessie felt comfortable enough to sing here. Singing's what women did at home.

The shop had quieted down by the time Sienna had finished stacking dishes. She thought of Liz and decided to check on her. The professor would need sobering up, but it was best to save face while offering a pep-me-up. She assembled a carefully laid tray with a clay pot, clay cups, a carved mother-of-pearl spoon in the shape of a turtle, an intricate bamboo whisk, and a jar of the finest matcha. Behind the bar, she stopped to fill a carafe with steaming water.

Harold looked up as Sienna approached. "Would you do us the honor of pouring?" she asked him. He looked at Liz in surprise, then smiled so that deep roots fanned out around his eyes.

"Yes. Thank you. I would be honored." He cleared a few empty wine glasses from the table between them and gestured for Sienna to lay the tray.

He began to make the tea. Silently, Liz reached up and grasped Sienna's hand. Liz smiled an apology, and Sienna smiled forgiveness. Liz squeezed Sienna's hand and pulled her into the empty chair. They accepted cups of bright tea from Harold when he offered. Sienna noticed that he gave Liz the cup of honor. She smiled into her own cup while she sipped. Perhaps not all the men in Liz's life were foolish after all.

After they were all served, Harold prepared more tea. He handed Sienna her second serving. When she sipped and smiled gratitude, he asked, "How *did* you know?"

"Liz was right in substance —"

"If not in style!" Liz, sobering, interjected.

"Yes," Sienna grinned, "I suppose. Though you're not the first person to fall prey to French wine."

"Look at that woman over there!" Liz thumbed toward the mother with the pixy cut, her stage whisper drawing attention to the frayed edges of her composure. "She blames at least half the Reformation on the effects of European booze!"

"Well…" Harold looked as though he was tempted to take on the question of booze and the Reformation, but he exerted himself. "Surely you don't mean that the wine turned you onto my love for matcha?" he asked, redirecting Liz toward a more sedate conversation.

"Hmm?" Sienna looked puzzled for a moment, then caught up to the turn in conversation. "Oh, no, of course not. As I was saying, Liz was right about it being a gift. Only the prayer is so automatic that I don't even think about it. I hear the answer before I ask the question."

"The question?" Harold asked, holding his clay cup gracefully.

"How do I love this person?" Liz answered. She was looking at Harold.

"Yes." Sienna composed her expression, not wanting to draw attention to Liz's flirtation more than necessary. After all, Liz was correct again, if a bit more forward in her expression than Sienna might have been. "Well. Thank you for the tea, Harold. I hope we see you here again." She rose and left him to

Tea & Crumples

his companion.

The children were tired, and families left in a large wave, just as they had entered. Sienna wished them well and began to gather their detritus. Most of the crayons were intact, but she separated out the ones with tooth marks. They would be fine after sharpening. On the table where the children had sat were drawings of rainbows, dogs, superheroes, a princess, and several teapots. She gathered up spent napkins and used cups onto a tray, and she stopped midway while piling dirty forks. The children had made a picture of her, or more appropriately, for her. There was a stick woman with dark hair and earrings as large as saucers. She held a pizza in one hand and a teapot in the other.

"Dear Miss Tea Lady, Thank you for the meal," it read.

Sienna bit back a huge grin. She tore the drawing in a square from the brown paper and put it in her pocket. It brushed against Bethel's note—*Susan was here.* Overcome, Sienna walked the tray quickly to the kitchen. She set it on the counter and walked to the handwashing sink. She ran the faucet to cover her giddy sniffles—that strange mixture of tears and laughter that comes when relief and joy collide—then rinsed her face with the cool water. She reached for a towel, and Jessie's song broke through to her, bringing forward her dashed dreams for Susan with an unexpected hope.

Come, ye weary, heavy laden, lost and ruined by the fall,
If you tarry till you're better, you will never come at all.
I will arise and go to Jesus. He will embrace me with his arms.
In the arms of my dear Jesus, oh, there are ten thousand charms.

Now that she was hearing the words, Sienna's thoughts of Susan shifted. A tiny baby, no longer still, but warm and cuddled close in strong arms of love. She tried to push the image away, afraid the comfort would only make her hurt, but it stuck in her mind like the caramel at the bottom of a sticky bun. She drew a breath and accepted it just as Jessie reached the final line of the hymn.

Grace washed right through her, sending a tingle of relief from her belly along her spine until her face, hands, and feet felt warm and relaxed. She leaned against the sink and heard the papers crinkle in her hip pocket. Joy and sadness overcame her so that she stared blankly until she felt a soft hand on her shoulder.

Sienna looked up to see Lettye's kind brown eyes. "Hey, there, boss, you okay?" Lettye asked in such a way that Sienna knew she would not judge her either way.

"It's just all too much sometimes." She swallowed, but a few tears surfaced. "I think I'd better go home."

"Do you need a lift?"

"No, I'll be alright. Thank you."

"We'll take care of things here. You take care." Lettye patted Sienna again and pressed lightly before lifting her hand away. Sienna felt sure that Lettye was blessing her.

She walked to her car and sat for a few minutes with the doors locked, waiting for the tears to subside. They ebbed out slowly, turning over the events of the day in the impartial way of the ocean; emotions took shape and vanished along with the salt water, leaving you no choice but to accept them. At length, she felt calm enough to drive. Her phone buzzed. It was an email notification. She tapped through to the message from Bethel. A photo popped up of Sienna and Savitri hugging, the warm tones of their hair and skin and smiles forming the perfect frame to the words on the paper they held.

Susan was here.

NOTES FROM SIENNA'S TEA FILES

Savitri, 57, restauranteur, social justice worker, prophet, friend. Masala chai prepared with 7 spices and blend of mellow Assam and Darjeeling. Or peppery coffee roasted to perfection and brewed strong in a French press, served with thick cream. No sugar, but dried apricots on the side. Warm and hearty, restorative.

Chapter Eight

Peter was awake when Sienna greeted him the next morning.

"I brought you a surprise," she said, holding up a white bag from the teashop. "We got in a special order bright and early from Pieman. It's your favorite, Shaker lemon pie."

Peter smiled and held Sienna for a long moment when she leaned in to kiss him. "Thank you. A perfect breakfast with the woman I love." He looked her over carefully. "What is it? Something's changed."

"That's not the only surprise." Sienna pulled out her phone and tapped the screen. She handed it to Peter. "Bethel took me to lunch and gave me a way to remember Susan's life."

"It's beautiful." Peter leaned back onto his pillows, a tender expression in his eyes. He held Sienna's hand and squeezed. Quiet stretched out into peacefulness as they looked from the photo to one another. At length, Peter spoke again. "When I get out of here, let's go to the other places, too. Let's get a photo of you in the bee balm, and at the other restaurants, and the make-out benches in Duke gardens." His eyes sparkled. "And of course, at the beach house." Susan had been conceived while they were on a particularly memorable vacation down in Charleston.

"Peter!" Sienna returned his mischievous grin.

"Well, she was."

"At least in the twinkle in our eyes, you mean."

"Yes." Peter smiled, then looked at Sienna soberly. "I'm very grateful to this Bethel, and I'm keen to thank her when I get well enough to leave. She has given you back the brightness in your eyes." He kissed her lightly on the tiny fine smile lines that stretched out from her eyes.

"It wasn't just Bethel." Sienna told him about the Jesus icon and the sweet, healing smell.

"So that's what it was," Peter said when she had finished with an account of her prayer for him the previous day. "The doctor who prodded me awake this morning said my numbers were looking far better than they expected and asked if I had been eating beefsteak and liver. He's from the old school, you know, that thinks organ meats can cure half of any ailment." He kissed her hand. "But it was you, bringing me myrrh from a hazel-eyed Jesus."

Sienna chuckled at the expression. Peter had a way of summarizing miracles into quippy turns of phrase. She supposed the ability was akin to his skill as an architect, indicating an entire way of life in the way a shelf or window framed a room. "Father Max comes into the shop to play chess with Cleotis most days. Maybe I'll see if he can come see you."

"That would be nice. I like being around people who dispense myrrh."

"Good. Because I think I might be drawn there, to the Orthodox church." She quirked her lips in a half-smile when he raised his eyebrows. "Even Marnie thinks so. She told me explicitly that she'd still be my prayer partner if we convert."

"Well, then that's that." He kissed her hand. "I know how particular Marnie can be."

"That's one way to put it." She grinned. Marnie had a habit of threatening to withhold prayer privileges if something displeased her. Half the parish had been threatened at one time or another, especially in basketball season. "If you root for that team, I'll strike you from my prayer list!" she would hiss in the coffee line. Usually, when Sienna teased her about praying for someone anyhow, Marnie would affect a sheepish look and say she had repented. "But I suppose even Marnie wouldn't argue with the Holy Spirit."

"Hmm," Peter grunted doubtfully.

"Well, Marnie approves, so it must be okay."

"Are you sure you're not just doing it for me?"

"You mean, am I trying to bargain with God to get you well?"

"Well, yes, that. But also, are you sure you feel a calling there? Before, when we explored the idea, I was more enthusiastic than you."

"I think at the time I was just overwhelmed at the prospect of so many changes at once. You know what they say about Orthodoxy?"

"Christianity, only harder?" Peter grinned.

"That's right."

Peter cupped her face. "You have had enough hardness already."

"We both have." She bent toward him, and they kissed.

"What we need is rest for our souls. I think we may find it there."

"I think so." She leaned back as an announcement in the

Tea & Crumples

hall indicated a code that sent footsteps running past the door. She tried not to think of such an alarm for Peter.

"What will you do today?" Peter deftly changed the subject. In the months since Susan had died, he had grown adept at distracting Sienna from her panic.

"I miss the dogs. I think I'll go to the shop through lunch, then go get the dogs and take them home." She breathed deeply and noticed that Peter's thumb was stroking her hand.

"That will be good for you. You shouldn't be alone right now." He looked at her with pain and compassion. "This is when we thought we would bring Susan home." Even though their daughter was gone, the remembered hope still pulled at both their mouths, making the half-smiles of sadness.

"I had a bit of a fit about that yesterday. That's why Marnie called and got me to listen till I saw Jesus."

Sienna looked at their interlocked hands and felt the warmth coursing through her from Peter's touch. She was surprised that even in a hospital room where nothing could happen between them, he could kindle her desire for him. It was his attention, she presumed, the way he knew her. She exhaled shakily and smiled. The biblical word for marital relations was so accurate. Her husband *knew* her; she wanted to *know* him. Peter must have been thinking along the same lines. He leaned forward with effort until their foreheads touched.

"I want to give you babies, Sienna." Which was far sexier than if he had focused only on the act of lovemaking and not the hoped for result. They were of a piece, as parents knew, the love and its desired fruiting.

They kissed until a nurse interrupted them with a loud knock. It was time for Peter's checkup, and time for Sienna to be on her way.

"I'll ask Father Max to visit you," Sienna said as she stood up.

"Thank you. Please do," Peter said, squeezing her hand. Neither of them were fond of kissing in public. Instead, they said, "I love you," and Sienna left.

The dogs were not pleased with her prolonged absence. Even Jonquil pressed against her legs to keep her from the door. Sienna had to stoop down to face the big yellow dog to make her understand that they were coming with her.

"It's okay, honey. You're coming home with me." Jonquil whined a little, recognizing "home."

"Ms. Bannock?" It was Jonathan, bringing the leashes. He held them out to her and looked on with sympathy for the dogs. "If you need us to look after them again, just bring 'em on back."

"Thank you, Jonathan." Sienna said over her shoulder. Pogo had gotten so excited at the sight of the leads that Sienna could hardly snap the leash to his collar. At length, she managed it and stood. "Alright, y'all. To the car!"

Jonquil walked close by Sienna's leg and bore Pogo's bumps with exaggerated patience. In the car, she whined.

"I know, girl," Sienna said to the dog's reflection in the rearview mirror. "You miss your daddy." She turned to look the big dog in the eye. "He's still in the hospital. But I know God hears your prayers." Jonquil barked once, quietly. It was a dog's amen.

Back home, the dogs wasted no time begging for food at their empty bowls. Sienna was glad that they bought dog food in bulk. That, at least, had not run out. She filled the bowls and set them in the dogs' customary places. Then she laid out the large stainless steel water dish before putting on the kettle for her own libation.

Tea & Crumples

"You two finish up here and then come help me weed the garden."

Sienna spent a pleasant afternoon drinking lemony mugs of tea, brushing and petting the happy(ish) dogs, and pulling a wheelbarrow full of henbit and crabgrass from the edges of the flower beds. When the air began to cool, she remembered that she had not eaten. She decided to call in an order at an Indian restaurant only ten minutes from her house. Savitri's Love and Lentils was her favorite for eating out, but she liked India Palace for take out.

She paced the thyme lawn while the phone rang and stopped in front of the bee balm to place her order. Distractedly, she pinched off a blossom in between specifying naan, a chicken dish, and a dessert of gulab jamun. She twirled the bright bloom between her fingers as she wrapped up the details, thinking of the rosewater syrup on the gulab jamun. Peter had kissed her for the first time with the syrup on his lips. Smiling, she tucked the bee balm flower in her hair and returned the phone to her pocket.

"Okay, you two," Sienna called to the dogs, "you hold down the fort, and I'll be back shortly." They panted happily from their favorite resting spots in the sprawling mint and lemon balm.

At the restaurant, Sienna chatted happily with the man who greeted her. As owner, he was always happy to hear from long time customers. She told him about the teashop's successful party the previous evening and hoped he could stop by. His wife joined him and promised to consult with Sienna on her chai when she visited, which both women hoped would be soon.

Sienna thanked them and picked up her bag, heavy with fragrant food—she wanted to have leftovers on hand so she would not have to rely so much on Tovah to feed her—and nearly ran into Greg, who was standing just inside the door when she turned.

"Oh!" she said, and self-consciously touched the flower in her hair. She stopped herself from looking down at her outfit, since at least the presence of a shirt differed from Greg's painting.

"Sienna," Greg smiled. "How lovely to see you. Are you going?" He was dressed in a slate blue cashmere sweater that contrasted just enough with his eyes to brighten them. He took his time looking her over, and the smile took on a pert edge as he lingered on the blossom.

"Yes, Greg," Sienna smiled tightly. The smell of the rosewater drifted up to her from the sack in her hand, and she felt her heart race under the man's open admiration. It would not do to engage him more than necessary. She raised the bag of food in answer to his question. "I'd better go before this gets cold."

"Of course." He opened the door and held it for her, then stepped graciously forward to open the outer door as well. "Let me walk you out."

"Um, thank you," She said, realizing that he already had.

"Any chance you would welcome company?" A bell rang inside the restaurant at the same time he spoke, and Sienna pretended not to hear him.

He was close enough for her to smell his cologne, a citrusy fragrance that she found pleasing. It wasn't as woody as the scents Peter favored, but it suited Greg. She tried not to pay attention to him, and she was grateful that she had parked close by.

"Enjoy your evening," he said when she stopped in front of her car. He stepped back and watched her get in, then waved when she drove away.

Sienna pulled to a stop sign while she waited to enter the freeway. Greg lingered outside the door to the restaurant, the last of the sunshine splashing him into sharp relief with the wall behind him. He was beautiful, framed in the oblong mirror. Perhaps he was more beautiful behind her, away from her. There were many lovely things in nature, she reflected, that were best observed from a distance.

She and Peter had hiked Yellowstone a few years before. They had marveled at a lake there that was as gorgeous as it was deadly, a gash of water in a rough land. Peter had noticed first. "It's mineral beauty. So different from living things. Mineral beauty only shows up in wounds. We get gems from mines and badlands and places that were broken." That night he had woven her a wreath of wildflowers. His meaning had been clear—to him, she was life and the glory of God. She was the living beauty that stood out against the harshness of yellow lakes and cold stones.

Perhaps that was why Greg liked her. She attracted him the way that trees and gardens appealed to wounded places. He must have wanted her near to tend him. She could feel his longing, feel the tendrils of desire in her flesh reach toward him the way a sweet pea climbs the highest sturdy stalk. These were dangerous thoughts, and she pushed them away. An old *Car Talk* CD was sticking out of the player. She pushed it in and smiled at the banter for the rest of her drive home.

The dogs met her at the door when she got home. They followed her to the kitchen, keeping sharp eyes on the food bag. Sienna retrieved a glazed pale-green plate and set it on the counter. She pushed the Indian food containers to the back of the counter, out of the reach of eager wet noses. The phone rang just as she bent to pluck a serving spoon out of the dishwasher.

"Hello. Sienna here."

"Sienna. Glad you are at home." Tovah's voice hid tension poorly.

"What's wrong, Tovah?"

"Well, I don't want to worry you." She paused while Sienna rustled the wrapper on the naan. "Are you eating something? Good. I was hoping you would remember to eat today."

"Tovah," Sienna said. She knew her friend was loath to give bad news, especially if she thought the recipient had other worries. "Let me hear it." She sighed at the long silence that followed. "Okay. You tell me some good news first, while I load up my plate. Then I'll sit down here amongst the dogs and a pile of Indian food, and you can fill me in."

"Deal." Tovah released a held breath. "Bethel was here today, and she left you an envelope. It feels like pictures. Your favorite envelopes came in, the ones with the poppy design on the liners. Oh, and Cleotis Reed had a stalemate with that priest. The tall, kind one with the black robe and the cross on his chest. Not the weasel." Tovah drew an agitated breath, but she managed not to go on a tirade about Greg, much to Sienna's relief. She wanted to think of Greg as little as possible. "Are you ready?"

"Yes," Sienna said. Whatever the trouble might be, it could not be worse than the fear that grew up in not knowing.

"Today a nicely dressed lady came in with a young man in glasses. Her son, I suspect. He ordered a salad and asked for fat free dressing. Lettye waited on him, and you know how she is. The height of tact. She told him we have the herbed raspberry vinegar, but also explained how we make all of the dressings in house with real olive oil. He chose the vinegar. The older lady, his mother, probably, asked if we had dishes with

Tea & Crumples

Brussels sprouts. Well, we happened to have some roasted, which is unusual at this time of year." Tovah paused and clicked a keyboard in the background. "To make a long story short, I believe they were friends of Elsie. Another two negative reviews showed up this afternoon. One complaining that there was no oil in the fat free salad dressing, one accusing the staff of withholding menu items that were clearly visible in the cold case."

"The cream cheese and Brussels sprout quiche again?"

"Yep." Sienna could almost hear Tovah nodding her head.

"You're kidding me."

"Nope. But here's the kicker. The sorority dinner that was scheduled for tomorrow called and canceled."

"Not Lettye's friends?!"

"No. They're coming for brunch. But there was a bridal shower from another sorority, and they made it plain that the review was what turned them off."

Sienna sighed. "Maybe we can—" she began, but beeping cut her off. She glanced at the phone's screen. "Tovah, it's the hospital. Do you mind if we strategize about this tomorrow? I need to take this call."

"Of course. Don't worry about this tonight, Sienna. You take care." Tovah clicked off.

"Hello?" Sienna answered, aware that nerves had edged her voice higher.

"Mrs. Bannock? Merrill Avery here. I'm the oncologist who has been treating your husband."

"Yes. I remember." Sienna's mouth went dry. "Is something the matter?"

"Mrs. Bannock, is it possible that you could come in tonight?"

"Yes, of course. Is Peter okay? Is he... is he?" The worst

possibility leapt to her imagination, and she struggled to express her fears.

"Peter's alive, Mrs. Bannock. But we need to consult as soon as we can."

"Is there anything you can tell me now?"

"We'll have a group consultation when you arrive, but our concern is tissue damage. The chemotherapy seems to be harming parts of Peter that it shouldn't."

"Oh." Sienna stared out the back window until her vision fogged. "Um, yes. I'll be there in about thirty minutes."

"We'll see you then. Be safe."

Sienna ended the call and dropped her hand to the counter, hard. The weight of the cell phone caused her knuckles to hit at an odd angle, and she sucked air through her teeth at the shock of pain. Her stomach grumbled, loud in the stunned silence.

"I'll be no good tonight if I don't eat something," Sienna reminded herself. She found the serving spoon where she had left it on top of the rice container. She scooped the food from her plate onto the naan and wrapped a piece of foil around the whole. She stuffed the leftover food into the refrigerator and retrieved her keys and purse. At the last moment, she tucked the small white tub of gulab jamun into her bag. If Peter was doing worse, it might be a food he could eat.

At the hospital, a clutch of doctors met Sienna at the nurses' station outside Peter's room. Dr. Avery spotted her first and cut off a colleague. She was not quick enough, and Sienna heard the very bad odds he had been giving for her husband's survival.

"Mrs. Bannock," Dr. Avery greeted her, extending a hand. "Please come this way." She began to walk toward Peter's room, but Sienna did not follow. She was frozen to the spot in alarm

Tea & Crumples

over the other doctor's words.

"I don't understand," she said to the doctor with the dire prediction. "This morning, his numbers were good. He was getting better."

"I'm sorry, Mrs. Bannock." The man extended his hand. "I'm Dr. Felix. Dr. Avery invited me for a second opinion. I was speaking generally when you came up, not about your husband's particular situation. He may have a better chance, depending on his test outcomes." Sienna noticed Dr. Avery's stern look. She thought she saw the older doctor shake her head toward Dr. Felix. He stopped talking and glanced down.

"Please, this way, Mrs. Bannock." Dr. Avery stood very still but for a gesture toward Peter's room. She waited until Sienna had gone into the room to follow.

Peter's color was worse, but Sienna knew there was cause for anxiety because of her nose. She could smell an edge of decay on Peter's breath.

The doctors arranged themselves in grim counsel on rolling stools brought in by interns. A part of Peter's jaw was necrotizing, and his kidneys were not well. They would have to stop the chemo, but the cancer was not yet gone. What followed was a series of what-ifs and contingencies that put Sienna in mind of one of Cleotis Reed's chess matches. He *might* recover from the kidney damage, and he *might* be spared further tissue damage, and the cancer *might* not grow in the meantime, and they *might* have gotten enough of it, and Peter *might* live longer than another month. But he might go quickly, and he might not survive the fortnight, and he should stay in the hospital to give his kidneys the best chance, and she should make sure his affairs were in order.

Peter slept uneasily beside her while the doctors gave the news. His hands were warm, but clammy. Gradually, Sienna stopped looking at the doctors and watched his face. It was more familiar to her than her own, a mirror that made her into her best self. He was beautiful, the light of her heart, and even in his illness, she still ached for the love of him. She would not waste a moment of looking at him while she could.

"We'll leave you now," Dr. Avery said quietly. "We'll know more in a few days."

Sienna waited till the physicians left, and then she kissed Peter's forehead. She pressed her cheek against his temple and listened, wanting to feel the peace that had always come to her when they were together. But along with the harmony of their bodies, a strident fluorescent buzz filled the room around them. It was dissonant and unwelcome.

NOTES FROM SIENNA'S TEA FILES

Tasting Notes: Oolong sample from Harmony Teas.

Provenance: Domestic US tea.

Liquor: Dull, ebony bark brown.

Astringency: Bitter rather than bite.

Body: Weak, watery, even when brewed double strength.

Fragrance: Dust.

Chapter Nine

"You look like Sheol," Tovah said after a quick assessment. "Sit down here, and I'll bring you something." Tovah pushed Sienna into the tufted leather chair and bustled out of the office, leaving the door open.

Sienna closed her grainy eyes and rubbed them till they stung a little less. The night had been horrible. She had left Peter sleeping, but she was too tense and anxious to sleep much herself. If Jonquil had not broken the rules and joined her in bed in the wee hours, Sienna may not have slept at all. She leaned forward and pressed her too-sensitive face against the cool of the wooden desk. Gradually, snippets of conversation reached her from the tearoom.

"So I decided to write a romance novel!" Liz's voice bubbled above the general murmur. "I figured it was about time to make money off history. Lord knows I am not going to make anything through scholarship."

Deborah answered in a lower voice. Sienna was not quite sure what she said, but the tone sounded amused. Tovah

Tea & Crumples

returned then, pushing the office door closed behind her.

"Drink this." She set a huge mug in front of her. It was filled with fragrant Keemun sweetened with honey and cream. The bouquet suggested that it was the top shelf variety. Sienna sipped, unable to resist the treat. "And then you need to eat this. The berries are good for your brain, even if half of them are technically out of season now." Tovah's mouth quirked as she placed a large slice of mixed blueberry and blackberry tart in front of Sienna, the fork sticking out at a jaunty angle. The blueberries were out of season locally, of course, but the blackberries were perfectly ripe and very much in season. One of the early jokes of their friendship was the superstition of blackberries, which were meant to have been kissed by witches after Michaelmas. They had speculated long into the evening about the effects of witch-kissed berries.

"And speaking of Michaelmas," Tovah said, in perfect sync with her memories, "I think we should press forward with the grand opening that weekend." She watched Sienna gulp her tea, saw the conflicted feelings pass over her face. "You should feel free to do whatever you need to do for Peter," Tovah said, cutting off Sienna's guilty expression. "We can handle it. I've been training Jessie on stationery, so she can cover if I'm needed for tea. Lettye is gold, as you know, and Nina is really showing her mettle. She's becoming a bit of a fixture around here."

There was a knock on the door. Sienna forced down an extra bite of tart in case she were needed.

"Come in," Tovah called.

Lettye smiled as she leaned in through a crack in the door. Her eyes were sparkling with amusement. "Excuse me, you all. Sienna, I think you are wanted by the professors. Apparently, the big climax to an important story is waiting for you."

"Thanks, Lettye," Sienna said. She couldn't help but smile

in return. "I'll be right out." Lettye grinned and pulled the door shut. Chin down, Sienna nodded to Tovah. "Thank you, Tovah." She pressed her lips together in a contrite smile. Tovah did not like carrying on, so Sienna left it at that. "I'd better go see what's up with the professors." She picked up her mug and walked out into the teashop.

"Sienna!" Liz called, waving her perfectly-manicured hand. Her fingernails were deep bronze and caught the light, giving the impression of a summons light. Sienna walked quickly to the table and sat between Deborah and Liz.

"Liz has decided to write romances," Deborah said by way of greeting, "and she has apparently inspired herself."

"You mean you have a romance of your own?" Sienna raised an eyebrow and smiled. "Besides unsuitable men?"

"Well, I wouldn't go that far." Liz smiled. She leaned in conspiratorially, but did not drop her voice. "You remember Harold? From the party?"

"Of course. Matcha," Sienna nodded and sipped.

"Yes." Liz paused and turned to Deborah. "Sienna did his tea while he was here." She drew herself up and went on, addressing them in a voice meant to carry in a hall. "Well, I told Harold about my romance idea. Why shouldn't I put all that research to good use and acquire some funds? Women love historical romances. They eat them up." Liz sipped her tea, waiting for Sienna to agree.

Sienna nodded. "And what did Harold say?"

"Harold doesn't say much. He's a man of action," Deborah interpolated, waggling her brows.

"Shush, you. Don't ruin my story!" Liz chided.

"Of course," Deborah muttered into her teacup. Her eyes danced with amusement. However much Liz might have protested that she was waiting to tell the story to Sienna, it was

Tea & Crumples

clear that Deborah had read between the lines.

"Well, I got to telling Harold my idea. When I got to the part about my heroine leaning up to kiss the hero at long last, I realized that I had no idea how to describe a kiss to an actual tall man. So I asked Harold how tall he was, and he said six, one. And he asked me how tall I am, and I said five, four. Which are about the same heights as the hero and heroine, you see. So I asked him, if just for research, I might put my arms around his neck, just to see how to describe it." Liz looked intently at the wall, a besotted grin slipping onto her face.

"And?" Deborah prompted.

"Hmm?" Liz asked, coming back to them. "Oh. Then he kissed me." She beamed and picked up her teacup. Then, into the cup, she murmured, "And now we're engaged."

Deborah choked on her tea and sputtered, "What?!" Then, recovering, "Way to bury the lead!" She smiled and squeezed Liz's hand.

"That's wonderful!" Sienna said. "It's one of the most romantic engagement stories I've ever heard."

"It is, isn't it? I should write it down, put it in a book," Liz grinned. Over her shoulder, Cleotis Reed caught Sienna's eye. He raised his cup in salute to the good news.

Sienna smiled at him.

Liz, interpreting her smile as wistfulness, seemed suddenly inspired. "Sienna, what is your engagement story?"

The smile faded from her face as she thought of Peter sleeping fitfully in the hospital. She looked down to conceal a sudden rush of tears and tried to cover her emotion by taking a draught of tea. The professors were unconvinced, and she felt them both skooch close and hug her.

"I'm sorry," she said, swallowing hard. "I'm very happy for you, Liz. It's just that my husband is very sick right now."

"Oh, Sugar, I'm so sorry," Liz soothed, rubbing her back. Deborah placed a quiet hand on her shoulder. Sienna sniffed and looked at her tea, unable to face talking about how fragile Peter had become. After a few moments, she looked up at Deborah. She was struck with the sudden awareness that Deborah was praying for her. She swallowed again, feeling calmer.

"There, now," Deborah said. "You've had a very difficult time of it lately, but now you're here. There's tea and chess, and we're here."

Sienna was grateful, but conflicted. "I feel awkward burdening my customers like this."

"Oh, come, now, Sienna!" Liz chastised, pulling herself upright. "You know better than anyone that tea is not like that. You joined us at the tea table, so we're your friends."

That drew a real grin to Sienna's face. "I hadn't thought about it like that, but I think you're right." A rush of warm memories filled her chest, all of the stories she had shared over and about tea swirling golden brown and hot into the hollow of her sadness. "Tea and sympathy."

"Tea and friendship," Deborah amended.

"Tea and friendship," Sienna repeated. From the corner of her eye, she saw Nina waiting to talk with her. "Liz, I wish you all the best," she said with as much happiness as she could muster. "Now, if you *Lady Professors* will excuse me." She rose to go to Nina, while behind her Liz exclaimed about her love of the "lady professors" moniker.

"Miss," Nina said when they had ducked into the kitchen, "I have a little problem. I'm going to need a ride home this afternoon." She seemed uneasy, and Sienna wondered what trouble had arisen that the girl was concealing. She would not press the confidence, but she sent out a quick prayer for Nina

Tea & Crumples

and her family. Whatever had caused the proud girl to ask for help must have been serious.

"Of course, Nina. What time will you be off?"

"I'm on till 4:00 today, unless it's busy. Jessie and I are overlapping the afternoon tea time." Sienna noted that Tovah had scheduled the staff to cover things in her absence and breathed a little sigh of gratitude.

"Right. Well, I plan to stick around till then myself. I would be glad to take you home."

"Thanks, Miss. I wouldn't ask, but the bus doesn't go near where we live, and…" she trailed off, embarrassed.

"It's no trouble at all, Nina. Really." Sienna cast around for a change of subject. Sensing that Nina was most at ease when she was useful, an idea struck her. "Now, Nina, I have a favor to ask. But first, I need to know if you bake."

"Bake, Miss?" Nina's eyes lit up. "Actually, yes. I make tortillas, pan dulces, churros, and cupcakes." She stopped and reddened. "But maybe you mean like French breads. I don't do those."

"Actually, it sounds as though you have a hidden talent. I'm glad it finally occurred to me to ask."

Nina brightened a little. "I cook, too, for my brothers and sisters and my other family. My mom has to work late sometimes. I love showing other people how to cook, too."

"I'll keep that in mind," Sienna nodded. "But the reason I asked today is because I need to pass on my gluten-free scone recipe to someone. You know that my husband is in the hospital?"

"Yes, Miss. We have a novena for him right now." She looked down, embarrassed as the intimacy of the gesture hit her.

"Thank you," Sienna said quietly, touched. "Peter can use

all the prayers he can get." She cleared her throat to keep from crying again. "So I may have to be out unexpectedly. I may need you to make the gluten-free scones if I can't be here. Lettye tells me a few customers have come to rely on them."

"Great, Miss. I'll get an apron and wash my hands."

Later, after the warm scones had been transferred to a tray, Sienna made her rounds of the tables. A.C. and Cleotis had paused in their game to talk. Their low tones warmed the corner of the shop.

"Well, howdy, Sienna!" A.C. greeted her. "May I just tell you that for a tea person, you make some right fine coffee?"

"Why, thank you, A.C." She smiled, mirroring the bright grin on A.C.'s face.

"Yep," he nodded, "I find it right interesting the way people can be good at things they don't prefer."

"I guess that's true." Sienna sounded doubtful, as though she was thinking out the possibility.

"Happens in church all the time," Cleotis interjected.

"That's for certain. I remember a fella in my congregation who taught Sunday school for fifteen years. Everyone thought he was so good at it, it took that long before anyone asked him what he thought of teaching." A.C. took a large drink of his coffee then examined the chess board closely.

"And what did he think of it?" Sienna asked after A.C. slid his bishop over a couple of spaces.

"He wanted to lead the hymns. Turned out, singing hymns was what really charged him up spiritually, not teaching. He had fallen into Sunday school teaching one week when the previous teacher was out, and what do you think he chose to talk about?"

"Hymns?" Sienna smiled.

"That's right." A.C. grinned and took another sip of his

Tea & Crumples

coffee. "Fact is, today there are hardly any bodies who would stick around a place fifteen years, so's they could figure out what they loved and what fed them spiritually."

"You mean, the way people church shop willy-nilly, or the way they just drift away?" Sienna fidgeted uncomfortably after she asked, thinking of how she had not been to her home church since Peter got sick.

"Maybe," A.C. considered, "May be."

"Sienna here has been interested in Orthodoxy lately, A.C." Cleotis said, not looking up from his consideration of the chessboard.

"That so?" A.C. lifted his eyebrows. "Did you grow up Orthodox?"

"No, but I find it comforting. I like the icons and the chanting." Sienna felt the lack of a teacup in her hands as she fidgeted. She finally settled on twirling one of the hard-won pawns from A.C.'s captures.

Cleotis lifted his queen and quietly replaced her on the board. "Check."

"Well, now," A.C. answered Sienna, as if he were not in dire danger of losing the match. "Sounds to me as though that's just God trying to get your attention where He can."

"What do you mean?" Sienna asked, her brow creased. She hoped he was not going to call her experience into question. The sweetness from the prayer service was so real and rich in her memory.

"Well, the Lord is in all parts of his body, whether we acknowledge one another or not. The way I figure it, is that sometimes we grow familiar and stop paying attention. So He catches us, right where He thinks we'll notice." He paused to move his bishop again. "Check."

"I'll be," Cleotis muttered through a smile. He moved a

rook, but remained silent, a grin gradually overtaking his face.

"So, maybe I have just stopped paying attention to God at my church, you mean? That's fair, I guess. I've been telling myself I was too busy to go, since my husband got cancer, but I used to be there twice a week."

A.C. glanced at Cleotis, exchanging the rapid communication of lifelong friends. He leaned back in his chair for a moment, considering Sienna. Then he picked up his coffee cup and sighed. "Ms. Sienna," he began, reverting to the Southern familiar formal address, "I've been on this earth for over four-score years, and I have seen a little of God and the ways He loves us in that time, I'm glad to say. What I figure is this: That when we live through a lot of hurts in a place, we start to go numb for a spell. We stop noticing the sweetness in the harmonies or the brightness of the flowers or the way the regulars dress and laugh. While we're bleeding, the color bleeds right out of the places we love. But by and by, if we stay there, we start to come back alive. We start to love the people and the prayers and the music and the place again, newer and deeper. And God catches our attention right where we've always been."

"But is it better, really, to stay there, even if He's caught our attention elsewhere?" Sienna swallowed a lump in her throat.

"That's just the thing, Sienna. God catches our attention after the sorrow because we realize later that he was always there right with us, in it." There was a silence as A.C. reached toward the board. "Checkmate."

"Yes, it is!" Cleotis beamed. He stood to shake A.C.'s hand. A.C. rose as well, and the men hugged across the table. Sienna, still seated, noted that only two tall persons could have hugged that way.

"Well, gentlemen, that calls for a round on the house!" Sienna smiled. She hurriedly gathered the empty teapot and

Tea & Crumples

carafe and walked toward the back. Her heart pounded against joy and pain as she replayed A.C.'s words in her mind. *God right with her in the sorrow?* The thought would have comforted her if it were not so frightening.

NOTES FROM SIENNA'S TEA FILES

Tasting Notes: India Palace house blend spiced tea (loose leaf black tea, orange peel, star anise, cinnamon, white pepper, dried ginger chunks, cloves, nutmeg).

Provenance: Black tea is Assam; spices imported; orange peel house made from Florida oranges; ginger from local growers.

Liquor: Warm brown like cherry stain.

Astringency: Clean bite; bracing, not overbearing.

Body: Surprisingly round; the orange and chunked ginger fills out the middle with unexpected brightness.

Fragrance: Rich, comforting.

Chapter Ten

Tovah and Sienna stocked a beautiful array of creamy cotton papers that afternoon, drawing paper lovers to the back of the shop. A mother bought her little boy his first set of notepaper to write his grandparents. He was the sort of boy people write about, all large blue eyes with an effusive smile. Her heart was glad after watching him stroke the smooth paper and look up to his mother with obvious joy and gratitude.

"Mama, can I even draw a planet on it?" he asked, clearly taken with the possibilities of blank pages.

"Yes," said the plump, round mother with a rich, warm voice. "You may write or draw anything that you love."

"Yippee!" he sang, just as the afternoon sun slanted through the front window and lit his straw-colored hair into a halo. Sienna was reminded of the sweet clarity of boy choirs in that moment, and she allowed herself to grin broadly at the recollection until Nina tapped her shoulder shyly.

"Oh, dear," Sienna said to Nina, "Is it 4;00 already?"

"Yes, Miss."

"Let me get my things, and we'll head out." She waved goodbye to Tovah, who was helping the little boy with his purchase, a smitten smile on her face.

In her car with Nina, Sienna turned to the girl and smiled reassuringly. "Where to?"

Nina gave directions, and Sienna pulled out into the slow traffic. Downtown was flocked with pedestrians for one of the cheerful street parties that had become a regular feature of revitalized city life over the past few years. Sienna watched as Nina's dark eyes grew wider to take in the colorful scenes. When they were headed toward the north part of town where Nina lived, the girl turned toward Sienna.

"Do you always listen to this kind of music?" she asked.

"Hmm?" Sienna had forgotten she had music on. She listened for a moment to the rich choral harmonies from a sacred music mix CD Peter had made her. A male choir was just finishing a glorious arrangement of Pablo Casal's "O Vos Omnes." She sighed in self-recognition. She had not noticed the music because it was narrating her heart. To Nina, she responded, "Sometimes. That particular song is from Lamentations. Do you know what it means?"

"Not really. At first I thought I recognized it, but it's Latin, isn't it, not Spanish?"

"That's right. It means, 'Is it nothing to all you who pass by? Behold and see if there is any sorrow like unto my sorrow.'"

"Whoa." Nina gaped. "It's so sad, but it was so beautiful. I felt like those voices were surrounding me." She looked down. "Or something."

"I think that's what they were meant to do. Church music is supposed to bear witness, not only to God, but to other travelers on the journey. We have to stand and sing to each other."

"Oh! I get it." Nina straightened, and she spoke brightly. "Weep with those who weep, and rejoice with those who rejoice!"

"Yes. Exactly." Sienna smiled a small smile. She did not want to pry into her employee's affairs, but she was struck with an urge to share more about the beauty they had both witnessed. She considered for a moment how best to broach the subject. "Nina, have you by chance ever gone to Holy Week services?"

"Every year. We at least go to midnight Mass. Why?"

"Maybe you'll remember that passage from the song. In Holy Week, we have the laments, and those words are spoken as though from Jesus to each of us sinners." She grew quiet, thinking of how the services would never be the same, now that she had passed through so much sorrow herself.

"I don't think so, Miss." Nina answered quietly. She trained her eyes out the window as they pulled to a stop at a shabby corner to wait for the light to change.

"How do you mean, Nina? You don't think so," she prompted.

"Oh, I have heard it. I remember what you're talking about. But I don't think it's Jesus talking to us sinners about what we did to him. At least, not only that." She blushed and looked at her hands.

"Go on, Nina."

"I think he's talking to you, Miss. About your sorrow, not your sinfulness. 'Is there any sorrow like unto my sorrow?' Because he will help you through it if there is. If you are in that kind of sorrow, then he's inviting you to let him help you carry it. That's why we say it when we talk about the cross. It's so we'll hopefully remember that other thing he said, about coming to him if we're weary and heavy laden. And he knows we are, and that's why it's '*all* you who pass by,' because he doesn't want us to think he doesn't get it." She had warmed to her theme, sounding more confident as she spoke with an authority beyond her years. "There's no one with sorrow like his, because he carries all of our griefs and sorrows." She paused, then turned in alarm. "Oh, I'm sorry, Miss, I didn't mean to make you cry."

"Thank you, Nina," Sienna managed. She blinked to clear her eyes as they pulled up in front of a shabby white house with brown shutters and dead, weedy grass. Though the property was run down, the yard was cut short, and the front bed by the house boasted a row of tall tomatoes in cages, still heavy with red fruits. Hanging baskets on the tiny porch overflowed with purple and green foliage, and pots of herbs lined the broken and narrow cement path to the door. Sienna turned to Nina with a smile that was only slightly dampened by her show of emotion at Nina's insight. "Is this your home?"

"Yes, Miss. Would you like to come in? I'm just going to be making supper, but my grandma and little cousin might be there."

"Oh, thank you, Nina. Ordinarily, I would love to, but I'm hoping to catch my husband awake this evening at the hospital."

"Oh, of course. Then, another time. I'll cook you and Peter my *arroz con pollo* when he gets better. It's a family recipe, but I make it better than my *abuela*." Nina winked.

"I'm looking forward to it. Please send my best regards to your family. Tell them they have a wonderful, well, you." She waved as Nina got out of the car and walked briskly to the front door. A small dark-haired boy threw it open as she approached, and Nina swept him up into a hug. She waved to Sienna just as the boy wrapped his thin arms around Nina's neck and kissed

Tea & Crumples

her on the cheek. The image stayed in Sienna's mind and, combined with the beautiful words from that surprising young woman, served to distract her as she tried to navigate her way back to the south of town.

She arrived home to very hungry dogs. After feeding them, she brushed them and gave them each a hug. Jonquil whined, as though she knew what Sienna was going to tell them.

"Now, little ones," she said, "I have to go see your daddy, and I have to work. You are going to have to be brave dogs and stay at day care for a few days again, just until your daddy gets better."

Pogo barked, and Jonquil sighed. Both dogs cooperated when she got their leads and took them to the car. Jonathan met them at the doggie day care, a deep sympathy in his dark brown eyes. He assured her that he would care well for the dogs, and she thanked God for the quiet, gentle young man.

The evening was waning as she parked in the hospital parking deck. The year was still warm during the days, but that night, a cool breeze blew on her as she crossed the street to the main building. She pulled a thin sweater closer around her and tried not to think of her cold hands and how they might never be warm if Peter didn't pull through.

Someone had made tea for Peter. He was sitting up in bed, a steaming melamine cup on the tray before him. He was pale, but the fragrant tea made him seem more himself. Sienna went to him and kissed him softly. Peter stroked her face with his right hand. His left was covered in tubes, and he kept it under the tray. She could tell he would have held her with both hands if not for those tubes; he did not want to worry her.

"My dear one," she said, and kissed the crinkles where his eyes smiled. It was a statement, not a question. A thousand worries had chased around her mind that day, but now she was there with him, she did not want to waste precious time on anything less than cherishing him.

"Beloved," he replied, his voice sounding weary.

She pulled up a chair and sat by him. She ran her fingers through his limp hair and brushed a strand behind his ear. He looked at her in the quiet way he had. His love was simple and present. He loved her, even if he was too weak to talk. After a few minutes of loaded silence, Sienna noticed that Peter was not drinking his tea.

"How is it?" She nodded toward the cup. It smelled fine, but that did not always indicate with tea. She sipped it. It was good. A thought crossed her mind when she saw the wry turn of Peter's mouth. She raised the cup to his lips, gently, and he sipped.

"Thank you," he croaked.

They carried on silently for a few moments. Raise, sip, rest, raise, sip, rest. Then Sienna fell into the familiarity of tea with Peter, even in this new form. She told him about her day, about A.C. and Nina, and how perhaps God would lead them right where they were. He nodded slowly and smiled.

"Yes," he said. "*Ubi caritas et amor*," he began, but he winced and went pale at the effort.

"*Deus ibi est*," Sienna finished for him. "Where there is charity and love, God is there." She raised the cup once more, and he finished the tea. "Do you mind if I move this?" She asked, palm extended to the bed tray.

He shook his head slightly. She scooted the tray aside and carefully climbed up beside him on his right side, avoiding the various tubes and wounds. She balanced on her hip and leaned up to kiss the pulse in his neck and the scratchy, unshaved cheek. So close to him, his low fever was more obvious. Sienna placed her head on his shoulder, held his right hand in her left between them, and placed her free hand on his heart. She closed her eyes and prayed as she and Marnie had prayed for so many. She let her fears and grief and worries fall away, and she became gratitude, she became love, she became the healing power of God for this person before her, her husband who was like her own flesh. The prayer was one, above all, of presence. Only this time, in addition to the usual sense of unheard music and unseen light, Sienna remembered the sweetness from the icon and the gentle instruction from Nina. She remained caught up in a long amen, and gradually Peter slept. She felt an ebbing away of the prayer that left peace in its wake, and she gently rose from the bed.

She straightened the blankets over him and kissed his face lightly. She was about to sit and watch with him awhile when the phone buzzed in her pocket. It was Fran from the altar guild, and it was far too late for Fran to call. Sienna dimmed the lights in Peter's room and answered the phone quietly.

"Hello?" she said in the low voice reserved for talking near sleepers, "Sienna here."

"I'm so glad I caught you, Sienna. I was just at the church setting up, and I noticed there were no flowers." Fran was a longtime teacher, and she liked to give information so that people could draw their own conclusions. Unfortunately, Sienna was too tired to understand the significance.

"Oh?" Sienna responded.

"Well, I just wanted to make sure that you were still going to be able to do them in time. I know it's late tonight, but I will be here an hour before the service tomorrow, if that would help." She meant the early service that started just before 8:00 in the morning. "I can open the sacristy for you then."

"Oh! Yes!" Sienna said, realization dawning. "Of course. I can bring them then. I'll see you at seven. Thanks, Fran."

"You're welcome. And Sienna," she said uncertainly, "I want you to know that we're praying for you and Peter." Fran was a very private woman, and her admission of prayer must have cost her. Sienna was grateful that she made the effort. It was so precious not to be alone.

"Thank you, Fran." They hung up.

Sienna looked across the room at the slow rise and fall of Peter's chest. He was lovely even in his weakness. She kissed his temple and turned to leave. The next day was their wedding anniversary, and she wanted to make the altar flowers glorious in thanksgiving.

NOTES FROM SIENNA'S TEA FILES

Fran Lehman, 63, altar guild chair, high school trigonometry teacher. Chocolate caramel blend: Keemun, roasted cocoa nibs, vanilla, toffee bits, steeped strong and long. Serve with plenty of demerara sugar and a dollop of cream. Or in a pinch, hot chocolate.

Chapter Eleven

Sienna rose well before dawn and dressed in a long, thickly woven coffee-colored linen skirt, a long-sleeved black T-shirt, and her batik blazer in reds, golds, and browns. She pulled her hair into a chignon and fastened it with a simple wooden hair stick. The mirror told her that she looked like a mourner, even with the bright jacket. She added several long strands of amber and colorful wooden beads and dabbed on lipstick. It would have to do.

The garden was dewy and peopled only by a rabbit and a few curious birds. They hopped away from her when she approached the various beds, shears and flower pail in hand. She worked quickly in the semi-darkness, clipping stems by memory and fragrance as much as by sight. The bucket filled with dark pink dahlias, tall mint, red and orange coreopsis, and the seven remaining sunflowers. She sketched an arrangement in her mind, but there seemed to be something missing. She set down the pail and paced the lawn, searching. The damp thyme filled the air with a bite that cut through the chill. An

Tea & Crumples

impression of red caught her eye in the porch light, and she nodded. Gathering the last stems, she hurried to get on her way to the church.

The sacristy was empty when Sienna arrived, but she was glad to see that Fran had set oasis blocks to soak already. She found the plastic liner for the tall, wide grapevine basket, settled in the saturated floral foam, and set to work. She managed to transfer the arrangement into the basket and wheel it to the table in the apse with twenty minutes to spare. Only the curate and an ancient parishioner were already in the nave, both making their way about their tasks slowly, the man to his arthritic genuflection, the curate to her candle lighting.

Sienna had never attended the early service, so she sat in a front pew. She bowed toward the altar rather than genuflecting and slid into the seat. Graduallly, other parishioners entered and knelt and opened prayer books and put them aside. The hush of soft page turns let her know it was nearly service time. She lowered the kneeler in front of her and prayed the prayer before worship. It had been the first prayer she memorized when she had joined the Episcopal church twelve years before. No sooner had she finished, than she heard the rumble of kneelers moving, people standing.

She stood with the others and reverently bowed as the cross processed past, carried by the curate. The rector and assistant followed. Then the service began. It was the Elizabethan service rather than the modern one to which she was accustomed. She tried to keep up with the unusual responses as the service clipped along elegantly. When they came to the Eucharist, Sienna found her eyes drawn to the flower arrangement framing the rector as he lifted the bread and wine. The tall red spikes of bee balm seemed to glow. There were five of them, bright as Christ's wounds.

Swallowing hard to keep her voice, she knelt with the others, priests and all, and spoke aloud the prayer before receiving communion. A line stood out to her, "Thou art the same Lord whose property is always to have mercy." It was old-fashioned, but it hit home. She began to weep hot silent tears. The same message as in the church under the icon, the same message as Nina brought her, the same simple truth of God's love that had sustained her and Peter through eight years of marriage.

Face burning and wet, Sienna went forward and knelt with the others to receive communion. She thought of A.C. as she waited her turn, of his wisdom. She said a silent prayer of thanks for him as she received, for he was right. God had caught her attention.

The day was young when the service let out, so Sienna made her way downtown for breakfast at the French bistro near Tea and Crumples. She broke from habit and ordered strong, sweet coffee, a plate of beignets, and an omelette. She relaxed into her chair by the window and enjoyed the effects of the early sun on the downtown building faces. A cheerful family chattered nearby, and she smiled at the towheaded children using big words to express small pleasures. Someone moved in her peripheral vision, and she turned toward him, expecting the waiter.

"May I join you?" Greg asked, an easy grin lighting his face.

She was taken aback by his sudden appearance. "But it's Sunday!" she exclaimed, surprised. Then, feeling rude for blurting, she opened her palm toward the seat opposite her.

"Thank you," Greg said. He settled into the chair, sending a waft of warm citrusy cologne across the table. He was dressed in another cashmere sweater, this one deep maroon. His gray eyes were clear and present, intelligent and sharp. He looked at her admiringly. "You are right; it's Sunday. I've taken a leave of absence while I work things out with my wife. Bishop's recommendation."

"I see," she said, and she fiddled with her fork. The server set down her coffee, and Greg ordered one for himself.

"Do you?" he asked. "I suppose I must seem very strange to you, my showing up so often in the shop and around town," he licked his lips subtly, "being open about my admiration for you." He gave no hint of contrition. Rather, his mouth pursed slightly in a sexy pout.

"You seem to like the idea of me thinking you strange," Sienna answered, meeting his eyes. She tried not to look at his supple lips or to notice the way her pulse raced when he looked at her. "But I think I have you figured out. You only want me because you cannot have me."

"Is that so?" he asked. The waiter placed his coffee in front of him, and Greg ordered breakfast, leaving Sienna to wonder whether Greg questioned her availability or her accuracy as to his motives.

"Is this your first Sunday away from the pulpit?" Sienna asked in an attempt to turn the conversation.

"Yes. At least, the first since recent events came to a head. I take vacations, of course. My family has a lake house in the mountains where we spend summers."

"Will you go there now?" She hoped he would. Distance would keep her head clear. When Greg was in front of her, she felt the pull of attraction. She did not like how it addled her thinking.

"No. I have a few projects to see to around town." He looked at her, let his gaze linger on her lips for a moment. She was about to look away when his eyes snapped back to hers. "Have you considered, Sienna," he leaned forward slightly, aligning his shoulders with hers, "that I admire you because you are admirable?" *And beautiful,* his look said.

"Greg," she began, clutching her coffee mug with both hands, "I—"

She was interrupted by the waiter placing their food in front of them. Then, for a surreal few moments, they bowed their heads as Greg prayed aloud the usual prayer before meals. She made the sign of the cross over herself out of habit, then straightened herself in the chair.

"Greg, about what you were saying, about—"

"Admiring you because you are admirable."

"Yes." She drew a breath and decided that firm formality was the best course of action. "Be that as it may, Greg, it's not right for you to say so. Not to me, not with my Peter sick and your wife—"

"My wife has nothing to do with it. And as for your Peter, I'm sure he would agree with me."

"Perhaps in sentiment, but not in your right to express it."

"And what do you think I'm expressing?"

"More like an offer." She poked at her omelette. "I think you're offering something you're not free to give, and I'm not free to receive."

"But if you were?" He poked his fork into a fruit slice and lifted it, considering. His focus shifted to Sienna's flushed complexion across the table. He seemed to interpret her blush as encouragement. "It's not an objectionable prospect, surely, spending time with me. Getting to know one another." An image seared into Sienna's mind of eager kisses and close bodies.

"Stop, Greg." She cleared her throat and leaned toward him, speaking low. "You should not do that, you know. You are misusing a great gift."

He sat back as though slapped. "You can tell?" He

considered her for a moment. At first she thought he would repent. His eyes seemed lighter, and he seemed to be listening. But the amorous expression returned to his features the next instant. "Well, another reason to admire you."

"Are you going to church this morning?" she asked, trying to wheedle him back toward holiness. "I went to the early service."

"No." He leaned back and smirked as though on to her. "No, too many awkward questions. I know all the other priests in the area, of course."

"Of course," she agreed, but she did not relent in her goal. "I had a bit of an epiphany in service this morning."

"Did you?" he flirted.

"I did." She took her time eating and swallowing. "You would have appreciated the flower arrangement today." She looked into his eyes and held her gaze steady. "You're very fond of bee balm, I understand." He looked down at his food. "There were five tall blossoms in the arrangement, bright dark red."

"Like the five wounds of Christ?" he asked, his tone almost mocking. "Is that the source of the epiphany?"

"'My heart is a five-petaled rose,'" she quoted rather than answering him. "'My heart is a rose with five petals.' Isn't that how Mechthild of Magdeburg described the way Christ's wounds had affected her psyche?"

"Psyche. Soul. Heart." Greg fiddled with a last grape on his plate. "Sounds about right. But what could she have meant by it? Hearts don't take lasting impressions like that." He stared into his coffee.

"Don't they?" Sienna challenged. She finished her meal and set her napkin on the table next to her plate. "I think that some impressions, when given the weight of good habits and holy meditation, can transform an entire person."

"No. I don't like that part of her writing," Greg said decidedly. A wounded expression haunted his eyes. "I prefer her talk of attraction, of God drawing the soul to himself like a needle pulling inexorably toward a magnet. Irresistible." He gazed hungrily at her face.

"Perhaps," Sienna said, looking away to gather her purse. "Perhaps a little sacred reading is in order. Somehow, I don't think Mechthilde meant what you imply." She laid a few bills on the table and rose to leave. "Happy studying, Greg." She decided haste was in order. Whenever someone looked at one that way, it was best to run away, especially if any part south of one's head wanted to stay.

He stood when she did. "Thank you," he answered awkwardly. He remained standing as she walked away, but she saw him sitting when she passed the window a few moments later. His head was tilted, and he stared blankly at her vacant chair. His bravura had collapsed, and he seemed empty.

She started to push away pity, knowing how easily it could be twisted into affection when one was vulnerable. But years of having Marnie as a prayer partner had taken hold on her mind. She heard her friend's voice in memory, describing the *pieta*, the pity of Christ. His pity was a stand-in for his great mercy. It was mercy one could see. She stopped trying to make herself not pity Greg and redirected her feelings toward prayer. "Lord, have mercy upon him," She said, and then felt her own vulnerability deeply. "Lord, have mercy upon us."

Once she had rounded the corner on her brisk walk toward the teashop, Sienna felt Greg's allure fade away. Gradually, she stopped thinking of him and began thinking of tea and of Peter. By the time she reached the shop a few blocks away, she was deep into a debate over which tea to bring Peter to celebrate their wedding anniversary. She decided on a top shelf Assam blend with a rich bouquet. That way, Peter could enjoy the fragrance even if he was not up to sipping.

Sienna busied herself preparing for the after-church rush, while in her mind she collated stories to bring Peter along with the tea. She would have to tell him about the flowers and how A.C. was right about God getting her attention. She hoped A.C. himself would stop by that afternoon so she could thank him, but as the hours between brunch and teatime ticked by, neither A.C. nor Cleotis Reed made an appearance.

Without Cleotis holding court at the chess table, the shop seemed empty. Sienna was ill at ease at his absence. She had come to depend on Cleotis Reed not just as a physical anchor to the shop, but also as a beacon of understanding and wisdom. She decided to leave earlier than she had planned. It would do her good to while away a few hours with Peter.

Peter smiled groggily when she entered the hospital room. "Hey, Beloved," he croaked, "guess who called me?"

"The dogs?" Sienna joked. She poured him water and held the straw to his lips. After a few sips, he nodded and spoke again.

"Marnie."

"Marnie?" Marnie was friends with both of them, but Sienna thought it strange that she would call directly to Peter.

"The same." Peter smiled, and his expressive eyes teased her for being surprised. "Seems she wanted to tell me about a shrine where she prayed for me. Hip deep in grass, but the spring that flows under the ruined shrine is said to help miracles along when they are a bit on the feeble side otherwise."

"Oh." Sienna knit her brows. If Marnie was talking about miracles, she must know that Peter was very sick. "And what did she have in mind for this shrine water?"

"She said she made tea with it."

Sienna laughed at the unexpected turn. "No!"

"Yes." Peter grinned broadly, winced, and grinned smaller. "Said it was the best way she could think of to pray for us, what with customs being suspicious of liquids and all."

"Is she coming back soon?"

"A few days, she said. She's sure the tea won't wear off before then."

"Well, that's good news at least."

"Which? The persistence of holiness in tea water, or Marnie's return?" His eyes sparkled in his gray face.

"Both, I imagine." She settled down next to Peter's bed and entwined his hand in hers. "We can use the help."

"Marnie said that help is already on the way. Says you know a miracle-working priest?"

Sienna's heart raced and her brow pinched. Surely Marnie couldn't mean Greg. If he was a wonder worker, his gifts were too inverted to help anyone till he got back on track. Her confusion showed.

"An Orthodox priest?" Peter prompted.

"Father Max!" Sienna relaxed and considered a moment. Yes, it was right there in her image of him. He was one of those whose Amen held authority. "You know, I think she's right. I didn't see him today, which is not surprising. Next time he comes in the shop, I will make sure to see if he'll visit."

"Not that I'm complaining about my favorite visitor, of course."

"Of course." She kissed him.

"I had big plans for our anniversary. Double massages, a fall garden tour, a little pouch of foolishly expensive tea." Peter's eyes closed slowly as he listed the surprises he would have given her.

"They'll keep till you're better."

"Sienna," Peter looked her in the eyes with obvious effort. "They'll come in here to tell you how I'm doing in a little while, and it won't be good news." He squeezed her hand. "I want you to know that I love you so much, with my whole person. Even if we don't have long together…" He swallowed.

"Then let's spend our time right." She pressed her lips on his temple and held his head to her chest. "I love you, Peter. I want to help you be fully alive for as long as you are here with me." They kissed gently, and Peter's eyes slipped shut.

"No pressure," he whispered. She pulled back, worried that she had held him too tightly. "I mean," he opened his eyes a little, "no pressure on picking the right way to spend our time."

Sienna sat up straight and knit her brows in thought. After a moment, her face relaxed into a small smile. "There's always time for tea."

Peter chuckled lightly.

Sienna opened the small tin she had brought along and held it near Peter so he could smell it.

"Wow," he said. He raised his eyebrows, though his eyes remained mostly closed.

"It's not foolishly expensive, but it will have to do." Sienna let Peter rest for a moment while she bustled with the tea. After a space of ten minutes, the room had filled with a warm, malty and floral fragrance. She poured the golden brown liquid into mugs and watched them steam. When she placed the mug on his bed table, Peter woke.

"Thank you." He smiled with his eyes.

Sienna held one mug up for each of them. "To us!" she said.

"To us!" Peter echoed. She held one cup to his lips, and they both sipped.

They had a space of quiet in the tea-scented air before it changed. The door swung open, and Dr. Avery entered. Her demeanor held the directness of one who brought news, but her eyes were sad. It would be bad news.

NOTES FROM SIENNA'S TEA FILES

Merril Avery, 56, oncologist, fabulous baker, hiking enthusiast. Jasmine and oolong tea with honey, brewed lightly but in quantity. Served hot or iced—when she's on the job, hot, but iced when she's hiking. The sweetness of clover honey complements best. Warm, fragrant, healing, relieves pain and eases tension.

Chapter Twelve

In her dreams, Sienna kept finding herself falling into lakes when the hiking trails sloped suddenly, removing her foothold. The splash of her last fall melded with a wash of heavy rain on the windows. She rolled over in bed and reached for her phone. It was not on the table. She sat up. She was on Peter's side of the mattress, and her phone buzzed lightly on her nightstand. It was Tovah, calling early. That must mean something was amiss.

"Sienna, I know the timing is bad, but I have to call in sick today," Tovah whispered hoarsely. "Can you believe it? Mumps. Who gets mumps anymore?"

"What?" Sienna blinked. "Oh, Tovah, I'm so sorry. Of course you have to stay home. Get well. Rest."

"I've had the vaccine, and they gave me a serum or something. Should just be a few days."

Sienna winced in pity at Tovah's pained whisper. "Oh, Tovah. No need to explain. I'll go in, or I'll get Jessie to cover."

"That's the other reason I called. Jessie is out of town at a

Tea & Crumples

bluegrass festival she's playing."

"Oh." Sienna rubbed her forehead. Peter might not have a lot more time. The doctors' percentages were lower than the fat percentages on her raspberry thumbprint cookies. "I'll do what I can."

"What is it?" Tovah's voice raised to a grating volume.

"Peter's not doing well."

"Two days, and I'll be better. I may still sound like Cerberus, but I'll come back in two days."

"Two days." That gave her another two weeks, maybe, with Peter. She knew she should say something to Tovah, but she was too shocked to feel her way through to speech.

She hung up the phone and stumbled to the shower. The sharp spray washed some of the grief from her eyes. She dressed in a soft blue batik skirt, a long white tunic, and coral beads. Then she remembered the cold. She dug in the cedar chest Peter had built into the back wall of the closet and pulled out a quilted silk jacket in a rich berry hue. It was under Peter's cream merino cable sweater, the one he wore while sketching in the autumn and winter. She fingered the ink and charcoal stains on the cuffs, remnants of their happiness. He'd leave blue and gray fingerprints on the teapot in the cooler months. When he kissed her in autumn, he'd leave dust in her hair. Her seasons relied on Peter.

She closed the chest and slipped into a sturdy pair of black leather Mary Janes. The shop needed her if it was to survive Peter's illness. It was painful to be away from him, but it would not be for long. For two more days, she would give the shop as much as she could. Then she would stay by Peter until he left the hospital. She would drink in his face, the strong length of his lovely hands, and she would hope. The hope would be her prayer.

The early morning routine at the teashop went smoothly enough until Nina arrived. The girl looked shaken, anxious, and wan. Sienna invited her to sit at the tea bar.

"Here, Nina. I think you and I could both use some breakfast before we get underway." Sienna set a mug of tea and a warm almond pastry in front of both of them. She ate quietly for a few minutes, observing Nina.

"Miss, I may need a ride home again later." Nina kept her eyes trained on the pastry.

"That shouldn't be a problem, but I won't be able to leave until we close at 6:00. Is that okay?"

"Sure. But I may have a ride already. I'm just not sure." The girl worried her lower lip.

"Is there anything that I need to know about, Nina?"

"I'm not sure, Miss. My sister may have had something come up, is all. I'm nervous for her." She was silent for a long space. She quickly finished her pastry and drained her mug and made to get up.

"Nina?" Sienna stopped her. "Would you like us to pray about it? You don't have to say what it is, but we might do better today if we ask for help."

Nina nodded, and Sienna reached for her hand. She breathed deeply and relaxed into the space within that was a prayer room, where she could see people in the light of God's love. She sensed the anxiety of pursuit. "Oh Lord God our protector, hide Nina and her sister and family under the shadow of your wings. Keep them safe from those who pursue them, and send the help they need when they need it. Give them a sense of your comfort and presence, through Jesus Christ our Lord. We thank you that this is so. Amen."

"Thanks, Miss," Nina said. She sniffled and wiped her eyes, then took their plates to the back.

Tea & Crumples

Sienna sighed, looking around the empty tearoom. Everything was clean and neat, but she walked to the manuscript table anyway, damp cloth in hand. It was clean, not even a sticky spot in sight. Her employees were very thorough. She retrieved a small pot of beeswax and orange oil furniture polish and rubbed the old refectory wood into a fragrant shine. Then she rearranged the pens in the central container, setting each of them nib down. Satisfied, she nodded at the table and went to check the tea stocks. The bins were all amply supplied, the clean teapots lined up, the hot water dispensers at their proper temperatures. Again, she noted the efficiency of her team.

The thought crossed her mind, "I'm not needed here except as an extra pair of hands," but she caught it by the tail as it passed. "No," she said to herself. "That's just guilt speaking because I have not been here much. The systems I set up are working well, and my team is doing excellent work. That's cause to rejoice, not berate myself."

Nina returned from the kitchen and slipped a tray of fresh tea sandwiches into the case. "Are we ready to open, Miss?"

"Yes!" Sienna said, noting the time on the clock. It was almost 8:00, and regulars would be along soon. "Thanks, Nina. Would you like to open the door?"

"Sure," she said, brightening at the small but authoritative responsibility. She walked quickly to the door and unlatched the deadbolts. She opened the roll shade, revealing a warm brown and red logo of a teacup with a feather quill across its saucer. "Tea & Crumples" marched above the logo in an Art Deco print. Nina flipped a carved wooden *Open* sign forward, just as the warm brown smile of Cleotis Reed, kindly smiling, filled the window between the logo and store name.

"Good morning, Mr. Reed," Nina said. She stood back,

holding the door for him.

"Good morning, Miss Nina," Cleotis answered. He doffed a tweed hat that he had clearly worn against the cold and held it in one hand at his side. He was completely still as he looked at the young woman, giving her his full attention. "And how is my favorite tea hostess this morning?"

"Well enough, Mr. Reed," Nina said. Her answering smile did not quite wipe the anxiety from her eyes and forehead. Standing near the tea bar, Sienna was sure Cleotis Reed noticed.

"Hmmph." Cleotis smiled back at her, a kind and gracious smile that seemed like a dose of strong blessing. It was contagious. Sienna felt her face stretch into a smile, and she saw the tension ease out of the girl's shoulders and face. "Well, praise the Lord!" Cleotis Reed said, and he went toward his chair at the chess table.

Sienna brought him his usual tea, and she added a few small chocolate wafers to the saucer as an afterthought. She placed them on Cleotis' right.

"Well, what's all this?" Cleotis asked, noticing the cookies straight away.

"Nina made them. They're wonderful. Like the chocolate part of Oreos, but better, and much healthier for you."

He ate a cookie and raised his eyebrows in theatrical appreciation. "These are wonderful, Miss Nina," he said toward the girl, who had lingered near the door after his entrance benediction.

"Thank you, Mr. Reed," she answered. She blushed a little and asked, "Will Mr. Whitmer be here today? I made those for him. He told me he liked nothing better than the cookie part of Oreos, and it was a shame they didn't make them separate."

"I don't believe we'll be seeing A.C. anytime soon, at least you ladies won't. I might see him again sooner than most."

Sienna and Nina stood near, confused expressions playing over their faces.

"A.C.'s with the Lord now," Cleotis said with a solemn nod. "I was at his funeral yesterday."

"Oh, no!" Sienna said, and she sank into the chair opposite Cleotis at the chess table. "But I wanted to tell him thanks, for what he said to me last week."

"I'm sure he knows," Cleotis said, his somber brown eyes a little darker with tears.

"I'm so sorry for your loss, Cleotis," Sienna said. "He was your oldest friend."

"Yes, that he was." Cleotis pressed the tea in the small pot next to him and poured out a cup. Nina, who had bustled away at the announcement, returned suddenly and placed a mug and teapot in front of Sienna.

"Thank you, Nina," Sienna said. She reached out for the girl's hand and squeezed. "Please, while we're the only ones here, would you like to sit awhile, too?"

Nina nodded and pulled up a chair. At length, Cleotis looked toward her again.

"That was very thoughtful of you, Miss Nina, making those cookies. And if I might make free to speculate, I'd say it was inspired, too. Here I am, coming for my morning refreshment without A.C. for the first time in five decades, and I get a reminder of his ways. These cookies may not do A.C. much good right now, but they would have made him happy, and that makes his passing easier on me."

"Five decades. So you met in the 60's?" Sienna asked. "You must have been some friends to get together in those days!"

"That's right. In fact, though not many knew so, A.C. and I were kin, related by marriage. His brother and my sister were married in 1964. When they both died in a house fire, A.C. and his family were the only white people at the joint funeral."

"A house fire?" Sienna asked, brows knit with doubt.

"To own the truth, it was arson. They were locked in, trapped by men with guns, and then burned up. Seems some people took exception to their union."

"The Klan?"

He nodded. "After the funeral, my wife and I invited A.C. and his wife and children over for the luncheon, and he saw my chess board. We had our first game right then and there. Had to push aside quite a few hams and plates of biscuits to do it, but we played together well enough."

"Did you win?" Nina asked.

"Of course." Cleotis smiled a little. "But I could see that he would be a good opponent. Didn't think like me, but had a good heart. And I was right about half of that."

"You did think alike after all?" Nina asked, leaning in.

"After all, I believe we did."

"He certainly had a way of sharing his thoughts," Sienna said, a sad smile on her face. "As unassuming as if he was talking about the weather, but in reality he was spreading the grace of God."

Cleotis nodded. "He certainly had a knack for speaking his mind. He would truck no unkindness, either. I have come to lean on his good sense like a walking stick. Come to think of it, I suppose I've thought of him as God's way of keeping me in line, one of the manifestations of God's shepherd staff." He looked down into the murky swirls of his teacup, then raised his face, brightening. "No telling what kind of mischief I'll get up to now."

"He's built in now," Nina said. "You don't have to worry about acting out. True friends are like trees that grow side by

Tea & Crumples

side. Even when you die you share the same roots."

Sienna raised her eyebrows at the girl's insight. The bell over the door tinkled, and Sienna rose to meet Bethel Bailey, who was already clipping along to the tea bar. "You stay, Nina. Y'all reminisce for a bit. I'll see to Bethel."

Bethel fidgeted with her peach tweed jacket, whose boxy cut looked a little too high for Bethel's stout frame. She fiddled with a brooch as Sienna came around the bar.

"This will not lay right!" Bethel said, looking at Sienna with knitted brows. "Granny insisted on me wearing this— contraption—today!" She gestured to take in her unflattering jacket, "Her friend Ms. Betsy is stopping by the office, and Granny told her years ago that the reason she never wore the brooch Ms. Betsy gave her was that I had fallen in love with the only jacket that went with it and insisted on having it for my own." She blew a puff of air out through her lips and shook her head. "I'm going to need tea today. Lots of tea." She leaned forward toward Sienna, who was already laying out the tea things in front of Bethel. Bethel's eyes narrowed and she grasped Sienna's hand as the tea mistress set out a clean silver spoon in front of her. "What is it?"

Sienna looked up into Bethel's kind eyes and almost burst into tears. "Peter's not doing well. He may not make it. They've told me to expect to say goodbye in a couple of weeks."

"Oh, Sienna!" Bethel gasped. She held tightly to the hand she had captured and looked at her, an expression of compassion transforming her features. After several seconds, she sighed and released her. "And here I forgot to ask Father Max about visiting y'all."

"You've already done so much to help me feel better about life, Bethel. Don't beat yourself up. Besides, I can ask Father Max to come see Peter when he comes in to play chess with

Cleotis later."

"So you're not mad at God?" Bethel asked. Her expression was open and bright, as though she had asked a simple question.

"Um, no," Sienna said, eyebrows raised in surprise. "I suppose I hadn't considered it. Don't give me too much credit, though," she smiled demurely. "I'm still a bit shocked."

"I don't know," Bethel said. She removed the leaf basket from her tea, set it on the saucer next to the teapot, and replaced the lid. "In my experience, it doesn't take much to get mad at God."

"What do you mean?" Sienna held her breath a moment, then went on, "I don't really think of you as someone who gets mad at God."

"Oh, I fuss at God plenty. But that's not what I mean. There are some people who get in a hard situation, and straightaway they start hollering. Why did God allow such and such to happen, and how could there be a God if there's this horrible thing in the world? And so on."

"So, more like having done with God altogether than getting angry with Him."

"I guess so. I hear so many people saying they don't understand how God could do such and such to them, and then maybe they don't believe in Him anymore. I'm glad that's not where you're going. That's a hard place to walk."

"Yes," Sienna said. She watched Bethel pour her tea before continuing. "But those people really think they do understand God, and what they think they understand, they just don't like. Only, what they think they understand is not God at all."

Bethel nodded.

Sienna leaned forward a little and lowered her voice. "You know what is one good thing about what I've been through,

Bethel? I know that God doesn't leave us in hell. If I have to go through hell again, I want Jesus with me." She and Bethel exchanged the pained look of those who have lost.

Bethel stood on the rail under the tea bar and leaned forward, hugging Sienna tightly over the expanse of tea things. There was a metallic thunk and a splash.

"Oh, shoot!" Bethel pulled back and looked down. She retrieved the brooch from where it had fallen into her half-full teacup. She set it on a napkin. "I think I'm going to need some more tea."

Sienna replaced the cup with a fresh one and eyed the brooch on the damp napkin. She gasped. "What *is* that?" She shuddered.

"I know," Bethel answered darkly. "Granny obviously felt the same way as you, or she would not have gone to such lengths to foist it off on me. But to answer your question, it's a tarantula. Ms. Betsy is a retired science teacher, and she thought this brooch—which is modeled on a real spider, if spiders could be gold with crystal green eyes—was just gorgeous.

"Well," Sienna said, wiping up the remaining mess from the splash, "bless her heart."

Bethel laughed, sputtering tea into her cup. "I'm glad at least it's done one good deed today—distracting you a bit."

Several grad students in corduroy and cotton filed through the door and headed toward the long booth seats with power outlets for their computers. Sienna smiled at Bethel. "I expect I'll see you again today," she said. "But for now, I have to go caffeinate the next great minds of academia."

Nina bustled into action as well, and between the two of them, Sienna and Nina got everyone settled quickly. A few more folks trickled in over the next hour, including Sienna's favorite stranger, a bearded man who wrote piles of postcards and notes at the manuscript table. Even though she was a little worried that the shop was not more full during the prime caffeination hours of early morning, she was glad to have the opportunity to meet the letter-writing man. He ordered a pot of citrusy green tea and a spicy brioche roll with candied fruit mixed into the dough.

"Here you are," Sienna said, setting the items to the side within his reach.

"Thank you," he said, smiling. "I don't believe we've met. I'm Michael."

"Sienna. I'm one of the owners here. I've seen you, but haven't had a chance to stop by before." She glanced at his notepaper, neatly stacked with a book of stamps and one of the rollerballs from the jar. "I'm glad you like the pens. They're the kind I use when I write letters."

"Yes," he said, and held up the pen, "I'm always leaving the house without one. I love the table here. It's perfect for keeping up with friends."

"You must write a lot." Sienna smiled.

"I have a lot of friends, all over the world. It comes with being a pilgrim." His blue eyes were clear and friendly, and his expression put her in mind of men from past centuries who followed long roads in search of God.

"A pilgrim?" she smiled. "I have a friend who's a pilgrim, too. When she gets back from her latest adventure, I'll have to introduce you. Y'all can talk about all the places you've found God."

He laughed. "I would like that, thank you. But you know, I haven't found God on my pilgrimages, or at least not in the destinations."

"No?" She looked again at the pile of notecards and noticed

a second pile beyond them, letters addressed to Michael with postmarks from all over the world. He followed her gaze and smiled.

"Yes, I've met a lot of fellow pilgrims. That's just the thing. No matter where I go, I'm always being surprised to find that God is walking with me all along." He broke into a grin that took over his broad face.

Sienna smiled, too, and she felt her heart lift. "Well said, Michael. And well met." She nodded again in parting and went to see to a lately-arrived graduate student.

The morning passed quickly with a steady stream of customers. Sienna and Nina worked behind the scenes and managed to spare a few extra seconds of welcome for each person who arrived. Even so, Sienna let out a deep sigh of relief when Lettye walked in just before noon. Lettye was swift to administer gracious welcome and service, and Nina seemed energized by the lunch rush. Sienna seized the opportunity to work in the kitchen, heating dishes, cleaning, and baking.

It was a relief to let her face relax from the forced expression of politeness. She felt her mouth fall into the too familiar lines of grief. The pull of the frown that overcame her when she was alone reminded her forcibly of the weeks after they lost Susan. How many hours had passed while the sun failed to penetrate her eyes? She had stared fixedly at the memory child, warm from her body but so still. Her mind was pulled in equal measures by awe and love at the beautiful girl in her arms and the shocking pain of loss. The teashop had saved her then, its need for her busy hands pulling her along until she saw that she could live despite the implacability of her grief.

But now it was not a help to her. Peter was still alive, and the shop was keeping her from him. She glared at the tea mug in her hand, a fine bone china confection of roses. Its beauty was obscene when Peter was dying alone. Sienna raised the mug above her head, opened her fingers, and watched it smash into pieces on the concrete floor. Belatedly, she noticed the noise. She looked up just in time to see Nina, who was rushing to find out what had happened.

"It's okay, Nina. Just averting the evil eye." She glanced down at the shards of china under the sink. "I'll clean it up." She pulled her face into what she hoped was a comforting smile.

"No, Miss, I'll get it," Nina said, already moving the broom across the floor as she came toward Sienna. "You have a visitor. A lady. She's asking for you. I think she said her name was Marnie?"

Hope washed over Sienna as she started toward the door to the front of the shop, but it did not last long. She remembered Marnie's words the last time her family was disintegrating. Marnie had been so sure that Susan would live. Anger jolted through Sienna, and she swallowed it in a heady rush as she stepped behind the tea bar. There was Marnie, glowing as usual, wearing a new set of silver bangles patterned in Celtic knots. She smiled when Sienna walked in, but the expression turned wary as she took in her friend's expression.

"Sienna! I'm so glad to see you. We just got in, and I came right over." She leaned forward for a hug, which Sienna returned stiffly.

"Why, Marnie?" Sienna asked without preamble. Her voice was almost a whisper, but filled with the low throb of pain that made it audible to Marnie over the clatter and murmurings of the shop. "Why did you tell me Susan would live?"

Marnie's brow creased with compassion, and she stared at Sienna for a moment, her mouth agape. She blew out a breath and glanced around the room. There was a table for two apart from the others, and her eyes lit on it. "Could we have some tea and sit? Then I'll tell you whatever you'd like to know."

Sienna nodded and started to put together a tray with two pots—a small clay one for Marnie's pu-erh and a glazed brown pot for the Keemun Sienna preferred and added a plate of sandwiches and almond pastries. She carried the tray to the table where Marnie was already seated.

"Thank you," Marnie said. She piled her plate with food and poured a cup. "How's Peter?" she asked. She lifted the mug so that the steam rose up before her face, and she inhaled deeply. But she did not take her eyes from Sienna.

"He's dying," Sienna said, returning Marnie's gaze. "But Tovah and Jessie are out, so I had to be here today." She poured a cup of tea and readied it perfunctorily, sloshing the cream a bit so that a drop made its way slowly down the side of her cup.

"I see." Marnie drew a deep breath and released it. She ate a tea sandwich, drank half her cup of tea, and looked around the shop. "I saw this. Before. The shop full of life and love and hospitality." She looked at Sienna, who stared straight at her, a blank look plastered over her face. "But as to why I said Susan would live, that was not a vision. Not exactly. It was a sound."

Sienna thought of the moments after Susan's birth, the quiet that had been so startling. Susan would never cry. She gulped her tea to keep her composure, then looked back at Marnie. "A sound?"

"I saw *something*. An impression of your rooms, yours and Peter's, the house, the shop, the gardens, the church, all the places you love. And Susan was there, but I never saw her. I only heard her. Her laughter. I thought it meant that she would live."

Sienna stared into her teacup, then drained it in three long gulps. She nodded without looking up, rose to her feet, and walked toward the kitchen. She stepped into the cooler and let the tears flow until her face ran cold with them. Then she wiped the puddle from her neck, stepped out into the kitchen, and left a note for Lettye that she would be back in the morning.

In her car, Sienna blinked at the sight of her hands on the steering wheel. Her fingers smelled like herbal dish soap and vanilla from baking. She drove to the hospital and parked without letting herself think about what Marnie's vision could have meant. But as she turned off the ignition and set herself to watch with Peter, she could not shake a remembered phrase from the prophets. "*Your young men shall see visions and your old men shall dream dreams.*"

"It was a dream," she said aloud. A dream and not a vision. It had been meant to be interpreted symbolically, surely, instead of looked for in real life. If Marnie could make such an awful mistake, what certainty was there of hope?

After Susan died, Sienna had dug into the garden and built up her business. There was always something to hold. The joy of roots and even weeding seemed blasphemous to her in the early weeks—all that life in her hands when she felt so empty. The happy clatter of cups and spoons seemed a sacrilege. But she kept going because she had known somewhere deep that God shows up where we are. She had hoped that He would find her there in the digging and the work, that she would look up at the end of some long day and see that He had been with her all along, working alongside her, or better yet, that His would be the face on the other side of the teapot. It seemed a half-baked fantasy now, the idea that God would pour for them and then let her cry it out on His shoulder.

Hope was not something you could see, was it? What was it she had read once in her prayer study? "Hope is memory

Tea & Crumples

remembering the future glory of God." Maybe it was faith that you couldn't touch. But that didn't work either. If you couldn't touch faith, then it was all a game, wasn't it?

This dilemma carried her through the parking garage and across the street. When she entered the hospital, she had come back around to the original sore question. Had Marnie only told them a dream? And was she only wishfully thinking when she said Peter would be okay? Was that another dream? She shuddered at the thought of Peter as merely a peaceful presence in her memory; she did not wish to be haunted by the ghost of his loss before it happened.

As she opened Peter's door, she decided there was only one thing for it. She would have to hold onto something with her hands again and hope that God would meet her there. Peter was asleep, but his long, warm hands were stretched out on top of the blanket. She sat down next to him and held those hands, waiting.

NOTES FROM SIENNA'S TEA FILES

Tasting Notes: Cocoa Yerba house blend, yerba mate with vanilla, cinnamon, and raw cacao powder.

Provenance: South American except for Vietnamese cinnamon.

Liquor: Opaque dark chocolate brown.

Astringency: Mild bite that mellows well with addition of milk.

Body: Rounded, with long-lasting substance.

Fragrance: Cocoa and holiday baking.

Serve with: Milk and sugar, stevia, or honey. Grounding.

Chapter Thirteen

Sienna woke up after dark. Someone had put a warm blanket around her shoulders and a pillow under her face where it leaned on the bedrail. She jerked upright, and Peter squeezed her hand. He was awake.

"Hey," she smiled at him. She could feel the sleep creases on her face stretch from the smile. She rubbed her cheeks with her left hand and yawned.

Peter looked at her quietly. She suspected he had been watching her for a long time. For years, even. Early in their marriage, she would wake up well after sunrise to find him smiling at her softly, that same peaceful vigilance on his face. She had not noticed him watching her the past six months, but she was immediately eased to see him now.

"When I'm better, will you feed me pears?" he whispered.

"Yes," she managed. Her throat was tight with sudden tears. After Susan died, when the summer fruit came in, Sienna had been too exhausted by grief to eat it. She bought bowls full of peaches that lay forgotten on the table until they were overripe and drew flies. One night she had come home from a long day of painting and hammering at the teashop and found Peter in the living room. He sat her down on the couch, handed her a pint of cold beer, and fed her sliced peaches with homemade whipped cream. It was the first food she had tasted in months, a sort of sacrament of healing. Peter's favorite fruit was pears.

He waited until she had swallowed back her sadness before he went on. "And oatmeal stout over ice cream. And that spice—what is it?"

"Cardamom."

"Cardamom," he nodded, "that goes so well with pears."

"I'll make you cardamom shortbread, then?"

"Yes, or it can be in the ice cream. You choose."

She nodded. The memory of cardamom tugged at her, bringing up thoughts of long autumns and cooler weather. "It's baking season, you know. I'll have to make the shortbread soon to warm the house." A Bible quote popped into her mind, one they had used to flirt with each other. *How can one keep warm alone?* She pushed back a quiver of fear. She did not want to be alone.

"And pear season soon," Peter said.

"Yes." She looked at him, not sure what to say. His deep eyes were lit from within, like sunlight in a clear brown stream. Sienna recognized the light as hope, and she raised her eyebrows. "Peter, the doctors? Have they any news?"

"No," he whispered. The light was not gone from his eyes. "But I've had a visitor."

Sienna knit her brows, remembering the conversation and confusion that had driven her to his bedside earlier. "Marnie?"

"Susan." He spoke her name quietly, but the joy of it squeezed her heart.

"Susan?" She breathed deeply, released the breath. "Our

Susan?"

Peter nodded. "At first I was dreaming, but then I was sure I was awake, Sienna." He followed her glance toward the morphine drip that he controlled with a tiny button. He shook his head. "I wasn't medicated at the time."

Sienna cleared her throat as her eagerness to connect with their daughter overcame her visceral fear of ghosts. "You saw her?"

"I heard her. In the dream, I was at my drafting board. The windows were open, and I heard laughter. Then it came into the room with me, and I knew it was Susan. I could see her whole, like a joyful light. But the laughter, it was here when I woke up. Her laughter filled the corners of the room."

Sienna gasped.

"I'm going to recover. I don't know how, but I know I will." His eyes grew brighter, and she could feel his pulse race in the fingers she held.

She shook her head, puzzled. "But Peter, how can you know? How can you be sure it was her?"

"Listen, Sienna. It's still there. Just listen." A glow of happiness suffused his face, and he closed his eyes, head slightly tilted as though heeding something precious.

She tried to open her ears, her spirit, to hear what he heard, but she was distracted by the sudden labored sound of Peter's breath. Alarmed, she sat forward and called the nurse's station. Before the nurse had answered, the door opened.

"Mrs. Bannock," Nurse David said, a serious but calm look on his face, "if you'll excuse us for a little while? We have to stabilize your husband." Another nurse and a young doctor followed him in—Dr. Patel, one of the residents she had met in passing.

She looked down at Peter then. His face was still happy, but his lips were bluish. She kissed his knuckles and stepped back as the medical team began to work and speak rapidly in their coded language. She went into the hall and nearly collapsed against the wall. A nurse named Lydia came up to her with a cup of ice water and pressed it into her hand.

"Here, Mrs. Bannock. Drink this." Sienna complied, not knowing what else to do. "I'll bring you a chair."

"Thank you, Lydia." Sienna said when the nurse had rolled a desk chair over to the wall outside Peter's room. She sat heavily and stared into the water. At length, the young doctor came out into the hall.

"Mrs. Bannock?" she asked.

"Yes?"

"Your husband is stabilized for now, but we've had to sedate him. If you'd like to go home and rest tonight, he won't likely be awake again until midday tomorrow."

"Oh," she said, suddenly realizing that in the suspense of waiting, she had not really considered leaving Peter's side.

The doctor seemed to sense her hesitation. "Of course, if you'd like to stay with him, that's fine, too, but you may be in for several long nights."

Sienna looked at the earnest young woman with eyes equal parts intelligence and compassion. "Tell me, Dr. Patel, is he likely to improve?"

"I'm sorry, but no." She frowned, waiting for the news to sink in. Behind her, the second nurse came out of Peter's room and lingered, obviously wanting a word with the doctor. Dr. Patel waited, quiet, to see if Sienna had any other questions.

"When he's like this, the medicines, are there side effects? Hallucinations, maybe?" Sienna asked.

"Not usually," Dr. Patel replied, hesitantly. "Mrs. Bannock, this is not strictly medical, but I have observed, and my older colleagues have told me as well, that when people draw near to the end of their lives, they sometimes have moments of… ecstasy. Or what some people call self-knowledge or revelation. Is that the sort of experience that prompted your question?"

Sienna glanced at the unfamiliar nurse, still lingering behind the doctor, looking a little impatient, then back at the doctor's kind eyes. "Yes," she nodded. "Thank you, Dr. Patel."

The doctor nodded, a sympathetic smile on her face. She placed a hand on Sienna's shoulder. "Please, go home tonight. Rest. Peter will sleep tonight, and you can keep watch again tomorrow."

Sienna nodded thanks, and the doctor turned away, walking some steps down the hall before she turned to the nurse and began to speak in low tones. Sienna watched them till they turned a corner. Then she stood and went into Peter's room. Nurse David was watching an IV bag and adjusting a drip. He looked up and gestured welcome when she came in.

Without the suffusion of joy on his features, Peter's skin seemed gray. But a smile lingered in the nascent crow's feet beside his closed eyes. She listened to his slow, regular breathing and watched his lips return to a washed-out pink. She kissed them and left for home.

That night at home, Sienna did not want to turn out the lights and go to bed. She ate a meal of cold leftovers from Savitri's, wrapped a well-worn shawl around her shoulders, and tried to sleep on the couch. The lamplight was comforting, but a moth had got in and would not stop hitting the bulb. The soft *thunk-thunk* of its body against the glass annoyed her. She left the moth to its fruitless quest and went upstairs, not bothering to turn out the lights on the way.

In the bedroom, she found the dark preferable to looking at Peter's empty pillow. She lay under the blankets on her side of the bed and tried to relax. Her thoughts had matted together into an impenetrable rug. She couldn't unravel the unspoken questions to resolve them, and she felt her mind muffled by the weight of them. She kicked off the blankets and rolled over, hoping the sharpness of cool air would shock her into clarity or soothe her into sleep. At length, the only discernable effect was that her feet got cold. She burrowed back under the covers and stared at the wall.

In the past, she would have tried to pray, but she couldn't think how. Prayer could not be done alone. Sometimes you had to wait for someone else's prayer to hold you. She hoped she was held in prayer now. Perhaps, if God was thinking of her, as always He was meant to be, it was enough. It would have to be enough, because she could not form a thought on her own, and the wall did not inspire any. She rolled over onto her back and let her eyes travel over the ceiling. The ceiling fan murmured quietly above her feet. The crown molding bridged the white expanse to the wall, and in the corners…

In the corners, she began to cry. She wept for love of Peter, of Susan, of Marnie, of Tovah, the dogs, Cleotis Reed, A.C., Nina, Lettye, Jessie, and the pilgrim at the manuscript table, for Liz and Deborah and every face she had seen. She wept for Nurse David and Dr. Patel with the compassionate eyes, for Lydia who brought her water. She paused her sobs to blow her nose, loudly, on the corner of the sheet, then gulped air hungrily through her nose and mouth.

The air was filled with a light pungent scent. Perhaps the smell had been there all along, or perhaps the tears had jerked it free from her swollen nose. It was wild bergamot, she was sure of it. Her tangled thoughts resolved into the single image of the red blossoms in the altar arrangement. She drank the memory like she had gasped for air, amazed at her desperate

Tea & Crumples

need for its beauty. The flowers were bright, almost too bright, behind her eyes, and she closed them, as much to shut out the intensity as to draw it nearer.

She must have slept, though it could not have been for long. There was light in the sky when the phone woke her, and her tears had dried. Her mouth was dry and gummy as well, but she managed to answer civilly. It was Tovah, her hoarse voice hesitant over the line.

"Sienna? Have you checked the emails lately?"

"Mmm? No. Why?"

"Look," Tovah croaked, "I know you have a lot on your plate, but maybe today before you go, could you leave the investors' files on the desk? I think I can be in tomorrow, and I'll deal with it."

"What?" Sienna sat up in bed, startled. "What's going on, Tovah?"

"Five more groups have cancelled. Those bad online reviews. We're bleeding money." Tovah breathed loudly through her swollen throat, and Sienna winced in sympathy to hear the misery over the phone. Sienna must have made a small noise of alarm as well, because Tovah rushed on reassuringly, "We're going to make it, Sienna, don't worry about that. It's just that we'll need more money to get through these first couple of months than we thought, at least until the good reviews catch up with the bad."

"Oh, Tovah," Sienna said, not knowing which of her problems to address. She settled for the immediate one. "I will leave the file on the desk, no worries. Now, you take care of yourself today."

"I will."

"And Tovah?"

"Yes?"

"Thank you for watching out for us."

NOTES FROM SIENNA'S TEA FILES

Julie Patel, 32, oncologist, knitter, reading tutor, loves coffee flavored ice cream: Darjeeling brewed with dried cherries, served in large mug with 1 teaspoon sugar and a splash of half and half. Rounded, calming, earthy sweet. Takes the edge off of bitter foods.

Chapter Fourteen

The day did not grow easier. Nina was late for the first time, and Sienna had to open the store alone. Fortunately, only Cleotis seemed to notice.

"Where's my Nina?" he asked genially when Sienna set down a tray laden with his usual order.

"Oh, I'm sure she'll be along soon," Sienna said in a placating tone. She caught the wry dark eye and switched to honesty. "I have no idea, Cleotis," she said in a lower voice, "but if you're set here, I'll go see if I can find out."

He nodded, watching her carefully, then turned to smile at a gray-haired woman in a pink sweater who approached the chess board. Sienna walked away quickly while he was distracted with a new challenger, but she felt he had seen right into her during their brief exchange. She hoped her anxiety did not show so easily to all the customers.

That morning, she had arrived very early and made sure to leave out the files on the private investors who had funded a large portion of the capital for the shop. She was mildly comforted to see that two of them had specified the availability of additional funds in their original agreements. Perhaps their situation was not too dire.

Curious and finding herself with a few minutes, she checked the business emails and accounts. It had not been a heartening experience. The online reviews from people they knew to be customers were positive and kind, but there was a string of bad reviews as well, all alleging terrible and argumentative customer service and noncompliance in event planning. Several of the cancellation emails cited the reviews, and two of them demanded a return of the nonrefundable deposit, in light of scathing online remarks. Her head throbbed after reading the emails, but she slipped quietly behind the desk to call Nina.

No one answered after several rings, but Sienna heard a knock at the kitchen door after her third try. She locked the office and rushed to the door, where Nina waited, her face pale and strained.

"Nina!" Sienna said, relieved. "I'm so glad you're here." Nina glanced warily over her shoulder and pushed forward into the kitchen. Sienna knitted her brows in concern. "Nina, what is it?"

"Sorry, Miss. It's nothing. My ride was late today." She went straight to the handwashing sink, washed, and looked around the kitchen. "Let me get caught up. What's first, Miss, dishes or baking?"

Sienna looked at the pile of cups already accumulated by the sink, then back at Nina. The girl was maintaining eye contact, but her chin was set in a stubborn pose that suggested she wanted to be busy. "I think we may not be able to do much baking today. How about you head out and see to the customers, and I'll do the cups and make tea sandwiches for a while? We can trade in an hour."

Nina nodded and headed out to the front area. Sienna had just finished drying the cups and arranging them on a tray when Nina returned.

"Are we out of mint?" she asked.

"Mint?" Sienna was exhausted from the night before, and she thought for a moment. "We have dried peppermint for tisanes, but I'm afraid I've forgotten to order the fresh mint, if that's what you mean."

"Oh." Nina's lips twitched. Sienna noticed her evasion.

"What is it, Nina?" Her stomach tightened as she remembered the bad online reviews. She hoped desperately that whoever was causing the trouble had not returned and demanded Morrocan mint tea. It was the only varietal they sold that absolutely required fresh leaves. "Oh." She echoed Nina as the penny dropped. "It's Greg?"

Nina nodded and rushed to speak. "I'll take care of him, Miss, but I don't know what to offer instead."

"Hmm." Sienna closed her eyes and thought for a moment, letting her anxieties slip away. *Show me*, she prayed. A fragrance came to mind along with the image of a sharp herbal tang. She opened her eyes. "Could you bring me the tins of catmint and lemon verbena? Wait. I think I was feeling fancy when I labeled the verbena. It's probably called vervain."

Nina returned shortly, and Sienna opened the tins, inhaling deeply. She crumbled leaves from both tins into a teapot and handed the lot back to Nina. They kept two hot water dispensers for making pots of tea that required different temperatures. In general, the black teas required boiling, the greens very hot, but the herbals had to be decided on a case-by-case basis, usually by Sienna. "Steep for three and a half minutes in the 195 degree water, add a tablespoon of honey to the pot, and serve it with a cucumber slice." Nina listened intently and nodded in the way that convinced Sienna the girl was filing the procedure away for future reference.

Sienna sighed as Nina took the teapot and tins back to the front. If Greg was there, she would probably have to see him. He tended to linger on any day, and she was sure he would scent her weakness today. She tried to put him out of her mind by making tea sandwiches, but the sandwiches would not come together. She had forgotten to set out the goat cheese to soften, so the first sandwich stuck and crumbled. The jar of roasted red peppers would not open under her exhausted hands. She was too frustrated to cut the fine slivers of red onion.

Lettye found her staring at the cutting board.

"I came in early, and it looks like a good thing, too." She lifted Sienna's elbow and led her to a stool by the dish station. "Listen, Sienna, I think you should consider going on home."

"But you'll be backed up," Sienna muttered. She blinked the glaze from her eyes and shook her head at the mess she had made of the sandwiches. "How about I have a cup of tea and man the dish station? I think I can manage that, at least."

Lettye nodded. "Fine, but I'm making the tea. You set."

Sienna managed a small smile in agreement. She liked the Southern inflection of Lettye's speech when she took charge. Mrs. Hopkins had been prone to that expression, calling on Sienna to "set" herself down on the grass to discern a miracle from a weed, to "set" down and crochet something warm to lay by till the wind called for it. She looked at her hands tenderly, remembering that they could make warmth and tease out goodness from the soil.

"Feeling better?" Lettye asked, observing Sienna's improved expression. "I brought you tea and, don't argue, the best almond pastry. I've already written it down for lost, so unless you want me to actually drop it on the floor first, best eat up

Tea & Crumples

without protest."

"Thank you, Lettye." She dutifully sipped her tea, which Lettye had made just the way she liked it. "I was remembering my favorite old lady from childhood. The first time I made a crochet scarf, it was like magic dripping through my fingers. Not that it was objectively pretty, you know. I dropped a few stitches and not one loop matched another. But it was useful and warm."

"A reflection of its creator?" Lettye smiled.

"I hope." She bit into the pastry. Lettye nodded, satisfied, and left her. Sienna had just finished the tea and pastry when Nina brought in a tray of cups to be washed.

"Miss, I hate to ask, but do you think you could give me a ride again?"

Sienna looked up, but Nina did not meet her gaze. "What's going on, Nina?"

The girl's face flushed, and she took her time setting each cup into the wash water. At length, she turned to Sienna. "You know that I have my citizenship. It's legal that I work here."

Sienna nodded, silent.

"Well, my older sister wasn't born here. She's being investigated. I usually ride with her to work, but she's scared right now."

"I see. Of course I can give you a ride. But the rest of your family, are they safe, too?"

"They're scared. Almost all of them are legal, but they don't have their papers in the house. My mom is afraid to go to the bank to get the birth certificates out of the safety deposit box, in case they are being watched."

"Almost all of them?"

"I have one aunt with an expired visa, but she doesn't want to leave her kids alone to go back and hope the paperwork goes through again."

Sienna nodded. "Where is your family? Do you think they are really being watched?"

Nina looked directly at Sienna and pursed her lips. "I know they are. I have had to do all the errands this week, because there's an agent just driving past the house every few hours. My family, Miss, my family is partly on the run. They don't have a place to go. Our neighborhood is patrolled now, and the family has been spending most of the day at church the past few days."

"I may be able to help." Sienna and Nina jerked their heads toward the door, where Greg was leaning against the frame. "I have a big, empty house in a neighborhood that is not patrolled. Plus, *yo hablo español*. And I'm a priest, so I suspect I'm already acquainted with the folks at your family's church."

Nina blushed deeply and examined her shoes.

"Greg, I'm sure you meant well, but this area is off limits to customers, and this conversation is private." Sienna stepped forward so that she was between Nina and Greg. She was furious that the confession that had so obviously pained Nina had been overheard.

"Of course," Greg said. He did not move, but he looked slowly between Sienna's grey face and the side of Nina's red one. "Excuse me for intruding. But please consider my offer. I would be glad to drive Nina to pick up any of her family and help them get settled for a night or two." He nodded a half bow and left the room before they could respond.

"Nina, I'm so sorry," Sienna began, touching the girl's shoulder lightly.

"It's ok, Miss." Nina sniffled, then touched the back of her hands to her face and looked up. "You know, I don't know him very well. Otherwise I might take him up on the offer. My aunt would probably let him help us since he's a priest. But, getting there, I would feel weird driving alone with a man I don't know." A small smile touched her lips. "Other than how he takes his tea and likes jam with pastries, I mean."

Sienna looked down at her arms, which she had crossed without noticing when Greg interrupted them. She made herself relax and took a deep breath. "I'll go with you to pick up your family, and then Greg can drop us, or me, off after they are settled."

Nina brightened. "Really, Miss?" She sighed in relief.

Sienna nodded. "Let's get through the main rush of the day, and we can close a bit early. Lettye can handle the closing. We can leave around 3:00?"

"Jessie was heading back from her festival this morning. I think she's coming in at 1:00." Nina nodded toward the calendar near the back door, where, sure enough, Jessie had made a note to that effect.

"Great," Sienna said flatly. "Then we can leave once she's here."

Nina scanned Sienna's face and drew a breath as though to speak. She nodded curtly instead and returned to the tearoom.

Sienna focused on washing dishes. She arranged the teacups by theme without noticing. Those with floral patterns sat together, while the plain or abstract ones kept company in separate rows. It was curious, was it not, that none of the teacups depicted overt religious symbolism. Yet they were central to the way she practiced faith. They were vital to how she loved. She lifted a deep bone china mug decorated with a botanical diagram of two herbs, catmint and peppermint.

Mrs. Hopkins grew catmint along an entire fence in her yard. It had been the subject of Sienna's first lesson in gardening and the one that seemed to have stuck with her best. They were weeding the flowerbeds together, and Sienna noticed that catmint was the main weed. Why, then, was it allowed to flourish in another part of the yard?

"Because, SiSi, it's a miracle." Mrs. Hopkins had plucked up a few stems in her green-stained fingers and laid them reverently in Sienna's little hand.

"But I thought it was a weed."

"Here, it's a weed, and there it's a miracle. Knowing the difference takes a lifetime. That's why I'm here, so you can have the miracle while it's ripe." The old lady winked.

Sienna thought of her garden at home. She had not quite sorted her plants, but there were some that were definitely miracles. The bee balm stalks that she had put in the church arrangement sprang to mind. On the other hand, there was Greg's drawing. A weed. And Peter's lifetime was pinching off too soon. Her thoughts swirled into confusion, and she set the teacup on the tray with the others to be returned to the serving area.

"I need a ripe miracle," she whispered, over the clatter of fresh water pouring into the sink. She reached out to God, to Mrs. Hopkins, and to any other garden saint that might listen in. "Please."

Jessie's arrival was heralded by her own bright singing.

"*And we'll understand it better by and by. By and by, when the morning comes…*" she trailed off with a grin at Sienna.

"From your lips to God's ears!" Sienna said, smiling back. "A good festival?"

"Oh, yes. We came in second place for the gospel category *and* we were the only ones in the top five with hair smaller than our faces, so you know the competition was stiff."

Sienna managed a tired chuckle. "That's great news.

Congratulations."

"What is it?" Jessie asked, the grin sliding from her face as she looked her boss over.

Where to begin? What to leave out? Sienna decided to start with the most urgent information. "I'm going to ride with Nina and our customer Greg for an errand for Nina's family. You and Lettye can handle things here, I hope."

"Of course. But what's making you so sad?" Jessie's question was innocently straightforward in a way that pierced Sienna's thin composure.

"It's Peter," she said quietly. Talking about her trouble made her notice how tired she was, and she closed her eyes to relieve the gritty feeling that had settled in them. "He's dying. I have to go back to the hospital tonight to keep watch, but it doesn't look good." Sienna felt herself embraced in Jessie's strong hug. The young woman's clothes smelled like caramel. She let Jessie rock her a bit, then stepped back and rubbed her eyes with the heels of her hands.

"I sing for the dying sometimes. If you think it might bring comfort or peace, I would be glad to stop by with my mandolin for a song or two."

"That would be lovely," Sienna responded absently, trying to restore her face into a semblance of calm. "But for now, I should go get Nina." She thought of Greg and felt a nervous squeeze in her stomach. "The sooner we get her trip over with, the better."

Greg's car was parked a few doors down from the front of the shop. Sienna slid into the back seat so that Nina could navigate. Greg and Nina fell into sanguine conversation. The road noise was steady and low under the gentle calm of their voices, and Sienna was bone tired from her long nights with Peter. She began dozing despite her wariness of Greg. She woke to quiet. The car was parked behind the largest Catholic church in the city, and Sienna just caught a glimpse of Nina and Greg disappearing into the building. A few minutes later, they returned, along with three anxious women with Nina's dark hair and bright dark eyes. The women bustled into their seats while Nina made rapid explanations in Spanish. She turned to Sienna.

"We're going to stop by Greg's house to get my family set up, then we'll go by my house to pick up the things they need, and then we'll head back over."

Sienna nodded at Nina and tried to smile reassuringly at Nina's relatives, who returned the gestures.

It did not take long to reach Greg's house, a restored bungalow with a well-tended yard and tasteful decorating. He opened the door and ushered them all into a foyer where they huddled, glancing around politely. On the wall by the door, a seascape hung on its side. Greg noticed it.

"Oh, this?" he asked, seeing that the women were all looking at the painting. "I call it, 'Sea Sickness.'"

"Really?" Sienna smiled a little at the whimsy.

"This way," Greg gestured into a large, warm living room. The women filed into the room, Sienna at the end of the line. "No," he said so that only Sienna heard him, "That just happens when a door is slammed too often." She hurried into the group, disliking his confidential tone.

In the living room, Greg's demeanor was hospitable. He offered Sienna a seat then broke into effusive Spanish while he showed the other women to the guest rooms and gave them a tour of the necessary places in the house. Sienna heard Nina's relatives giggle and respond from somewhere behind the swinging door that led to the kitchen. The group emerged through the dining room like a small flock of chipper ducks

Tea & Crumples

surrounding a jocular goose. Sienna smiled to see the women so at ease.

Nina approached her while her relatives continued chatting with Greg. "Are you ready, Miss?"

"Yes, whenever you are. All sorted here?"

"I think so." Nina spoke briefly to the others and nodded to Sienna.

Greg led Nina and Sienna back to the car and asked directions to the credit union where Nina would pick up the important documents. Sienna tried to stay awake as they wound slowly through city streets. In the front seat, Greg entertained Nina with stories of his own family.

"My mother always knew the right food to make everyone feel at ease. One time, Dad invited a business client to dinner, and Mom made meatloaf with peas and carrots and mashed potatoes and gravy." He glanced at Nina and raised his brows. "Now, she was a great cook, but she made that simple food because she just knew. And what do you think? When the man arrived and found out the menu, he about melted in gratitude. He was used to plain English food, and it was the first meal he'd been able to really enjoy on his whole business trip."

"My mamá is a great cook, too, but she's a little more bossy about it. If she says you need *sopa* or *arroz con pollo* or tacos, you have to eat it. She's usually right, but it's not like she leaves it up to you to decide." Nina chuckled a little. "I think that's why I like baking so much. Mamá never interferes in it, since she remembers growing up when it was usually too hot to bake. And even Mamá won't tell people they have to eat *churros* or *dulce de leche*, so I get to dictate all the sweets, too."

Sienna fought against dozing while her car mates chatted about the best way to make hot chocolate and coffee. She pulled her head upright when the door closed. Greg was watching her from the front seat. She sat up and tried to relieve the ache in her neck and shoulders without drawing too much attention.

"Tired?" he asked, his gray eyes steady on her face. For the moment, he seemed calm and peaceful, and Sienna felt drawn to confide in him. Then his eyes shifted slightly, hungrily, to where she rubbed her neck. His hand on the front seat moved slightly toward her in unspoken invitation to comfort her. She dropped her hand and tried to feign alertness.

"Just some late nights, thanks." Sienna smiled tightly. "I'll be fine."

Greg looked over her sleep-warmed skin. She colored more deeply at being observed. "You look as though you've been keeping watch," he said casually. Sienna blinked but did not answer. "And who is watching out for you?" It was an offer, not a question.

Sienna drew a sharp breath and faked a smile. "Oh, lots of people, I assure you. Not least Tovah and," she grasped for a change of subject, "Nina. Thank you for helping Nina, by the way. It's very kind of you. I suppose you help a lot of people in distress in your line of work."

"Some. But I'm also here for my friends." He shifted toward her. "If I can help…"

"Well, Nina and her family are wonderful, aren't they? I think that this is just what they need to get over this little rough patch." Sienna looked toward the building, where the opening door heralded Nina's return. She sighed in relief. From the corner of her eye, she saw Greg flinch. "And here she is!" she said too brightly as Nina got into the front seat.

"Mission accomplished?" Greg asked in his casually confident way.

"Yes!" Nina smiled. "And I got the phone numbers we'll

Tea & Crumples

need to sort out my aunt's papers. If we can just go pick up a few things from my house?"

"Of course," Greg replied, putting the car into gear.

Nina gave Greg directions, and they fell into banter about families again, this time about kitchen gardens and dishes. Greg described his mother's china pattern and her herb patch.

"Don't tell me about herbs! My family thinks that you can cure anything with something from the garden. None of us get sick because we don't want to have to drink something gross."

"Tell me about it," Greg countered. "You know in Peter Rabbit where he has to take chamomile tea after eating too much? That was my mother. She kept a chamomile bed alive in the Carolina heat just to have something to threaten us with if we sneezed or ate too much candy or just needed an attitude adjustment."

"Ha!" Nina scoffed. "Try peppers and mint. Not peppermint. Peppers. And. Mint."

"You win," Greg smiled. They pulled into Nina's drive, and she bounced up the walk. Greg and Sienna watched her till she entered the house. As soon as the door closed behind Nina, Greg turned to Sienna. This time, he did not hesitate. He reached for her hand and held it. His warmth shocked her.

"Greg," she began. He cut her off.

"Sienna, I want to help you. I want to be here for you. Maybe you can't accept my offer now, but you must see how I could be there for you."

"No, you can't, Greg. You aren't free, and I'm not free, and that's beside the point."

"I don't think it is. I think the point is that I see you. Your warmth, your insight, your kindness. I think that in the near future, we're both going to need someone to see us, intimately. And I want to let you know I'm here for you when that time comes."

Sienna looked at their hands. He held her fingers firmly, distracting her. *God, give me the words to say that he needs to hear.* She was quiet, staring past their hands, waiting for some word or vision that would put an end to Greg's pursuit, to her own temptation to avoid her grief by using Greg. After several long moments, what came to her was a fragrance, the aroma of spicy food being cooked in a nearby house. From a backyard, a child's laugh reached out to her. She looked at Greg then and saw him clearly for the first time. Of course. His banter with Nina told her all she needed to know.

"Greg," she squeezed his hand and pulled her fingers free, "you don't love me or need me or want me. I remind you of your mother."

He drew a sharp breath and sat back, stunned. His brows knit, raised, and lowered again. He nodded briefly and turned to face the steering wheel. Greg did not speak to Sienna again, and he was quieter with Nina on the way back to the teashop.

"You're sure you're fine?" Sienna asked Nina as they pulled up in front of the darkened shop window.

"Oh, yes, Miss. Thank you for going with us today! Mamá will have cooked us a big dinner to say thanks to Padre Gregorio here," she joked.

Seeing the girl at ease, Sienna nodded and got out of the car. Greg was, after all, a pretty decent person, even if he had been way out of line where she herself was concerned. She waved goodbye as the car pulled off, then turned to find her own car.

Couples and small groups walked past her to the various restaurants and bars that made downtown one of the best places to eat in the country. The cold air brought her the hoppy smell of microbrew beer, the tang of richly spiced sauces, and a warm afterthought of almonds and vanilla. It was the sort of night that Peter would have loved. They would have held hands on their way to dinner, kissed in front of windows on the way to dessert. She squeezed her left hand over the memory and the wish and the sweetness. Perhaps she could bring them with her to his bedside.

NOTES FROM SIENNA'S TEA FILES

Nina Hernandez, 19, teashop waitress, cooking teacher, prophet: chocolate malt black tea with milk and sugar. Hot or iced. Served with her churros. Revelatory.

Chapter Fifteen

As soon as she entered Peter's room, she felt time shift. Like she had always felt at the holiest times of the church year, the very air beckoned her into the longest night. Longest nights were nights of death, of change, of resurrection. God works at night, she thought. A shock ran through her and she made the sign of the cross over herself.

She looked at Peter and saw him for all the love they shared. Swift, dim memories of Peter in the light of morning, at sunset, by candlelight, raced through her mind. Then stillness came. She noticed, as it left her, the aching dull thunk of grief. She was left with Peter, the palpable bodily Peter. He was really there and not only a thought that could be pushed aside or beaten down or worn at the edges like an old photograph much handled.

"Peter," she almost whispered. It was the voice of recognition. He was the other half to her sacrament. She needed him the way bread needs wine. They had been woven together into the dwelling place of God, and all the small graces of cups and

Summer Kinard

spoons and blankets and baking were stocked with the joy of their union. She bent and kissed his gray, dry face, astonished at his beauty.

Now that it was almost too late, she cherished the touch of him. "Thank you," she voiced in low pitches. "Thank you for him. Thank you." She kissed his hands and laid her head on his shallow breathing, let his quiet heart reverberate through her. Limned in gratitude for his presence, she fell asleep.

A man in dark clothing stepped into the room when his knock went unanswered. He walked to Peter's bedside and made the sign of the cross over the sleeping man and wife. He waited in near silence, the only sound the gentle susurrus of wool prayer knots through well-worn fingers. Sienna did not stir, though her dreams were peopled with soft, kind voices and the light one only recalls from childhood—like sunlight through pink springs, but unburdensome for all its brightness.

Another knock went unanswered after midnight. Marnie entered, then hesitated when she saw the priest standing by the bed. "Are you—? Forgive me for asking, but are you really here? I mean, in the body? Only, saints often dress alike."

The priest nodded and smiled understanding. "I'm Father Max from the Orthodox Church. Sienna invited me to pray for her." Seeing Marnie's continued hesitation, he added, "Yes, in the flesh."

Marnie walked around the bed to stand beside him. "There's something we must do, Father. Only, I will ask you not to mention it later except that you leave me out of the tale. It must be for God's glory alone."

"Of course."

Marnie looked at Peter with a studied eye, then held her hands out above him. "The cancer is here," she moved her hands, "Here, and here. But the part that is killing him is here." She paused her hands again. "I will need you to touch him, and then perhaps I might lay one hand on his chest and one on your arm?"

They moved into place. The prayer beads slipped whirring through the priest's hand. Gradually, in her dream, the light changed for Sienna. It was bright golden as sun through a magnifying glass. In the room, Marnie's bracelets burned her skin and the wounds beneath them throbbed. Joy poured into the room like the smell of incense in air pealed by bells and candlelight. Father Max's hands shook, and the prayer rope thumped against the hospital bed, which shifted its load on a preset timer. Marnie's face contorted with compassion but glowed golden over the fluorescent room lights. Soft thrumming wind stirred Father Max's beard, and he remembered all the baptisms he had performed as well as the birth of his children.

In their sleep, Peter and Sienna smiled at one another under a canopy. They were wearing crowns made of pale flowers. Someone was smiling at them just outside their peripheral vision. They could see the echo of the joyful countenance on one another's faces. Music played, and they walked toward the sound of singing.

Sienna had forgotten to pull the shades in Peter's room. A ray of morning light caught her left eye and troubled her awake. The music from the dream continued. She lifted her head, careful of her achy neck muscles. Jessie was playing a mandolin softly at the foot of the bed.

"*Nada te turbe, nada te espante, Quien a Dios quiere, nada le falta,*" the girl's warm voice chanted low and clear. She watched Sienna rub her eyes, then drew the song to a close. "*Solo Dios basta.*"

"Is that a Taizé chant?" Sienna smiled. "I thought you only

sang bluegrass and Appalachian hymns."

"Not at sick beds. It's not fair to make people want to get up and dance when they have doctor's orders to rest." Jessie raised an eyebrow and nodded toward Peter. "Though if you ask me, he looks near enough ready to dance, for all the fuss he's made." Jessie lifted her mandolin into its case and busied herself with preparations to leave.

A low chuckle ran under Sienna's hand. She caught her breath and turned sharply to see Peter, his color healthy, his smile brilliant, if a bit watery around the eyes, and his laugh unfettered by pain.

"Forgive me, Jessie," Sienna said, not turning back to the girl, "but am I dreaming? Are you really here?"

"That seems a common question the past few hours." Peter said with a chuckle.

"What do you mean?" Sienna asked.

"Only that I met other visitors on their way out when I was coming in," Jessie supplied. "Tovah and Deborah and Liz and Bethel Bailey. Only Tovah was wearing a mask due to her recent illness, so we had to verify her identity. And they apparently all arrived on the heels of your priest friend Father Max."

"I slept through all those visitors and no one woke me?" Sienna looked from Peter to Jessie and back again.

"I'd better head out. I don't want my boss to catch me coming in late to work." Jessie winked at Sienna, waved goodbye, and left them to talk together.

"I wouldn't let them," Peter said succinctly. "Your face had peace for the first time in ages, and I didn't like to disturb you."

"What about you? You were asleep, too." She touched his face, first with a few fingertips, then with her outstretched palm. "You look... well. Peter! You look well!"

He kissed her palm and breathed deeply. "I feel it, too. No doubt the doctors will want to look me over again soon. Let's see what they have to say about it." He reached up and cupped her hand with both of his warm ones. "But if you want my opinion, I haven't felt this well in years."

"It sounds as though we had a string of miracle workers last night."

"Bringing in grace by the handful?" When Sienna became a Christian, the parishioners at her tiny church filled the baptism font with water that they carried handful by handful. Each of the ninety-eight people, and some of the children three times, added water with their own hands.

Sienna smiled, "Yes." The memory lit her face. "Exactly like my baptism. The Holy Spirit working through what each person brings. Or brought, rather."

Peter's stomach grumbled.

"Hungry?"

"Very. I ordered breakfast, but it takes an hour to get here."

"Tea?"

"Yes, please."

Peter watched the ease take over Sienna's movements as the familiar ritual restored her from sleep. When the tea was steeping, he drew a deep breath.

"Mmm."

"It's your favorite."

"Not the tea, but it is my favorite. It smells nice, but you smell edible."

Sienna lifted her hair to her nose and sniffed. Cardamom, green tea, dark China teas, and fenugreek. "Oh. It's all the Indian food I've been eating."

"Comfort food." He reached out and took her hand. She relaxed her fingers in his grip, relishing its refreshing warmth.

"You must have been really stressed out by this. And the shop opening at the same time."

"And maybe closing."

"Closing?"

"I shouldn't be so melodramatic. There have been a lot of bad reviews, all apparently started this by one person who didn't like how we described the quiche or something. Our sorority parties keep cancelling."

"And you rely on the big parties and events to make ends meet." Peter frowned.

Sienna sighed in reply.

"What will you do? I saw that Tovah is making herself recover quickly as usual. Does she have ideas?"

"We have to contact our investors and see if they can front us a little more to get through the next two months. We had to pay extra to get some of the dishes and furniture rush delivered, and the plumbing in the ladies'... well, you know about that." A pained expression pinched her eyes. The baby friendly bathroom and lounge had required expensive pipes to be moved into expensive places. They were expecting Susan when they approved the changes, giddy with parental joy. "We made our quarterly budget based on the pre-booked event schedule. All that work, *poof*."

"Do you think the investors will help?"

"Two of them might. One of them we've never met, actually. She said in her emails that she would be glad to invest further if she believed in the business. I think she's our best hope."

"A true community builder?"

"Yes. Dream investor. Strange name, though. Xenia R. Maris."

"Strange name, ha. Xenia means stranger, doesn't it?"

"I think so. But maybe in this case, she's an angel unawares.

Tea & Crumples

I'll set up a meeting for her to visit the shop, and we can just hope she believes in it. But why am I going on about that, when you're awake?"

"Agreed. Let's spring me from this joint, and then we can work together to sort out the teashop."

"We've always worked well together, haven't we?" Sienna looked at Peter with the newfound sense of oneness that had come over her the previous night. She had not let herself feel how she missed him these weeks while he was in the hospital. Her hazel eyes shifted toward green. Peter's dark eyes responded. Desire and love sprang up in her belly like a plucked string. She bent and kissed his hand playfully, letting her lips pull at his knuckles a little. "But first, tea?"

"Yes," Peter answered low and swiftly. "Always tea."

Sienna poured the tea and gave a mug to Peter before taking up her own. Peter watched her in silence with a smile playing around his eyes. An unobservant intruder would have noticed the politeness and ritual; Peter and Sienna felt the seduction in old courtesies. All the latent playfulness and bodily awareness of ritual woke up between them. It breathed in the bouquet of the tea and glanced between their modest eyes.

The intruder, when she came, was not unobservant. Dr. Patel glanced between the couple, saw the casual joy of tea ceremony, and relaxed the knot in her lower back. "Mr. Bannock, you're better!"

She was met by two satisfied smiles. "I hope so," Sienna and Peter said.

"Well, let's find out, shall we?" The young doctor smiled at them, confident that the tests would show what her instinct told her already.

NOTES FROM SIENNA'S TEA FILES

Tasting Notes: Golden Monkey black tea. Top shelf tea, perfect for celebrating.

Provenance: Fujian region of China, direct shipped to the shop.

Liquor: Dark honey color.

Astringency: Mellow.

Body: Round.

Fragrance: Honey and peaches.

Chapter Sixteen

"The preliminary tests show no cancer." Sienna beamed at Tovah. Tovah handed her a mug of her usual, along with a brownie. "A brownie? For breakfast?"

"Just eat it. You're celebrating."

"Mmm. This is delicious. New?"

"Nina. Her mom's recipe. Mexican chocolate. Now, you were saying?"

"No cancer. It's gone. All that's left is scar tissue. But they don't want to be hasty."

"So he's in for another day of observation?"

"I think so. As Peter said, they are bound to run out of stuff to pick out of him to test before long. Then they'll have to let him go. Not that I'm ungrateful for the awesome care he's received. Just eager to get him home with me now that he's well."

"Of course. You want to tuck him under your wing and make sure he's held in fluff and comfort till you're sure of him."

"Is that what Marc did when you came home after your

bout with meningitis?"

"Marc, our mothers, our oldest. Everyone. My advice, should you choose to accept it, is to coddle the snot out of him whether he likes it or not. He'll be tired even if he doesn't want to admit it. Put him on that Andirondack deck chair out back, tuck a blanket around him, and administer tea and soup till he floats."

"That's very specific advice."

"Good advice always is." Tovah picked up a few crumbs on a fingertip and ate them. "You were right about the brownie, though. It's great, but not breakfast. Peanut butter pastry?"

"We have those in stock?"

"It's autumn, so I told Hearth to send any and all nut pastries our way."

"Yes, please."

The back door opened, and Lettye came in through the kitchen. "Welcome back, Sienna!" She hugged her boss. "I'm so grateful to hear about Peter. My Bible study group *and* Granny have been praying."

Sienna returned the hug with gusto. "Well, tell your Granny we said thank you, and thanks be to God! He's coming home tomorrow."

"Have a peanut butter pastry." Tovah slid a plate in front of Lettye and turned to pour out tea when a small timer dinged on the counter behind her. "And your tea, ma'am."

"Well now, what are we going to do about these cancellations?" Lettye asked. She draped her cashmere sweater over the back of the pink barstool and slipped into the seat. "I've been able to convince my college sorority, my Bible study group, and Granny's prayer group to continue to engage us. But those reviews are hurting us. Whether they meant to or not, the ladies who wrote them echoed some of the same language a

Tea & Crumples

lot of church folks use to indicate indirect prejudice."

"Oy ve. I, too, have been able to bring in a few bookings from people both loyal to me and skeptical of the Internet."

"But we don't have enough, do we?" Sienna asked. Her rhetorical question was met with silence as they each tasted their tea and pastry.

"I contacted Ms. Xenia Maris." Tovah consulted a notepad. "She can come next week for a visit. Nina can start her Mexican sweets cooking classes next month. What else can we do?"

"Deborah mentioned a wedding shower," Sienna said. "Has Liz booked it yet? If not, I'll remind her."

"What about our regular customers?" Lettye asked. "How can we expand our services that tap into what they already love?"

"Like what? A paper touching party instead of just a tea tasting?" Tovah asked.

"Actually, yes." Lettye shook her head for emphasis. "Have you *seen* the paper lovers? We could ask some of the local letterpress artisans to use some of our papers to demonstrate their art. Or we could make special orders from them, with our logo. Have a featured artist once a quarter, set up orders of custom stationery from Durham artisans as well as the big three catalogs we already have on offer."

Sienna and Tovah, both paper lovers, gasped eagerly.

"That's a great idea going forward," Tovah said. "Let's put it in our business plan and try to get the first paper party going before the holiday season."

"Is there a way we could get things moving sooner?" Sienna asked. "Michael the postcard pilgrim guy comes to mind. Could we have a write-in special? Maybe a few of them in October? Fall into writing, or something?"

"What do you have in mind? Tea discount? Paper swap?"

"Oooo, paper swap!" Lettye said. "That's a great idea. Bring your remnant stationery for a paper swap, write a letter, drink some tea, get a free first class stamp?"

"Well, that would be less expensive than free tea," Sienna said. "I like it. Stationery swap with a free stamp for participants. We should pick a date soon and spread the word among graduate students and Jane Austen fans."

"How about we have two of them over the weeks for the universities' fall breaks?" Lettye asked.

"Yes. Great idea," Tovah said, scribbling down the plan.

"What about chess, Miss?" Nina, unobserved while the others were absorbed in brainstorming, leaned forward next to Tovah. "Mr. Cleotis Reed would probably be willing to get something going for us."

Tovah glanced toward the front of the store where the chess table held pride of place in the window. "Let's ask him." She smiled as she spotted Cleotis' warm smile at the door.

Dogs can smell joy. They licked Sienna's face in relief when she picked them up. Pogo leapt and even Jonquil squealed when she saw the relaxed set of Sienna's shoulders. They sniffed around her neck where Peter's touch had been. Jonquil licked her ear.

"Okay, you two. Yes, Daddy's coming home today," Sienna smiled and rubbed the dogs' ears. She stood up to go to the door, but Pogo was too, too happy to stop the celebration. He wiggled through the air a few more times, until Jonathan the dog handler quietly extended a hand to his side, bringing the lab to heel. "Thanks, Jonanthan."

"I'm glad to see them happy again. Please tell Mr. Bannock we're glad he's home." The large young man spoke calmly, but his eyes smiled sincerely when he glanced up at her. Sienna

Tea & Crumples

saved him the embarrassment of unwonted eye contact by shifting her gaze around the room.

"You know, if it hadn't been for this place, we might not have caught the cancer." The thought overwhelmed her, and she breathed a sigh of gratitude. Jon let her struggle a moment to contain herself, then laid his large hand on her shoulder. She couldn't help but notice the similarity to the gesture he used to heel Pogo.

She thanked Jon again, gathered the leads, and took the dogs to the car. The day was cool, so she let the back windows down a little. She caught a glimpse of Jonquil's fur ruffling as the dog turned her face into the wind. Sienna approached the turn off to their house and passed it. The dogs were at the beginning of Peter's medical emergency; they should be there at its end.

Peter met them at the hospital door. His wheelchair attendant wished him luck and praised God before rolling the ugly cart back into the building. Peter, a little slow from the broken leg and the time off his feet, met Sienna at the passenger door. She kissed him and held the door while he worked his way in. Her hand shadowed his back as he leaned into the car with the heavy cast. The cancer was gone, but the bone still had some weeks to heal. It was a grace, Sienna thought, to have an injury she could help with.

They drove home in giddy silence broken only by the dogs' frantic alternation between window joy and licking Peter's neck over the back seat. Sienna had brought home Peter's blanket and the other household items from his hospital room the night before. She had washed the afghan in cedar wool soap and left it on a clothesline by the lavender to dry all day. When they got in the house, Peter sat in his favorite chair to rest. The dogs curled around his feet. Sienna ran outside to get the blanket, stopped on the way in to make up a tea tray, and brought the lot briskly to the living room.

She tucked Peter in, poured out his tea, lit three beeswax candles, and popped outside to gather a few herbs with old blossoms on them. These she brought in a small vase to sit beside her husband, who dozed briefly under the dual administrations of his wife and the dogs. He woke up when Sienna handed him a mug of tea.

"Thanks." Peter inhaled deeply, looked from the tea to the candles, the afghan to the herbs, and he chuckled. "Trying to put the smells back in the right place?"

"Yes." Sienna picked up her cup and sipped. Peter drew several larger gulps from his mug, then leaned forward and set it on the edge of the table.

"You've forgotten something," he said, letting his eyes rove over her face and catch at her eyes. "There's no me without you." He held out his arms, and she came to him. With a little delicacy regarding his broken leg, she managed to sit comfortably on his lap. Peter pressed his face into her hair and breathed deeply. "Better," he said. She kissed him. "Much better."

"Do you think you can make it upstairs? Or shall I make up our bed down here?"

Peter answered her with a more urgent kiss. At length, he whispered, "Down here." The dogs sensed the change in mood and took their opportunity to play in the backyard while the sun was out.

Much later, Sienna woke up on the couch, pressed against Peter's side. The afghan, redolent with cedar and tea and kisses, tickled her nose where it had come to rest after their frenzied reunion. She lifted her head and smiled into Peter's amused face.

"What?"

"I didn't know you would be so enthusiastic about making me feel at home. But I guess it makes up for the lack of detail on bed making."

"I'll get you more bedding later."

"Promise?" He pulled her closer and nuzzled her. She answered in kind. "I like your answer." Peter mumbled between kisses. "But," he kissed her chin, "I think," he kissed her décolletage, "we should eat first."

Sienna pulled away reluctantly, taking the afghan with her. She wrapped it around her middle and let it fall off her shoulders. She paused at the doorway and smiled over her right shoulder at Peter, who grinned back at her, covered in only his cast and a few throw pillows. A few minutes later, she gave him back his blanket.

"I'm afraid we only have leftover Indian food and yesterday's leftover pastries from the teashop," Sienna adopted an air of solicitude as she laid out plates of naan sandwiches stuffed with spinach and curried chicken alongside a china serving dish piled high with chocolately rustic tarts. "What will you have?" She smiled, indicating the abundant table. Peter was not looking at the table.

"Come here, please." She went to him. "Wait. Bring one of those chocolate tarts." She did. "Perfect."

"Agreed."

"So, how was Peter's homecoming?" Bethel Bailey sipped hurriedly on her tea. Sienna blushed a little at the memory of the previous evening, which had extended late into the night.

"Um, it was good." She tried to hide her discomposure by fiddling with a tea basket.

"Oh, I know you don't have time to talk me through it. I'm

only on break. I'll come back at lunch, and you can tell me more then. What I am really asking is, how did the dogs take it?"

"They were very happy."

"Good." Bethel nodded once and leaned her head to the side. "What did Peter think of Father Max? Did he say?"

"He liked him." Sienna heard the shortness of her replies, but she couldn't think of what else to say. She was still too overwhelmed by the miracle of Peter's recovery to talk coherently about it. Bethel had inadvertently hit on the one time she had come close to expressing her joy, but of course she couldn't really talk about experiences so integral to marital intimacy. She could scarcely speak of Father Max with more clarity, since his words were the ones that came to mind over and over again the night before. "God is great and loves mankind," she said quietly.

"Well, yes." Bethel beamed. "He is, and he does."

"Beg pardon?"

"God is great, and He loves mankind," Bethel repeated.

"Oh! I didn't realize I'd said that aloud." Sienna swallowed and hoped her other memories had not slipped out unawares. "Forgive me, Bethel. I'm distracted and not conversing well."

"Well, it's understandable. You know how after Jesus heals people up from the dead, sometimes he tells them not to tell anyone. Well, I reckon that's to let them off the hook as much as anything. Because how can you talk about things that are so full of love they make words give out?"

Sienna wanted to hug Bethel. "Yes, exactly." She added another raspberry cookie to Bethel's saucer in lieu of trying to hug her across the counter. "Thank you, Bethel."

Bethel grinned and ate the cookie in two quick bites. She drained her tea in one last gulp. "I'll be back at lunch. See if

Tea & Crumples

you can talk about it then. If not, *I* have something to tell *you*."

"I'm looking forward to it." Sienna waved her off and gathered up the used tea things from the counter.

"Looking forward to what?" Liz's voice was a paradox of loud volume and conspiratorial tone.

"Liz! It's so good to see you. I missed you the past few days." Sienna walked around the counter and gave Liz a hug.

"Well, I'm here, and I tell you what, it was *not* easy to lose my tail to get here alone."

"Your tail?"

"Deborah. She can positively scent an intention for taking tea. And it's not like I have an excuse for putting her off. I only got here without her today because her friend who's making her wedding dress has a baby that won't nap through loudmouths. She's at a dress fitting for now, but she'll join me here in a few minutes." Liz produced a folded half sheet of linen parchment and slid it across the counter to Sienna. "Which is why I wrote it down."

Sienna looked over the list. "Deborah's bridal shower? But I thought she knew about it already."

"Just because she's too picky to let us surprise her about the place doesn't mean she can't be surprised about the details." Liz turned her head sharply at the jangle of the doorbell. "Darn. And here she is already. You think you can manage all this? My number's on there if you need to check in."

"It shouldn't be a problem." Sienna smiled and tucked the paper into her apron pocket. "Let me get you a tray going. Your usual?"

"Oh, surprise me!"

"Me, too," Deborah added as she joined Liz at the counter. "I love surprises."

Sienna didn't trust herself not to give anything away if

she spoke, so she smiled and nodded. Liz and Deborah took their usual table near the stationery section and set to talking and laughing. Sienna watched them for a few minutes, then decided to take them in a new direction with their tea tray. She assembled two pots, a chocolate flavored black tea with nibs of toasted rice and a lemony vanilla-scented green tea, both blends she had concocted. To go with the teas, she chose a plate of arugula, goat cheese, and pickled melon sandwiches alongside nutty maple pastries. She grinned as she approached the friends' table.

"And I have not read a lick of fiction in a week!" Liz lamented. "Oh, what's this? It smells divine. Here, let me pour. Oh, it's green. You take that one, Deborah. I'll try the bulletproof stuff. Oh my gawd! This is amazing. I'm going to have to taste everything. The only problem is what to put in my face first. Do you have a minute to sit with us?"

"Oh, please do join us," Deborah added. "And tell me what's in this tea! This one, too. No, Liz, you can't hog it. I'm sure I smell rice, and I never pass on tea you can eat."

"Good guess," Sienna chuckled. "The black tea has crushed chocolate nibs and toasted brown rice, plus cocoa extract to round out the flavor. I want you to guess what's in the green tea. You've proven you have a nose for it."

"Vanilla."

"Yes."

"And lemon?" Deborah sipped again. "No, it's the tea itself, isn't it? It's just a citrusy leaf. How did you find it, and can I take it home to bathe in it?"

"I told you the stronger tea was wasted on her. Now, Sienna, tell me about this stationery swap meeting. Am I going to show up and have somebody try to pass off her returned-to-sender wedding invitations as postcards?"

Tea & Crumples

"Well, no—" Sienna began.

"But that would be a great use for them!" Deborah smiled. "I hate throwing out the two that came back to us. I think if we resend them as postcards, at least our judgmental relatives will have to keep them. No return address and all that." Her face was bright, but her voice strained when she mentioned the relatives.

"Deborah! I'm so sorry to bring it up like that. My big mouth. There's a cost to being intuitive, you know. Here I was picking the most random problem I could, so I thought, and I accidentally landed on your sore spot."

"Insight is a double-edged sword, isn't it?" Deborah sniffled a little and sipped her tea to recover. "Even when everything goes well, at the very least, one finds oneself dropping intuition bombs on one's friends when they are most vulnerable."

"Gaw, I know! Don't ever take me shopping. I have made seven out of ten shopping partners cry by noticing her avoidance of a flattering color that reminded her of her beloved granny or telling a little story about her fragrance that brought up all of the self actualized moments of her youth."

Deborah stared. "'Self-actualized moments of her youth?' You do need to read some fiction. I have the latest Pullitzer winner in my car. I'll pass it to you when we head out."

"You know what I mean. As in, 'I knew I wanted to be a doctor when I smelled the sea lavender by the light of the new moon' or what have you. People, correction, *women*, are always telling me their coming-of age-stories. Mostly when I compliment them on their jewelry."

"Or tattoos?" Deborah deadpanned.

"Exactly. And thanks for the book. I'll take you up on the offer. Now, Sienna, what's all this about a miraculous cure, and does it work on wrinkles?"

"I don't know how to describe it except to say that Peter was dying and now he's well. Apparently, half a dozen miracle workers trouped through the hospital room last week and handed over their unused grace."

"A hand-me-down cure?" Liz asked. "Deborah, you'll like that. Cheap as free. Used the once?"

"Free, maybe, but not cheap." Deborah smiled. "Hand-me-downs have the advantage of being given by people who got a lot out of them the first time around and know you'll love them, too."

"However it happened, we're so grateful. I'm so grateful." Sienna's eyes crinkled in a huge smile. "I'm happy."

"Let me pour you a cup," Liz said, and did so. "Tea and sympathy."

"Sympathy is even better when you are sympathizing with joy," Deborah added. She sipped her tea and tilted her head to the side as she watched Sienna take up a cup. "Something else has changed. You're lighter now." Her eyes flicked to the manuscript table, where Greg usually sat, and back to Sienna. Sienna caught the motion and nodded.

"Oh. Yes, that's easier now, too. Greg backed off. He just needed a little perspective."

"Perspective?" Liz asked, motioning an upper-cut punch with her free hand.

"Not like that." Sienna smiled. "He just needed some context."

"Don't make me invent the reason."

"No, please don't. We don't want her to start in on the self-actualized moments of *your* youth, too."

"Haha, Deborah. Seriously, what made the difference? Hidden cameras? Restraining order? Threatening a lifetime ban from the shop?"

"None of that. I just pointed out that I remind him of his mother."

"And his natural repugnance of Oedipus did the rest?" Liz asked.

"Clever," Deborah said. "And talk about insight. He must have been hurting and ran to the nearest woman who fit his archetype. You, ma'am, are wise. I mean, beyond your wise way with teas. Most people who study psychology and family systems don't notice the patterns when they see them in their own lives. What put you onto it?"

"I wish I could say I was just observant. But all I really noticed was my own tendency to sin. I felt tempted by him because I was afraid I would never have the things I wanted in life with Peter—children, companionship, love. He was an easy answer, and I knew he was the wrong one. I guess I figured maybe I was his easy answer, too, but he had a different question."

"Dang," Liz sighed. "I am so going to ask you for advice once I'm married. Now that you say it, I know what you mean. Children and love and intimacy aren't like market goods. You can't just go into a store and make an exchange. I suppose it's because of that little quirk that I held out from marrying until Harold. When you're single, everyone wants to tell you how to pick up the sex or the child or the love substitutes as though they are all the same. All those biddies asking me when was it my turn to get married or have kids—they came across as holding me cheap."

"And love isn't cheap," Deborah said, "But it is free."

"Exactly," Sienna said. "And that's the other thing. If it's not integral, part of the whole of our lives and best choices, how could it be free? That's how I first spotted the lie in Greg's attentions. Neither of us were free. Of course, it didn't stop my mind from playing through a few scenarios at the worst possible times."

"Exits are here, here, and here," Deborah mimicked a safety announcement. "The body is that way. Always with the backup plan. Great in a fight, bad in an emotional crisis."

"Grief confuses our spinal cords, is what it is," Liz said. "It's in one of these articles I read this week—"

"Instead of fiction," Deborah interrupted. "Now, don't start spouting the articles again. Sienna has to get back to work, and we never let her answer your question about the stationery swap."

"Right," Sienna put down her teacup. "The swap will be of blank writing or correspondence cards or note sheets, all high quality. Everyone brings three sets, enough for three letters, and you leave with three new ones."

"Perfect for using up the end of a stationery set that familiarity has made contemptible," Deborah said.

Liz raised her eyebrow at Deborah. "You need to read more fiction, too. I think we both need a little flutter before we have to grade midterms and papers next week."

"We should do a book club here."

"Now, that's an insightful idea!" Liz patted the table in excitement. "Sienna, is that something you all would allow? I mean, with the understanding that the book club would be made up of a bunch of loudmouth, educated women, half of whom only read along to see if there were any racy bits in the plot?"

"Of course. Just pick a time, and we can reserve space for you." The murmur in the store had grown louder while Sienna sat with her friends. She looked up and saw a few women gathered by the door. One of them seemed very familiar. "Excuse me, ladies. I have to see to some folks. Y'all tell me

Tea & Crumples

what you think of the tea once you've had a chance to really try everything together. And come up for a free refill." She smiled at them, and Liz shooed her off with a friendly wave.

"Good afternoon," Sienna greeted the cluster of middle-aged women by the door. "May I show you to a table?" The women gathered closer at her greeting. There were five of them. One of the women smiled at her in recognition. Sienna smiled back, but couldn't quite place the face.

"Mrs. Raines?" Nina bustled up to a frosted blond woman with dignified eyeglasses on a chain and a pumpkin-colored tweed jacket over a crisp cotton shirt and wool trousers. The woman's wizened face brightened into a huge grin, and she embraced Nina warmly.

"Why, I didn't know you work here! Nina, dear, it's so good to see you. Is this what you're doing during your gap year?"

Nina blushed and tilted her head forward, not quite nodding. She turned to Sienna. "Miss, this is Mrs. Raines, my favorite teacher in high school. She taught me chemistry and home ec and business."

"*AP* chemistry, *four* years of home economics cooking, and *advanced* business accounting," Mrs. Raines corrected. She beamed proudly at Nina. "Nina was my star student," she said to the women with her. "I hope she goes back to school so she can apply all she learned." She raised her eyebrows authoritatively toward Sienna. Nina glanced downward then recovered herself.

"Mrs. Raines, this is my boss Sienna Bannock, the shop owner."

"Mrs. Bannock!" Mrs. Raines reached out and grasped her hand in a warm two-handed shake. "I have heard so many good things about this shop that I just had to come."

Sienna looked toward Nina and smiled. "I'm glad Nina has

told you good things. We certainly love having her as part of our team here."

"Oh, not from Nina, though of course she's wonderful and I'm glad you value her contributions." She smiled again at her former pupil. "It was my dear friend Elsie here," she gestured toward the familiar-looking woman in the group.

Sienna felt a wave of shock. Elsie was the woman who had ordered the cream cheese and Brussels sprout quiche that had caused them so much chagrin online. Sienna managed a tight smile and nodded toward a table behind the women. "Please, sit here and rest yourselves. Nina can go over the day's menu while I gather a few teas for you." The women took their seats companionably while Nina and her teacher exchanged pleasantries.

Sienna loaded a wide tray with four pots of tea, cream and almond milk, two types of sugar, a jar of honeycomb, and a few stevia packets. She breathed a quick prayer before she returned to the table and laid out the tea. Mrs. Raines watched her carefully as she placed the pots in front of three women and between the other two.

"Well, that's a very specific placement," Mrs. Raines commented. "And very specific condiments. What inspired you?"

"I told you they know what you want here," Elsie smiled. "It must be a God thing, because last time I was here, they turned around one of the worst days of my life with just a mug and a slice of quiche."

Sienna gaped.

"I see you don't recall me, Mrs. Bannock."

"Oh, please, call me Sienna."

"Sienna. I came in a few weeks back to ask about a TEA sorority event. You all had thought I meant a tea party like

Tea & Crumples

we're having here instead of donated goods, but you still treated me so kindly. I hadn't eaten all day when I got here because my first sorority scouting appointment canceled last minute, and my mother, bless her heart, had just had another one of her spells, so I hadn't slept much, either. I couldn't even remember the name of the quiche y'all served me!" She chuckled. "But you fed me and gave me good strong black tea, and I came back to myself by the time I got home."

"She's been pestering us ever since to come try out her magic teashop!" Mrs. Raines added with a wink toward Elsie. The other women at the table smiled or laughed. "But I think maybe we ought to call it a holy teashop instead."

Nina stood quite still beside the table, her arms filled with trays of pastries and a tea stand of rich sandwiches and cheeses. "But I thought you hated this place?" Nina blurted.

"Beg pardon?" Elsie raised her brows in polite inquiry. "Oh, please, dear, go ahead and set those things down. I guess I shocked you a little, I was that out of myself that day."

"You had been running too fast, and your soul couldn't keep up with your body," one of the women said. "That's *wasiwasi*, as they say in Swahili. You had to stop so you could literally get yourself together."

"Well, yes," Elsie said, taking up the nearest teapot and pouring out a dark stream of rich tea. She added a couple of white sugar lumps and stirred. "But is it that surprising, dear?" She smiled at Nina, whose shocked expression must have answered her, but Elsie's smile only warmed. "Or at any rate, can you forgive me that day? Look! I've brought you four more customers. Shaken together and running over, from your one day of being kind to me."

"I'm sorry for our confusion," Sienna said. "It's just, we thought perhaps, because of the negative reviews, that you had a bit of bad feeling toward us."

"Reviews?" Elsie blanched. Mrs. Raines reached across and grasped her hand to comfort her.

"Oh dear," Mrs. Raines whispered.

"You didn't write them," Sienna said, realization hitting her.

"My mother." Elsie set down her teacup and covered her forehead with her free hand. When she looked up, her eyes watered with barely-contained tears. "I am so sorry. My mother suffers from early dementia. She heard me tell the story to my husband and must have gotten the wrong end of it. She still has lots of friends among the older generation of TEA alumnae." She saw the tension ease from Sienna's shoulders. "How many?"

"Fourteen as of yesterday. All from women claiming ties to sororities, complaining of negative service experiences and food that wasn't what was advertised." Sienna stood still to let Elsie process the information, but she wanted to do something to comfort her. She decided to bring a new pot of tea, one with special orange blossom overtones. It was more in line with who Elsie really was, now that Sienna was seeing her in a truer light.

"I will go through her address book tonight and try to find the women she called. I'm sure they'll take them down if there's a way. But last time she did something like this, we weren't able to remove the reviews. My mother doesn't understand a great deal about the Internet, but she's heard us talk so much about consulting online reviews instead of looking in the paper that she remembers about them. I really am most terribly sorry."

"Tell you what," Sienna brightened. "You ladies agree to spread good news about the shop by word of mouth, and we'll forget all about it. Now, please, enjoy your tea. Mrs. Pinkwater, isn't it?" she asked Elsie.

"Call me Elsie, please."

"Elsie, I have another tea I'd like for you to try. On the house." She smiled and went to the kitchen, leaving the table of women to their eager exploration of the tea treats.

"But Miss," Nina asked after following Sienna into the kitchen, "the cancellations? We are just going to forget about them, too?"

"To be honest, Nina, those reviews not only hurt the business, they hurt my feelings. When Tovah and I envisioned this shop, it was with the idea that hospitality and graciousness would rise to the top of every experience here. The reviews Elsie Pinkwater's mother influenced portrayed our business in the exact opposite light, and did so in public for strangers who didn't know they were wrong. But holding onto hurt feelings isn't going to help me get back to that vision of hospitality and graciousness."

"Aren't you mad, though? Just a little? I mean, giving someone free tea when they've made your life miserable. That's pretty weird."

"If we're just people in the South in America in a business that has been slighted by a customer, though unwittingly, then it's weird. But what if we're an outpost of the kingdom of God? Then we're perfectly normal. Everything weird we do here— your cooking, Cleotis Reed's chess mastery, Tovah's taste and organization, Lettye's grace and creativity, Jessie's music, my tea sense —is normal in the kingdom."

"Hmmph." Nina did not sound convinced. "I like the idea, but it still doesn't seem fair. I mean, she lost you so much money."

"It's not Mrs. Pinkwater's fault that her mother's friends flamed us online, or that people cancelled." Sienna turned toward Nina and nodded to the front of the shop. "Besides, it may be that God used this unfortunate event to bring about better things for us. Just think of how many opportunities we would not have pursued if this hadn't happened. Would we have asked our investor for help? Would you have spoken to Mr. Reed about chess events?"

"Mr. Reed! Oh, Miss, I have to take him a sandwich. I'll be right back." Nina rushed off to care for her favorite customer, and Sienna set about blending a fragrant orange and herbal Darjeeling for Elsie.

By the time she returned to the front, the ladies were in full swing, cackling and giggling like girls over their enjoyment of the tea treats and sandwiches.

"Do sit down, please," Mrs. Raines demanded in a friendly tone, "and tell us how you knew just which tea to give each of us. How on earth did you know about Lynne's diabetes?"

"Her diabetes?" Sienna plastered a wary smile on her face as she ran through the tea tray inventories in her mind.

"The sweetener packets, dear," Mrs. Raines prompted.

"Oh. Of course," Sienna relaxed. "To be honest, I didn't know about her diabetes. I only knew that I had to put it on the tray and that the lady in moss green needed to have the stevia packets alongside her orange spice tea and almond milk."

"You knew that how?"

"Oh, you know as well as we all do how she knew it, Margaret," Lynne, the lady in green, said. "It's like Elsie told us. She has a gift. And I mean a real gift. Dear, I have taught Sunday school for longer than you have been alive, I reckon, and I have seen my share of spiritual gifts." She touched the side of her nose and winked at Sienna. "Just keep asking God for wisdom when you use that discernment and knowledge, and I won't worry over you knowing about me."

Sienna looked at Lynne and prayed. Sure enough, the gifts of teaching and exhortation and wisdom shone out at her,

Tea & Crumples

and with them, another strongly expressed grace. "You have a powerful, deep way with discernment yourself, ma'am," Sienna demurred. "And you know why. God loves people." Lynne answered with a knowing smile. She nodded around to the other women at the table, then at the shop in general.

"I like this place," Lynne said. "It will do very well indeed."

"I'm so glad to hear it," Sienna said. She popped up as a stream of women dressed in warm, bright clothing walked in. "Please let me know if you need anything else." She smiled. "Enjoy."

The brightly dressed group turned out to be chess enthusiasts. They clustered in the tables and chairs around the board and argued amongst themselves as to who would challenge Cleotis next. Sienna opted to bring them a group tray of cookies and Assam with milk and sugar rather than attempt to distract their attention from the current chess match. She went to the kitchen to pull the tray together.

"What's this?" Tovah indicated the two plates piled high with raspberry thumbprint cookies and mini ginger cream scones.

"Cleotis has attracted a gaggle of young women followers. I figured a chess player rate of $5 per person should cover their stay. I'm giving them the big pots with Assam."

"I like the idea. Group rates for groupies. I'll add it to our business prospectus for the investor."

"Is she still coming?"

"Oh, yes. I mentioned that Cleotis was planning to pull together a last minute tournament, and she insisted on coming out that day to see who wins."

"She's a chess fan?"

"Seems so. Says maybe she'll challenge the winner herself."

"So long as she doesn't predicate investing on her ability to defeat Cleotis Reed, I think we can be alright with that plan."

"We'll need to have everyone on call for the tournament. There may be a crowd."

"That's a good problem to have." Sienna smiled. She thought of the worse problems that had burdened her of late and sighed relief. "If we break fire code, we can always ask chess fans to watch through the window."

"I think you think you're joking, Si, but that may happen. Apparently chess people talk. At least, they email amongst themselves. It may be last minute, but this tournament could draw hundreds of people a day."

"Hundreds? We max out at ninety-five." Sienna smoothed her hair back from her face. "What should we do? Sell tickets?"

"I have another idea. Is Deborah still out there?"

"She and Liz never leave before an hour and a half or so. Why?"

"The art gallery across the street. If we could live stream the tournament games, at least on the last day, I wonder if they would host an overflow site? We could ask the Hearth people to cater the food and have Jessie man a table with some of our big samovars. Deborah would probably help with the tech setup. When you were out so much with Peter, she helped me fix our Wi-Fi."

"I like it. Will you talk to Deborah?"

"Of course. You take care of the groupies. And hey, Sienna, it's good to see *you* again."

Sienna's heart clutched in bittersweet appreciation of the compliment. It was good to feel herself again, but the recent pain still smarted. She smiled with her eyes as she took up the tray. "Oh, Tovah, it's good to be back."

NOTES FROM SIENNA'S TEA FILES

Elsie Pinkwater, ~~bitter old crow. Lipton tea from bag. Or an astringent breakfast blend. Serve with white sugar. Puts teeth on edge but can be tolerated~~. Philanthropist, community and TEA sorority organizer, caretaker to aging mother: Elsie's blend—my recipe (orange blossoms, top grade Darjeeling, a little orange mint, a sprig of thyme). Layered, gentle blend with astringent edge and sweet finish.

Margaret Raines, public school teacher, philanthropist: Gunpowder green tea served a little hotter than most greens (190-200 degrees F). Serve with local honeycomb. (Clover honey is best.)

Chapter Seventeen

Sienna's phone rang as she wrestled grocery bags from the passenger side of her car. "Hello?" She tucked the cell between her cheek and shoulder and walked toward the house, two heavy bags dangling from each hand.

"Sienna!" Tovah nearly yelled. "What did you say to those women today? Did you have any idea who they were?"

"Which women? The chess fans? Don't worry. I didn't call them groupies. They loved the group rate arrangement. In fact, Nina said they left a huge tip, too."

"Margaret Raines and that Elsie Pinkwater and company."

"Maybe Nina said something to them? Mrs. Raines was her high school teacher."

"I forget that you entirely lack social ambition. Sienna, every one of those women is on or chairs a board for one of the local private schools. After we closed, I received emails booking us for about $100,000 in business over the next six months."

"Lord have mercy!" Sienna gasped. "'This place will do,' she said. I guess Lynne meant for something other than just having

Tea & Crumples

a ladies afternoon tea party."

"Meet the Parents teas, more like, for several elite schools. Mother's Day at one of the most prosperous churches in the area. And two legislative meet and greets, one for mental health awareness and another on care options for elders with dementia."

"Lord, have mercy," Sienna repeated. Peter opened the front door and raised his eyebrows. She set down the bags and put the phone on speaker. "Tovah, tell Peter how much business you just booked."

Tovah repeated it. Peter balanced on one leg with his crutches tucked under his arms and clapped. "Way to go, ladies."

"And all because Sienna refused to hold a grudge. She was kind to some very influential women today. Listen, I think I hear grocery bags crinkling, which means Sienna finally went to the store after a month. I'll let you go, and we can discuss this in the morning. Peter, give that woman a kiss for me!"

"I'll make it a good one, Tovah," Peter laughed. "Take care."

Sienna ended the call and put the phone in her pocket. She grinned at Peter. "Not bad for a day's work."

"Not at all." Peter leaned forward and pecked her cheek. "Now, will you come inside so I can make good on my promise to kiss you proper?" He stooped and grabbed up two of the grocery bags.

"Peter! Your leg."

"I'm balanced. Besides, you can't deny me this opportunity to demonstrate my chivalry. Especially when I intend to let you cook for me."

"How generous of you."

"Oh, I'm very generous." He winked at her as they carried bags through the living room side by side. "I've even arranged for dessert."

"Oh?"

"It's a surprise." He hobbled ahead of her and managed to set the bags down in front of the sink without clunking them.

"I like surprises."

"I know."

The dogs ran in from the backyard and snuffled Sienna's jeans, licked her hands, and nosed the grocery bags.

"No treats in there unless you want butternut squash," Sienna said to Jonquil. Pogo licked his lips and whined a little when he sniffed out the cheese bag. "That's not Pogo cheese. That's people cheese."

"Here, Pogo! Jonquil!" Peter called. He held up two peanut butter dog biscuits to catch the dogs' attention. "Go get it!" He threw them into the yard, one toward the fence, one toward the middle. Jonquil and Pogo raced outside, tails wagging. Peter smiled after them and laughed to himself when the sound of happy crunching came through the open door. He half turned to Sienna, keeping his eyes on the yard. "This weather is perfect. Not so cold we have to close the door at twilight, not warm enough for lots of bugs." He looked at Sienna, and the smile dropped off his face. "What is it?" He hobbled toward her and pulled her close.

"I had forgotten this," her voice was thick. "How great a team we are. The little ways. I put up groceries while you distract the dogs from the cheese. I used to love it. I didn't let myself think…" She trailed off.

"I'm here now." Peter held her tightly against his chest and braced her neck with his warm hand.

"I always said to myself that you would be such a good father, that we would be great parents, because of how well we work together. Then I made myself forget it. When Susan… it

Tea & Crumples

was too painful. To lose her and to lose that vision of us." She raised her face to her husband and looked into his kind dark eyes. "It's like I had amnesia."

He kissed the top of her head and wiped her tears with his thumb. He kissed her eyes and sighed. "We all have amnesia, Sienna. It's always like this."

She raised an eyebrow in question.

"I've had a lot of time to think and pray lately. And to visit with some pretty holy people. One of the things Father Max said stuck in my spiritual craw."

Sienna smiled. "You always find new ways to get your craw jammed up."

"Well, this was a good craw stick. He said he would remember me at the liturgy. And I asked him to tell me about the liturgy, what with me not having a high prospect of going at the time. Or so I thought." A low laugh. "He used the word *anamnesis*, remembering. The opposite of amnesia. We remember in the prayers and give thanks. We were interrupted before he could go into detail, but it stuck with me, like I said."

"In your craw. Excuse me, your *spiritual* craw."

"Yes." He kissed her hair and continued, "And I started to remember. How would it be if you loved someone, if you really knew them, and they you, and you forgot, but they didn't? And then one day you start to come back to yourself, and you know enough to remember that you were in love. How do you regain the intimacy and make it even better than before?"

"You mean, us, me? When I was depressed?"

"We were both terribly sad, Sienna, don't blame yourself. But I'm talking about even bigger. Like with humans and God. We used to walk with him in the cool of the evening, so in love that there were only two rules in all of creation— be fruitful and don't eat the fruit of one tree. Breaking those rules gave us amnesia, but God gave us a way to remember."

"The liturgy?"

"The whole life in Christ."

She nodded under his chin.

"And you and I are part of it, too. Our marriage is a place of recollection."

"Our marriage and our kitchen."

"Yes." He laughed and leaned down, holding her from him so he could look into her face. "I want to remember with you, Sienna. Always. Even when it hurts."

"And give thanks no matter how much it may hurt. Peter, I don't ever want to forget you again."

He kissed her. When they came up for air, his unbalanced crutch fell over with a clatter onto the counter. "How about I put away the cabinet things and you do the fridge?"

They fell into an easy rhythm of housekeeping. At length, Sienna paused, a jar of marinated feta in her hand. "I don't mind, you know. I like our parish, but I don't mind. A.C. said God gets our attention where he can, and maybe that's all that was attracting us to Orthodoxy. Maybe he's right, but maybe there's more there. If it cures amnesia?"

Peter sat clumsily in a wooden kitchen chair and propped his hurt leg catty corner to the next chair. "I think I'd like to explore it. It's just a hunch right now, but I think it might be the way we're called."

"I agree. Only, I worry. Are we running from our parish because we don't want to face the grief we experienced there?"

"The way it seems to me, Sienna, is that the little tastes we've had of Orthodoxy have helped us face grief better. But not alone. Facing grief while looking into the face of God. That's not running away."

"I guess not. Every person who has spoken to us from that

tradition has only helped us remember things, not run from them. Like Bethel Bailey helping me. *Susan was here.* It's so simple, but that was such a healing day."

"I want to go with you. Record all the places she was with us."

"Smile into the camera in all the corners where she laughs."

Peter nodded and turned to face the garden. A breeze brought the rich fragrance of late-season herbs into the room.

"They go together, Peter. Thanksgiving and remembering. But not necessarily one before the other. I remembered Susan and felt really grateful for her life. Like the thanks made a place apart from the fog of grief where I could be so happy she was here. And you. I gave thanks for you, and then you came back to me. I mean, yes, you were healed and came back to me. But also, I gave thanks and could embrace you again. I remembered you."

The dogs came in then, dragging with them the scent of thyme and chocolate mint. The mint was present in more than scent, Jonquil having caught some in her tail. Peter ruffled the fur behind the dogs' ears while Sienna cooked dinner. They fell into happy banter until the food smelled almost done.

"I'd better go wash up," Peter said. He hitched himself up and made his way to the powder room, the dogs following on his heels.

Alone, Sienna watched herself stir the sauce in front of her while her mind wandered. She thought of each spoon in her kitchen, starting with the wooden one in her hand, and touched them each with thanksgiving. She thanked God for the robin's egg blue teapot, for every frail cup and sturdy mug, for the jar of clotted cream in the fridge door, and for the bricks on the patio that loved to warm in the sun. Peter came up behind her and wrapped his arms around her waist.

"I thank God for you, Beloved," he said into her ear.

She put down the spoon and turned into his embrace. When she looked up, he was smiling at her. "What?" She matched his mischievous smile with a curious one. "Peter Bannock, what are you up to?"

"Just thinking of dessert."

She laughed. "I think I know what you were thinking. But about dessert. I bought you pears. And I hope you don't mind, but I bought the canned whipped cream. They were out of the good whipping cream at the store."

"And I found the jar of dulce de leche I had been saving for you."

"Wonderful. It will go with the dessert tea."

"It will go with dessert."

"What do you mean? The pears—"

"We can have the pears, too."

"And?"

"And these." Peter pulled two small silver teaspoons from his pocket. They were antique, authentic, and perfectly polished so that the bowls shone but the pattern had patina.

"Oh, my!" Sienna reached for a spoon, but Peter held it just out of her reach. "And what did you plan to do with those spoons?"

"Feed you caramel with them, one bite at a time."

"Oh?"

"By candlelight."

"Mmm." She nuzzled closer to him.

"But first," Peter stood straighter and sniffed the air. "Dinner."

Nina rushed in two minutes late the next morning. She looked at the clock and groaned. "Almost!"

Tea & Crumples

"Trouble with your ride again? Is your family okay?" Sienna relaxed when she saw the happy flush on Nina's face.

"Oh, no, Miss, it's just that I thought I could get here on time by taking the bus. There's a stop by Father Greg's house. Only, I was wrong. Two minutes late."

"Or the clock is fast."

"No. I set it. I'm late." Nina seemed exhilarated at the prospect. "But it shows that the buses are almost on time, so I can tell my aunt to use the bus without worrying. She leaves early for everything anyway."

"Things are going well with your family now?"

"We have the papers at hand for my parents and me, and Tamsin agreed to sponsor my sister for citizenship."

"Tamsin?"

"Father Greg's wife. She's back."

"Oh." Sienna felt a small jealous twinge. It annoyed her, but she knew herself well enough to observe the feeling without believing it. "That's great. When did she come back?" She heard the hard edge to her voice and hoped Nina did not misattribute her discomfiture. She was annoyed with her own jealousy, not with Greg for reconciling with his wife.

"A couple of days after we got there. I think Mamá talked to him. Not many people can resist Mama's wisdom. She won't let you. She's Mamá to everyone, whether they like it or not." Nina smiled, and Sienna matched her expression. She was pleased that Greg had found the mother he needed in a healthy way. "What is it, Miss? Why are you smiling like that?"

"I'm just so glad that everything is going so well. Your family is getting the help they need, and your Mamá helped out a very wounded man."

"Mamá says he's a good man, but he needed someone to remind him. Like he had forgotten himself, and she showed

255

him a mirror."

Sienna stopped and leaned on the counter, taken aback by how closely Nina's words echoed her conversation with Peter the night before. "Nina, has anyone ever told you that you have a gift for truth telling?"

"Um?" The girl reddened.

"It's also called evangelism. Telling good news. Speaking good words."

"Like a preacher?"

"Like a wise woman." She patted Nina on the shoulder. "Now, tell me what you've been planning with Cleotis Reed."

"Tovah told you about the overflow site? Well, Mr. Reed says that if we don't get the crowd to need it right away, he will offer a raffle for people to play against him in a match, even if they aren't registered for the tournament."

"That will attract a lot of people for sure. Yesterday there were twenty or more people here just to watch him play; only a handful dared to challenge him."

"But the raffle, Miss, Mr. Reed says that he will donate the proceeds to the shop."

"What? Why? That's so kind."

"He says he has a vested interest in seeing us succeed. Says he won't discuss it further with us till after the tournament, but he does not plan to take no for an answer."

"Speaking of which, we will need a lot of extra food laid up. We can't do most of the food ahead of time, but we can freeze quiches, scones, and thumbprint cookies. Today, when we're not too busy, I'd like you to make quiches. I'll make a double set of mini scones when I prep for the afternoon tea crowd."

Nina nodded and turned sharply toward the door to the front of the shop, where Tovah leaned in. "Did Nina tell you, Si? We're going to need another samovar to serve the tea at the

Tea & Crumples

tournament. I'm going to send Jessie to get one this afternoon."

"Tell her to get two. We'll do an Earl Grey and a breakfast blend in each location."

Tovah narrowed her eyes at Sienna and Nina. "The two of you look a bit piqued. Get in here and have some breakfast."

They complied and walked to the tea counter, where Tovah and Lettye grinned over a small chocolate cake with three lit candles. Nina smiled shyly.

"I read your personnel file," Tovah said. "Happy nineteenth birthday! *Happy birthday to you!*" she sang. Sienna and Lettye joined in. When they were finished, Nina blew out the candles while the others clapped and laughed.

"We got you something." Lettye slid a glossy page across the counter toward the birthday girl. Sienna knit her brows in question. Lettye mouthed, "You'll see," and nodded toward Tovah. If the two had been in on the present together, Sienna was sure the gift would be perfect.

"Thanks," Nina said. She lifted the paper and read. Her brows rose, her face brightened, and finally her mouth dropped open in surprise. She jumped up from her seat and hugged Tovah, who was nearest. "Oh, thank you! Thank you! Thank you! My own cooking classes? Is this really happening?" She waved the poster in the air a little. "You're advertizing for me?" The poster had the shop logo, Mexican breads, sugar skulls, and a beautiful candid photo of Nina smiling behind the tea counter. It advertized a cooking class in traditional Mexican sweet breads in preparation for celebrating *el Día de los Muertos.* "But we have to do churros, too. You can't tell someone about Mexican pastries without churros."

"Did we give you enough time to prepare?" Tovah asked.

"Oh, sure. Do you think it would be okay if my cousin comes to help, too? He's a real baker. His sister-in-law bought a tortillería and bakery, and everyone on that side of the family works there during the busy times."

"If you'd like," Tovah said. "But I don't want you to feel as though you are not enough. We've seen you work. You're competent and clear as a communicator. I think you teaching this class will be a great experience for everyone."

"Thanks, Miss." Nina's eyes filled with tears.

The women ate cake and drank an astringent Assam fixed with cream and unrefined lump sugar. Everyone was excited about the upcoming changes and expansions of the business. They fell into brainstorming.

"What about you, Sienna?" Lettye asked. "Do you think you could teach people about how you choose teas for them?"

"Only if it's a prayer group," Sienna laughed. "Seriously. I could probably teach a small class on blending seasonal ingredients into a few standard tea blends. Like, which leaves to use along with lemon and mint or basil for summer iced teas. Or how to make spiced teas strong enough in winter with no artificial ingredients. But I can't really take credit for the gift of knowledge."

"I see what you mean. It's a combination of your skills and experience and direct spiritual insight," Lettye said.

"Or what some people might call a powerful intuition," Tovah added.

"Why don't you teach a class on setting up an afternoon tea?" Nina offered.

"Now that, I can do."

"You can print out your scone recipe on cotton cards from the store," Tovah said. "Use our logo stationery so there's no mistaking it. Then if someone wants to pass the recipe on, it advertizes for us."

Lettye nodded eagerly. "And you can show them how to

Tea & Crumples

make good tea from what they have available. If they can't take custom teas home from here, show them how not to oversteep a bag or understeep some of the weaker teas."

"The decaf teas are tricky," Nina agreed. "If you don't show people, they always mess it up and complain."

"My scones, the teas, and what else? Do people really need to be shown how to make sandwiches?"

Lettye laughed. "You have clearly never met my ex-husband. Which is to say, yes. A lot of people, and not just men, cannot make sandwiches. How do you think McDonald's keeps in business?"

"True. Sad, but true," Tovah said. "We should show how to make a basic butter-based sandwich, plus one of our chevre sandwiches, and Lettye's chicken salad, maybe."

"Oh, yes. The tea ladies always love that chicken salad," Nina said. "I always have to bring those groups of ladies another plate of just the chicken salad sandwiches."

"Do you think I should show them the thumbprint cookies, too?"

"No. Just give them the recipe. Those take too long, with the refrigeration and everything. I'll print that one on the same cardstock. But we should keep Lettye's recipe a shop secret. Give them something to talk about and bring their friends in to try."

"Quiches?" Sienna asked.

"No. That can be another class. In the spring. Easter quiches, maybe," Lettye said.

"What about you, Lettye?" Nina asked. "Do you have any ideas for a class?"

Lettye and Tovah exchanged glances. "Actually, we," she gestured between herself and Tovah, "want to do an ongoing series of lessons on social graces in stationery."

Sienna nodded. "I love the idea! Do you think you might add the manners of the tea table as well? How to have tea with a friend, from inviting her to pouring out?"

"Or him," Tovah smiled. "Invite your young man to tea."

"Win over your crush with tea." Nina smiled shyly. "I like it. Sign me up!"

They had just finished their cake when Tovah focused on the door. "Look who's here. Sienna, you want to let Marnie in? I think we can trust her in the place for the four minutes before we officially open."

"Hmm?" Sienna turned and saw her old friend. "Oh, yes." She got up to open the door while the others cleared up the remains of the breakfast party. She hadn't seen Marnie since the day of her meltdown over Susan. So much had happened since then. She hoped that she had not been as abrasive as she recalled. At least she hoped that Marnie would forgive her. She unlocked the door and opened it.

"Sienna." Marnie stepped forward and hugged her. "It's so good to see you."

"You, too." She hugged back. "Thank you for going to see Peter."

Marnie looked startled.

"He told me how you talked about Susan. I think I understand now."

"Oh." Marnie looked relieved. "I'm glad." She stood awkwardly in the entrance and eyed her friend warily. Susan was a sensitive subject, and Sienna had often been put off by reminders of her.

"Come in and let me make you some tea." Sienna shut the door behind Marnie and ushered her toward the tea bar. "I wanted to thank you for praying for us and for talking with me last time you were here. I know I wasn't very receptive."

Tea & Crumples

"It was a lot to take in. Susan was your daughter, and I misled you about her. I didn't mean to. I didn't even know I was doing so. But that had to hurt."

"It did, but it also helped. You gave me another way to remember her. Another way to be grateful."

"That's a relief." Marnie let out a big breath.

"Peter said you came to pray for him on the baptism night."

"Baptism night? Who was baptized?"

"I mean, the night so many people came to visit and pray. The night he was healed. I had a dream about you, but I didn't know it was real."

"Is that where baptism comes in? Was I *laying down my burden down by the riverside?*" Marnie sang the last bit in deference to the hymn. She knew all the old Southern baptism hymns, even if she was about the highest church Episcopalian of Sienna's acquaintance.

"Hmm?" Sienna was distracted by the music. She got caught up in memories of summer church services and had to stare at Marnie for a moment to recall the conversation thread. "Oh, sorry. No. It's just that the night reminded us of my baptism, when so many people helped bring the water to the font. We figure Peter was healed the same way. Healing by the handful."

Marnie laughed. It was a deep, warm sound that shook her belly. "I guess—" She reached into her jacket pockets and brought out two handfuls of dried red petals and pale green leaves. She caught her breath around her laughter and tried again. "I guess that's why I felt nudged to bring you these." She moved her cup off her napkin and put down the blossoms. "Dried bee balm from our garden. Two hands full."

"Two hands full of grace." Sienna smiled and fingered the delicate dried herbs. She decided to put them into a new blend she was making. "Seems appropriate. You have been there with us through this whole ordeal. Through these ordeals. The shop, and Susan, and Peter. Bringing healing by the handful. Only, I didn't notice right away what was happening. You've kept me sane, Marnie. Thank you."

"Oh, Sienna. My dear friend, you are a joy to me." She touched the delicate pink and yellow chintz china cup that Sienna had set in front of her. "I'm glad to be able to give you something with my hands."

The bell rang at the front of the shop, and Bethel Bailey marched in, followed immediately by a rush of graduate students toward the bank of booth tables.

"You must be Marnie," Bethel said, extending her hand. "Bethel Bailey. Regular customer, Orthodox Christian, friend. Father Max said you prayed with him the other night, and I was to satisfy my curiosity about you in person as soon as I might."

"Did he?" Marnie smiled. "Glad to meet you. Though, I hope I'm not too much of a curiosity."

"You're a pilgrim and a praying person, which makes you odd enough, I suppose." She burst into song, "*To be a pilgrim*! And all that. Well, you are the type of stranger that God kept back as a little treat, as my granny says. I expect we'll get on perfectly."

Marnie grinned without even stopping to consider whether she was being flattered. "I couldn't ask for a better recommendation than that. Do you go on pilgrimages?"

"Bethel is the one who gave me the 'Susan Was Here' pilgrim assignment." Sienna placed a cup and a fresh pot of Bethel's favorite tea on the counter in front of her. "She goes to Father Max's church, and her husband is studying to be a priest."

"But I used to be Baptist, which is why my name sounds

Tea & Crumples

like a church name. Well, that, and Granny's ornery streak." Bethel launched into the story of her name while Sienna went to the kitchen to retrieve the cream and cream pitchers. When she returned, Bethel had just concluded, "It's better than being called Second, I suppose. Secundus, isn't that what Romans called their second sons?"

"You're right. Your name suits you., Marnie said. "I've been to Bethel. It's where Jacob dreamed the ladder to heaven. The front gate to heaven, some think. I guess that means you are a face that people see when they knock on God's door."

Sienna smiled at Bethel's expression. The women would doubtless get along well; they were the very picture of iron strengthening iron. She busied herself nearby so she could enjoy the happy opportunity of watching them.

"You're a healer and a seer," Bethel said. "Oh, I hope you don't mind my coming out and saying it. I don't mind beating about the bush when it's needed, but I think you know I know."

"I'm on the healing prayer team at church, yes. And I pray that God will show me the way."

"Tell me about your bracelets," Bethel said, her tone casual, her eyes sharp. "The patterns are beautiful. I noticed them in the photo Sienna showed me. They remind me of bandages."

Marnie, who had extended her wrists out of her long sleeves to show Bethel the bracelets, flinched and pulled them back at her last words. "Do they?" she asked. "I designed the patterns based on Celtic knotwork in some of the manuscripts of medieval Gospels. Have you seen the Book of Kells? I try to go see it at least once every few years. We like to travel to the Celtic isles. A lot of the saint sites escaped the Reformation. Of course, there wasn't much to destroy, what with the simplicity of the hermits. The great church paintings are gone, of course.

263

That pains me."

Bethel reached out and touched the silver band around Marnie's right wrist. "I imagine it does pain you. But what a gift to see them. There are certain losses that are restorative when we see them." Her words were neutral enough not to draw the attention of the people around them. Bethel might have been lamenting the loss of church art, but Sienna could tell that Bethel was talking about something more immediate. She relocated the bowl of tea she was blending so she could watch her friends more closely.

Marnie nodded and looked Bethel in the eye. "You know."

Bethel nodded once.

"Father Max?"

Bethel shook her head. "I knew before. He didn't tell me, but I do math for a living and figured it out. There are certain types of math that you get used to when you walk among people becoming like God."

"I see."

Sienna stopped her work sniffing bins of tea and stared from Marnie to Bethel, to Marnie's wrists. She remembered the bright light from her dream on the night Peter was healed. Marnie had a burn mark showing around the edge of the bracelet Bethel had touched. Surely not. Surely her friend did not bear the marks of Christ. Marnie turned to Sienna and looked at her. A wave of deep love welled inside Sienna. It brightened her memories of the days with Susan, with Peter, even memories that might have been of the future. The feeling bubbled to her lips. "Thank you." Sienna said, and she remembered.

Susan was lying in her arms, frail and still warm. Sienna heard her own voice, the words she had spoken to the child before the cord had been cut. "My dear little girl. Susan, I love

Tea & Crumples

you so much. I am so grateful to be your mother. I love you so much, you wonderful child." She had repeated it over and over, touching the miniscule fingers. She had kissed her daughter's tiny head, her unopened eyes, the perfect ears.

It was the worst day of her life, but now that she recalled it, it was beautiful. She was smiling; she was crying; gratitude and memory were one. Marnie reached out and squeezed Sienna's fingers, wiped her cheek with the back of a healing hand, and pulled her friend into a bear hug. Bethel joined in, squeezing them both so hard that Sienna laughed. She looked around, worried that she was making a scene. Cleotis Reed caught her eye and smiled, nodded. Her embarrassment melted away in the warmth of the hugs and memories.

"This," Sienna whispered. "Here." She hugged Marnie and Bethel harder. "Susan is here. This is what I wanted for her, had she lived. And she does."

"For nothing shall separate us from the love of God in Christ Jesus," Marnie said.

"To God, all are alive," Bethel answered.

"It's true," a deep masculine voice affirmed. Sienna looked up and saw Father Max standing at the counter.

NOTES FROM SIENNA'S TEA FILES

Tamsin Tippett, 37, lawyer: Rooibos with brown lump sugar (or caramel if available). Strongly brewed, can withstand long exposure to heat.

Chapter Eighteen

Sienna pulled away from the group hug. She smiled at Father Max, at Bethel and Marnie and said, "Tea," then bustled to the kitchen to wash her hands and face and put together a tray.

She pulled out the silver teapot from its flannel cozy, preheated it, and brought it to the front. Father Max was not the type to tell tales, but she wanted to thank him for being so gracious. His face reddened over his beard when he looked up from setting up the chess table with Cleotis and saw the silver pot, the pile of cookies and pastries on the best china, and small, intricate silver teaspoons alongside a Russian tea glass held in antique silver.

"On the house," she said. He nodded acceptance and glanced toward the tea bar where Bethel and Marnie sat in animated conversation. When he looked back to her, she thanked him simply and left him to his match.

At lunchtime, Nina emerged from the kitchen with a wave of sweet-cinnamon scented air. She carried a tray of mini churros around to all of the customers and told those who accepted one about her upcoming class. The shop buzzed with the warm fragrance of churros and the buzz of hungry minds and bellies. Sienna, Lettye, Jessie, and Nina were all busy with tea customers before the lunch hour was out, and Tovah seemed to be making a bride and her mother very happy in the stationery area. Sienna walked toward the paper alcove to find out the reason for the laughter. She had reached the journal stand when a commotion by the front door called her attention back to the shop.

Four children stood by a tea table full of ladies-who-lunch. The children craned their heads eagerly toward the tea stand of desserts. A tall woman suddenly filled the frame of the door. She spoke quietly, and the children withdrew to a polite distance and smiled at the table of ladies.

"Maria!" Sienna rushed forward to welcome her. "You made it! Let me get you a table. Or here, come to the tea bar. All the larger tables are filled right now, though of course you are welcome to go watch the chess table any time." She laughed as the little boy and one of the girls nipped straight over to where Cleotis and Father Max were deep in a match. "Of course you know Father Max. Come, come. Let me make you something. No, don't worry about the children. They are most welcome here." Besides a little extra twirling and dancing, the children blended in well with the shop as though they were accustomed to civilized settings.

"My children create their own weather." Maria smiled. "Still, they will probably be relatively calm, especially with Father here. Oh, what's this? Peanut butter pastry? The peanut butter makes it healthy, right?" She assisted a little girl into the high pink barstool while another girl pulled herself up in a neighboring spot.

Tea & Crumples

"What will you have, mademoiselle?" Sienna asked the smallest girl.

"Tea, please."

"With cream and sugar?"

"Yes, please!"

Sienna raised her brows in question to Maria, who nodded confirmation. Sienna prepared a large pot of malty Assam for the family and paired it with raspberry thumbprint cookies and a plate of the peanut butter pastries sliced into smaller servings. She placed the tray of tea things in front of Maria, who, now that Sienna had a chance to look at her sitting, sported a growing pregnant belly. Sienna added a bowl of fresh fruit to the tray.

"Now, shall I pour for you?" Sienna held up the pot over Maria's stein. Maria nodded, and Sienna smiled in approval as the rich orange brown filled the glass cup and contrasted with the brightly painted design. "Oh, that is lovely. I can see why you prefer it over ordinary cups."

"Plus the lid keeps the tea warm a little longer." Maria brought the stein toward her and breathed the fragrant steam. "This smells amazing."

"Shall I pour for the children, too?"

"Yes, please. They take extra milk."

"I'll leave room." Sienna filled two pale pink cups halfway and set them by Maria. Maria looked at her girls' eager faces and sat up straighter, simultaneously composing her face.

"One lump or two?" Maria asked in a precise voice.

"Two!" the girls chimed simultaneously. Their mother added the sugar and some milk, handed the cups to the girls to stir, and placed a few treats on each saucer. "Thank you," they said, and set to eating.

"Bethel will be here soon. Do you know her?"

"Bethel Bailey? Yes! She's the one who convinced me to make the trip out to try this place. She told me you had a real gift for picking teas. She was right." Maria inhaled the steam again and sipped from her stein. "This is wonderful."

"Mommy, I have to go to the bathroom," the youngest girl said. Maria excused herself and took the little girl's hand. They set off toward the ladies' lounge. When they returned, Maria's face was bright.

"That is the most child friendly restroom I've ever seen. Do you have children?"

"I had a little girl, but she died at nineteen weeks gestation. We planned the space with her in mind, though."

Maria's hands flew to her belly, but then she reached out to Sienna. "I'm so sorry for your loss. We lost one child, as well— a little boy. Of course, he died too early to know it was a boy, but I thought he was a boy. We named him Isaac."

"I'm sorry you had to go through that, too. But I'm glad to hear Isaac's name. It feels good to honor the love we have for babies, even when they don't grow up."

"One of the things I love about Orthodoxy is that I have a relationship with our son even though he's gone. There's a connection through prayer and the liturgy and saints. He prays for us, and we for him."

"For to God all are alive." Sienna repeated Bethel's words from earlier that day. Maria nodded and looked into her tea. Sienna gave her a moment to recover. "It's so strange. I just had a conversation about this very subject this morning with Bethel. But I don't want to upset you by dwelling on loss. You strike me as someone with a lot of joy."

"Well, they go together, don't they? The disciplines of motherhood bring us joy and sorrow. But mostly joy. A sword pierced Mary's heart, but she fell asleep in the joy of the resurrection."

They were joined by the two children who had gone to the chess table. The boy held Father Max's hand. "Mama," he said, "Father Max is going to be in a chess tournament, and he says I can watch if you want to bring me."

"Me, too," the oldest girl chimed in. Father Max greeted the seated members of the family and made the sign of the cross over them in blessing.

"Is there a child category in this tournament?" Maria asked.

"I don't think so," the boy said.

"Oh, can there be?" asked the girl.

"That's a very good idea," Sienna answered. "We don't have plans for a youth tournament this time around, but let me get with my staff, and we can set one up for future. When are y'all out of school?"

"We homeschool," The oldest girl answered matter-of-factly and climbed onto a barstool. She accepted a cup of tea and plate of pastries from her mother, then turned back to Sienna. "You can find the calendars of the local school systems on the Internet, though. That's how I plan my sleepovers. Public school kids don't get much time off, so you have to plan carefully."

"Thank you," Sienna said. She turned to Father Max. "So you'll be joining us this weekend? Excellent. I suppose you'll be in the higher tier of players, but you are welcome to come earlier to watch the other matches. We probably won't have to use the overflow site until Cleotis starts accepting challengers that afternoon." Father Max nodded acceptance.

"Actually, I was hoping you would join us now at the chess table. We have been having a most interesting discussion on miracles, and I think you will like seeing the resolution."

"If your chess game has gotten to the degree of miraculous,

I think I'd better go see." Sienna excused herself to Maria and commended the family into Nina's capable hands. Nina immediately plied the children with churros and drew Maria into conversation about the best oils for cooking Mexican cuisine. Sienna paused on her way to the chess table long enough to pour herself a mug of tea, then made her way through the tables of low conversation to the front window.

"What is this miracle that I'm meant to see, gentlemen?" Sienna smiled and approached the chess table. Cleotis and Father Max stood as she drew up a chair. They resumed their seats and took up their own teacups.

"You aren't afraid of miracles," Cleotis said to her. He waited.

"Um, no," Sienna said, flustered at the sudden leap into the depths. "Well, yes, really. They aren't exactly tame things."

"But you've seen them."

Sienna nodded, thinking of her years on the healing prayer team. "Yes. Peter is alive." The men regarded her in peaceful silence. "Peter's a huge miracle, and very special to me, of course. But yes, I've seen others. Most of them are more gradual." She looked at the board as Father Max moved a piece several spaces into the fray. "I think about most miracles like I think of the garden. You have soil and roots and stems and leaves, and sometimes a flower. Most of the story of a blossom is told before it appears. The flower is just the amen of the garden."

Cleotis regarded the board and moved a piece. He turned his gaze back to Sienna and nodded for her to continue.

"What's awful," she swallowed, "what's awful is the pain. It doesn't seem to go away. Like, miracles are wonderful, but they don't make suffering end. It's hard to explain."

Father Max moved another piece, then looked up at Sienna.

Tea & Crumples

"It's like we're all Lazarus," Sienna continued. "We might be raised, but we have to die again before the last day."

Cleotis moved another piece. "Check.

"And God may make them beautiful, but miracles are also deniable. I've heard women cured from cancer tell people how glad they were that the multiple MRIs and biopsies were somehow mistaken. Or a little boy who was unharmed after being run over by a truck, because his head was crushed into the mud from recent rain. The family thanked God for the rain, but they didn't seem to see the gritty way God had saved their child."

Father Max made a move. "Check."

"One time a woman came to us worried her mother would commit suicide. The next week, she said her mother had made an attempt, but the gun had jerked to the side when it fired. Her mother shot herself in the elbow instead of the chest. The blow had stunned her out of her suicidal thoughts. That woman understood, though. She came to us rejoicing over God's guerilla tactics. Her mother refused to accept the grace of God insofar as she determined to shoot herself, but God's grace prevailed in that an angel knocked the gun out of her hands. You see, that was the woman's prayer all along. She asked God to please help her mother not to shoot herself, but that if she tried, to please make her miss."

Cleotis moved a piece. "Check."

"And there was a man who prayed for his drug addict son to run late every day so he would miss his meetups with dealers. That man and the woman who prayed her mother would miss, they had a grasp of the way grace is rooted in everyday things. Schedules, and meetings, and the basic physicality of effort."

Father Max moved a piece and leaned back. He didn't speak, but Cleotis tipped over his king. The men shook hands and sat back in their seats, grinning.

"I suppose you two wanted me to come talk about miracles for some reason," Sienna said, looking between them.

"Did you see it coming?" Cleotis asked.

"The miracles?"

"The checkmate."

"No."

"I did. It didn't have to happen, but I saw the possibility. So did Max. That makes him a good opponent."

"But a better partner," Father Max said. "To be able to see the way to victory through the fogs of war. Chess is a war game."

"You wanted me to see your chess match?" Sienna knit her brows and looked from one game piece to another. She wasn't an expert player herself, but she enjoyed the ambience of the game and the chivalry of its rules. "What does that have to do with miracles?"

"Just a reminder," Cleotis said. He sipped his tea and let the quiet stretch out like a basking cat. Sienna, wary to the way the men's prior silence had prompted her to talk at length, sipped her tea, too, and waited.

"The Christian life is filled with joy and love and peace and all the fruits of the Spirit," Father Max said. "But it is also war and struggle. We don't always see the miracles coming, but the victory is a foregone conclusion."

A few tables cleared and a fresh wave of customers came in. Sienna grew antsy seeing Lettye and Nina try to juggle them all. She wasn't sure what the men had wanted her to say or to see, but she was anxious to get back to her work. "I'm not sure what I'm supposed to see here. It's too much to take in from a distance."

"We can talk again," Father Max said. "You'll want to get

Tea & Crumples

back to your customers."

"Thank you." Sienna started to get up, but a question niggled at her. "What were you two talking about before I came over, that you wanted me to hear?"

"Ah." Father Max nodded. "A small question. Whether miracles usually remind people of God's greatness or his love."

"Or if they ever notice that the love and greatness are the same." Cleotis' eyes twinkled.

"So nothing deep or anything." Sienna smiled. "Thank you for letting me talk. Next time—" she pointed a stern finger at each of them "—*you* have to tell *me* about miracles." The men agreed, and Sienna returned to the tea bar.

Maria and her children had moved to the stationery area, where they were examining sketchbooks and thick sheets of premium wrapping paper in elegant prints. Bethel must have sneaked in while Sienna was at the chess table. Her customary tea was sitting at an empty seat next to where Maria's family left their half-finished cups. Sienna could hear the energetic clip of Bethel's Southern accent in the stationery alcove. The children seemed to regard her as a favorite.

Sienna waited on a few graduate students, a grassy green tea drinker and two jasmine oolong lovers, and went to the kitchen to check stores for the tournament. She prepared a dozen large trays of cookie dough and put it in the refrigerator to chill. She stepped out of the cooler to see a familiar face peeking around the door to the shop.

"Greg!" Sienna said. She had forgotten all about Greg. Part of her had wondered if he would stop coming to the shop now that his temptation had subsided. She found that she was glad to see him. She wanted to tell him about Peter's recovery. It might be awkward at first to remember her mixed feelings over the past several weeks, but her earlier insight had been right, too. Greg had strong spiritual gifts, and she hoped that they could strengthen each other in friendship once the gifts were properly directed. Greg smiled so that his grey eyes lit like light in clear water. *Eventually*, she thought, *but not quite yet.* They could be friends eventually, but her body's memory queue needed to clear first.

"Sienna," Greg said. He fixed a smile at her, but the fox was gone from it. "I've brought someone for you to meet." He gestured toward the front. "Please."

Sienna followed Greg to his accustomed spot at the manuscript table, where a honey haired woman sat in front of creamy pages of stationery, scritching along with a silver pen. "Tamsin," Greg began. The woman looked up, her deep blue eyes sharp and kind. She stood. "This is Sienna. I told you about her tea." He turned to Sienna as Sienna reached out to shake Tamsin's hand. "And her good sense." Tamsin had a strong handshake that brooked no lies but implied impeccable good breeding.

"Glad to meet you," Tamsin said in a chocolatey low voice that made Sienna wish that Tamsin were singing. "I'd like to try the tea you choose for me." She looked at Sienna levelly, then tilted her head slightly, humbly. "I'm rather in need of a new habit. If tea is to be my vice, I'd like it to be an enjoyable one."

"Well." Sienna said, taken aback at the woman's frankness and clever humility. Tamsin and Greg were a good match. She wanted to honor that in her hospitality. "Let me see what I can come up with. How about one for you, one for Greg, and one to share?" Tamsin nodded and turned to Greg, whose eyes were on his wife. They sat down, and Sienna went to make them tea.

She prayed as she went, and a brisk smell came to her mind.

Tea & Crumples

She tried to sift it into its components. Caramel, mint, green, sweet, and sturdy round sunshine. She smiled and pulled down three pots. One for Greg's usual Moroccan mint, one fragrant orangey rooibos for Tamsin, and a clear glass pot for the tea they would share. Into the last pot, she scooped a handful of the flowers Marnie had brought her that morning. When the tea was brewed, she set the pots on a tray with extra cups, dark sugar, and honey.

"Caffeine free," Sienna said, setting the rooibos in front of Tamsin. "But let me know if you want something stronger. The advantage to this one is that it can stew all day in hot water without growing bitter." She turned to Greg and put a pot in front of him. "Your usual. Cool Morrocan mint with extra sugar. I've put extra cups so you can share with Tamsin." She lifted the last pot from the tray and placed it between them. "But this one is for you both." They looked at the flowering herbs floating in the delicate pot. A red petal flipped in the current from Sienna's movement.

"Bee balm," Greg said.

"Yes. Or wild bergamot. It's a classic American tisane. Grows in the hot weather, restores year round. Perfect for rebels and people of high principles. Good for people who speak for a living, as it soothes throats. Good for headaches, too, for when people get to be a little much." While she spoke, their faces brightened and their eyebrows raised. They turned to each other and smiled. "Enjoy," Sienna said, and started to walk away.

"Sienna," Tamsin said. "Thank you."

NOTES FROM SIENNA'S TEA FILES

Tippett Couple (see Greg and Tamsin's cards): Bee balm tea, served hot and plain alongside brown sugar. Restorative.

Chapter Nineteen

The day of the tournament dawned cold. Sienna exclaimed at the chill when she got up to turn off her alarm. Peter pulled her back into bed.

"Stay here where it's warm." He nuzzled against her neck and found her ear.

"Mmm." Sienna turned toward him. "I wish I could. But potentially dozens of chess enthusiasts will be waiting for their tea this morning."

"You don't want to disappoint the chess enthusiasts," Peter said. He hugged her closer so that she wanted to do just that. Sienna groaned a little and pulled away.

"No. I shall exert myself and resist your charms." She leaned toward him and kissed him on the lips. "Just this once." She winked and got back out of bed. "Besides, you don't want me to get on the bad side of the chess people. They're Machiavellian. In the best way, but still."

"I thought you said the likely winners were an old man and a priest."

"Yes. Well, them, especially."

Peter grinned and pulled himself upright.

"Will you stop by the shop today?"

"I don't think so. I have a client meeting, and I'm not quite up to snuff enough to make two big trips in a day. My energy's great, but healing bones takes time."

"Tomorrow, then. I want you to see it in action. We have a surprise bridal shower coming in. It'll be a fun group."

"After the service, before a nap with the dogs. I think I can work it in."

"Great." They made their way to the kitchen, where Peter started the kettle and Sienna started toast. "I don't know why I bother eating breakfast at home. Tovah is always finding an excuse to feed me again when I get to the shop."

"She was worried about you."

"I guess. Bethel showed me a photo she took of me a few weeks back. I looked worrisome. Pale, distraught. Like a pining heroine in a nineteenth century novel."

"That's good news, isn't it? Those heroines all had happy endings." He paused and set the blue teapot on the counter. "Well, most of them did."

"I'll keep that in mind." Sienna planted a smooch on Peter's neck.

"Was it one of the *Susan Was Here* photos?" Peter held the tea-infusing basket in his left hand with a tin of leaves suspended over it. He never measured the leaves; he had a knack for getting the amount just right. Sienna leaned on the counter next to him and nodded, and he continued sifting in the tea leaves in small, fluid motions. "Because I was thinking. We should go to those places sooner rather than later. I'm getting better with my leg. I should be able to go out with just a cane in a week or two. Let's go hiking before it gets too cold.

Tea & Crumples

I hear that decrepit old men with canes feel the cold in their mended bones."

"I don't know. I wouldn't want you to get hurt. It might be emotionally painful. And if you reinjured your leg, we might make the wrong kind of memory."

"I'm well, Sienna." Peter held her hand in his and cupped it to his chest. "The X-ray showed knitted-together bones. I'm just sore, is all, so I'm taking things slowly for another week." He kissed her hand and looked into her eyes. His expression shifted, and he leaned in for a long kiss.

"I like it when you take things slowly," Sienna sighed. She looked up at him and smiled. "Okay. You get into a smaller cast, and I'll take your decrepit-cane-walking self hiking with me. Only, a walking stick would probably be better for hills."

"True." He leaned over as a quantity of dog brushed against him. "And Pogo would like that, too, wouldn't you, boy?" Jonquil walked calmly up to him and sniffed his leg. She snuffed approval and bumped his hand with her head. "Alright, girl, I'll let you out. See, Sienna? Even Jonquil can see I'm better. She's letting me open the door for them again."

Sienna grabbed a piece of toast straight from the toaster and munched hungrily. "Too hot!" she panted around the chunk of too fresh toast, then swallowed and resumed her meal, crunching through the toast as fast as she could without choking. "Needs tea," She said when she had finished off the first slice.

"And butter." Peter smiled. "Slow down, there, Speedy. I don't want you to choke. Or are you really in a terrible hurry and I've held you up with my irresistible romantic advances?" He looked as though he were going to make another one. His expression changed to one of mild concern when Sienna grabbed a second piece of toast and wolfed it down, too.

"Seriously, Si, are you alright?"

"Yes," Sienna nodded, dusting toast crumbs off the front of her robe. "Just a sudden rush of nerves. Jumpy stomach. We're going to be so busy today." She attempted a sexy smile. It was queasy but sincere. "But I like your advances." She looked out the window, where the sky was lightening. "I'd better go get ready. There will be a crowd early today. Could you maybe bring me a mug of tea for me to drink on the drive?" Sienna put her arms around his neck and kissed his lower lip.

"You've persuaded me." Peter returned the kiss. "I'll do it."

When she drove past the shop, a line of men, women, and a few older children was stretched down the block outside the door. She had to park a block away. Tovah and Nina were in the kitchen when she walked through the back door.

"Did you see the line?" she asked.

"Did you see this?" Tovah responded. She held up a section of the local newspaper, which heralded the tournament on its front page. "Listen to this. 'Notoriously reclusive chess grand master Cleotis Reed convened the chess tournament in support of his favorite café, the tea and stationery shop Tea and Crumples.' Then it gives our address and says spectators can pay a flat fee to enjoy refreshments for each level of the tournament." She pulled a tray of fresh cookies out of the oven and slid another in. "I got here early and made more cookies. Luckily, Nina saw the paper, too."

"'Notoriously reclusive?' Can you believe that, Miss?" Nina wore an apron over a starched blue oxford as she removed piping hot churros from a large pot of boiling oil. Sienna noticed that Nina wore pearl earrings that drew attention to her face. She smiled at Nina's newfound confidence reflected in her dress and bearing. "Mr. Cleotis as a recluse." She harrumphed. "I mean, he's quiet, but it's not like he's hiding."

"Not from us, anyway," Sienna said. She slipped an apron over her head and jumped into the fray. "Do you know when Lettye will be here?" She addressed Tovah as they worked side by side to count out plates of cookies.

"Oh, she and Jessie are already here. They're setting up extra game tables and chairs in the chess area. I had them take down the larger round tables to make room."

"Good." Sienna raised her eyebrows at the evidence of her team's competence. "Then we might be ready for the crowd. We may need the overflow site before noon, though. I don't know what the fire department will think of Cleotis Reed's fan club out there."

"Well, now that you're here, we can manage."

"Tovah. You know you would manage with or without me."

Tovah turned Sienna toward her and held her by the shoulders so that she had to look into her friend's face. "You listen to me, Sienna Bannock. When Peter was sick, when you were recovering after Susan, when you were out of your mind with grief and fear, even then, you were always necessary to the success of this business. You are the soul of this place. Do you think I would open a shop with just anybody? We need Lettye. We need Nina. We need Jessie. But we also need you. I need you." She hugged her friend, strong and warmly, then pulled back just as suddenly, all business. "Now, don't you forget it." She glanced sideways at Sienna, taking in her appearance head to toe. She reached across to the other counter and turned Sienna to her again. "Here." She opened Sienna's hand and placed an almond butter pastry in her open palm. "Eat this before we go out there. You look piqued."

Sienna complied and went to check the hot water carafes. She turned on the samovars and hoped they would heat quickly enough for the crowds. Nina opened the door, and

Cleotis Reed walked in, followed by forty-something chess players. Jessie directed traffic in the tournament area, while Lettye explained the menu options to those who were seated at tables around the shop.

The morning clipped along to the quiet clink of chess pieces and the occasional polite, "Check" or "Checkmate." After the first hour, the contenders had thinned significantly; the less experienced players seemed to rush to their own detriment. Most of the players stayed on after they were eliminated, so that the crowd reached capacity by midmorning. They opened the overflow site and invited spectators to cross the street to watch the main tables in high definition streaming video, but they were reluctant to leave.

"We have to get people out of here or the fire department is going to cite us." Tovah ran her fingers through her hair and tugged the bottom of her crisp white oxford. It was rare to see her friend flustered, but Sienna was secretly happy to be of use to her.

"I have a plan." She nodded toward the nearly empty pastry case. "Since we've done so many extra food sales this morning, we can float an offer. Free tea and cookies for anyone who will go to the overflow site voluntarily. Plus a reminder that the tournament will be called off if we receive a fire code citation."

"I like it." Tovah reached out to catch Sienna's attention as she turned to go spread the word. "Oh, and I've asked Nina to start making churros. I'm going to shut down custom stationery orders for anyone who hasn't already made an appointment today. That will give me leave to make quiches. Please tell me we have eggs. I'll call Marc and have him bring in some cheese from the farmer's market."

"Quiches." Sienna blinked and tried to remember what was so important about them. "Oh! Yes. I remember. After Elsie

Pinkwater brought in her friends, I made half a dozen of the artichoke heart and chevre quiches and froze them. I was going to give them to her next time she comes in, as a very small thank you for connecting us with so much new business. Let's hope she isn't a chess fan."

"Good. That will get us through another hour or so. Who knew chess fans ate so much?"

"It's their giant brains."

Tovah rolled her eyes. "Well, go tell the big brains our offer, or we're going to be so crowded that they knock heads."

Thankfully, enough of the chess fans were frugal that they accepted the free tea and cookies offer and made their way across the street. The shop still milled with lunching chess enthusiasts and players, and the air grew thick with the smell of sweet dark tea and cinnamon, with an undertone of baked cheese and raspberries to round it out. Lettye circulated with trays filled with mugs of breakfast teas. She brought an empty tray back behind the counter and looked around, concerned. She turned to Sienna, who was measuring out leaves into tea baskets for the samovars.

"How are we supposed to find her?" Lettye asked.

"Beg pardon?" Sienna poured a huge pitcher of hot water into the samovar and turned to look over the packed shop. She followed Lettye's gaze, but didn't take her meaning. "Find whom?"

"Our chief investor. Xenia R. Maris. Will she approach us, or wear a nametag? Is she in the tournament?"

"Good question. I hadn't thought of that." Sienna riffled through the list of participants. She gasped. "There *was* a Xenia Maris in the tournament. Early this morning." She cast a worried look at Lettye. "I hope I didn't kick her out when I went around enticing people across the street."

"I'm sure that if you did, you were very polite about it."

"That must make up for it. Thank you for giving us the money we need to expand our business and accept new commitments. Now, please leave. Here's a cookie."

"Exactly. Who could be mad at a cookie?"

Sienna saw Cleotis Reed making his way toward the tea bar. She set the list on the counter and straightened up. "Could you make Mr. Reed's usual?" She turned to Lettye.

"I'm already on it." Lettye smiled and decanted boiling water over the black leaves. The scent of fire and barbeque wafted up from the pot. Lettye reached under the counter and pulled out a tin of cheese straws. She held it up to Sienna, who nodded eager approval. The cayenne in the cheddar straws would round out the smoky lapsang souchong that Cleotis favored. Lettye set the steeping tea, a fine china mug, and a plate of cheese straws in front of Cleotis' seat. "Here you are. On the house, of course."

"Thank you," Cleotis said. He ate a cheese straw and sat back a little with a relieved expression. "Perfect." He poured himself a cup of tea over lump sugar and nodded toward the tournament list. "Who were you all looking for on that list?" He sipped his tea.

"A Ms. Xenia R. Maris. She competed this morning, but we missed her somehow," Lettye answered.

"And I may have accidentally asked her to buzz off across the street," Sienna added. She blew out her lips, exasperated. "A fine way to treat someone we've been eager to meet."

"What do you all want with my granddaughter?" Cleotis leaned forward a little, his expression inscrutable. Sienna got a sudden impression of how tough an opponent he might be at the chess table.

"Your granddaughter?" Sienna asked.

Tea & Crumples

"Xenia Reed Maris," Cleotis said. His eyes softened with suppressed mirth. Sienna blinked as the penny dropped.

"Your granddaughter. The little girl who was at the history department party. She competed in the first three rounds. I remember thinking how she must come from a chess playing family to do so well against adults." A smile spread slowly over Sienna's face. Cleotis matched it. "You. Cleotis Reed. You're our chief investor."

"Glad to make your acquaintance." He reached across and shook Sienna's hand. Lettye shook her head and laughed, then went to tell Tovah the news. Tovah rushed to the tea counter.

"I should have known," Tovah said. "You knew too much about tea to be disinterested." She set another plate of cheese straws in front of Cleotis. She frowned and added one of the chocolate pastries she had hoarded for Ms. Maris. Tovah looked level at their patron. "It must have cost you a lot to let people know you frequent this shop. The paper said you were known to be reclusive."

"The paper only said that because I don't usually let them know about my little gatherings ahead of time."

"Secretive, then, and not reclusive."

"Private, maybe. But as regards my granddaughter's investment, I have some good news and some bad news for you ladies. The good news is that I can give you the money you requested. But not to cover expenses. That's the bad news. I want to see expansions if I'm going to extend the investment."

Tovah exchanged smiles with Lettye and Sienna. "It just so happens," Tovah said, "That we have plans for you to review. Only a little more big equipment costs, mostly advertizing, extra inventory, and tools. When are you wrapping up the tournament?"

"Around about 5:00 Father Max is coming in. I reckon I'll

be called upon not too long after that."

"Good. Let's go to the office, shall we, and I'll show you our expanded business plan." Tovah placed the tea things on a tray and led the way to the office. She smiled at Sienna through the door as Cleotis Reed tugged up his trouser legs and graciously sat in her grandfather's chair.

"Lettye just told me!" Nina said. The girl bounced at Sienna's elbow. "The shop is saved!"

"Well, it would have been saved anyway, after today. I think Cleotis had his little surprise in mind when he agreed to the tournament," Sienna grinned.

"It's like what Father Max and Cleotis were saying about miracles," Nina said, returning the smile. "They have already happened by the time you think to ask for them."

Sienna turned to Nina and, on impulse, hugged the girl around the shoulders. Nina beamed under the positive attention. "I think you're right, Nina." Sienna smiled. "I think you're right."

The next morning, Tovah met Sienna and Nina at the back door. They had arrived early to set up the surprise bridal shower Liz was throwing for Deborah. Sienna was carrying three life sized cardboard cutouts of characters from BBC Jane Austen films. Nina had a basket that held, among other things, four TARDIS teapots and a piñata that looked suspiciously like a handsome actor who played Sherlock Holmes.

"Set those things down." Tovah took the basket from Nina and leaned Mr. Darcy, Lizzie, and Emma against the wall. "We need to celebrate."

"I thought we celebrated last night?" Nina said. When Cleotis had defeated Father Max and the congratulatory crowds had finally cleared, the five women of Tea and Crumples had

Tea & Crumples

turned on a jazzy soundtrack and cleaned hard for over an hour.

"Did we?" Tovah stopped in her tracks and stared at Nina as though groping for a memory.

"Well, we danced while we cleaned."

"We have got to have more fun around here." Tovah looped her arm through Nina's and pulled her toward the front of the shop. They were met with a pitcher of mimosas, three plates of eggs benedict, fresh fruit, and pastries.

"Tovah, this is a feast!" Sienna said. "The news must be better than I thought."

"It's wonderful. All of our classes, the extra ovens, the upstairs office relocation. All approved. We can expand the stationery area and have room for three extra group tables. If the new business comes through from your teacher friends, Nina, we can even plan for a private party room upstairs in a year and a half."

"Wow." Sienna sat back and sipped her mimosa. "Those were our dream expansions! I didn't think we'd get to even seriously consider them for years."

"Yep. Eat up." Tovah pointed at their plates with her fork. They ate as she went over details. At length, they covered the schedule of classes they wanted to offer.

"Now, Nina, there's something I've been wanting to ask you." Sienna lifted her teacup and regarded the young woman beside her. "College. You're very capable and clever, and now we have evidence that you also excel academically. Do you want to stay with the shop long term, or…?"

"Or?" Nina swallowed and looked nervous, though she managed to keep her tone even.

"Or would you like us to help you invest the extra money from the classes you teach, so you might return to school later?"

"Wait. The extra money from the classes? You mean I get to keep it?"

"Yes. I though that was understood. We'll have to cover expenses, but then of course the teacher gets a big cut of the tuition fees."

"But that would be enough money for me to save for anything! I could buy a car or help my sister go to college."

"Your sister? Not you?" Sienna asked. She looked to Tovah, who shrugged one shoulder and narrowed her eyes at Nina.

"I've always wanted to cook and teach. Maybe that means I'll go to culinary school one day, but I'm not really interested in regular college. I like reading, but that's not the same as wanting to write assignments on someone else's schedule. I love math, but I like doing math, not reading about it and jumping through someone's hoops just to prove it to them for no reason."

"Okay, then," Sienna smiled. "It sounds as though you've given it thought already."

"You know," Tovah said, her gaze still narrowed on Nina, "I could use help with the bookkeeping now that business is picking up again. It will mean you working an extra half day each week. Are Sundays really fine for your schedule? I mean, today's a special occasion. But weekly?"

"Oh, yes, Miss," Nina smiled. "I always go to the Saturday evening Mass. The night before counts as the next day."

"You don't say," Tovah smiled. "Very well, then. We'll set up your schedule after Deborah's party. We'd better get those props into place."

Her last sentence was interrupted by a cacophony of knocks at the back door. Sienna rose quickly to answer them, but she swooned a little. She steadied herself on the tea bar and nodded toward her barely touched mimosa. "I'm a lightweight," she smiled. Her laughter echoed back to the rest of the team when she had opened the door. "Tovah didn't tell me!"

"What is it, Miss?" Nina asked Tovah.

"You'll see." Tovah winked. "An extra little surprise for Deborah's party."

Sienna returned to the tearoom wielding a puppet version of a mouse in a teapot. Three children rushed past her to Tovah, each wearing an elaborate hat. Marc Rosen followed, sporting a Mad Hatter-style tophat.

"My dear," he said, stooping to kiss Tovah's cheek.

"Mommy! Mommy! Can we have some?" The children pointed at the pastries still stacked between the women.

"Yes, but you'll need to eat them off plates so you don't get crumbs all over the clean floor."

"I've got them," Marc said. He passed a small stack of fancy plates to his wife.

"Okay. Here you go. Both hands—" Tovah began. But her middle child had already dropped a plate on the floor. It crashed with a tinkling shatter, and Tovah shook her head. "Oy vey," she muttered.

"Here, let me," Sienna said, grabbing a small dustpan and hand broom from behind the tea counter. She knelt next to Tovah and began sweeping while Marc and Lettye ushered the children to seats.

"You know, SiSi," Tovah said, a half-smile playing over her face, "delicacy with china is not a hereditable trait." She placed a large shard of broken plate onto the dustpan Sienna held, then leaned back to look at her friend. "You should remember that, now that you're in a family way."

"In a fam—? What?" Sienna gaped.

"Hungry, swooning, staring off into corners. I know that

look."

"Oh." Sienna lifted an eyebrow. "Maybe."

"Well, when the time comes, just remember. There's no shame in making the kids eat off plastic for a few years." Tovah tipped the shards from the dustpan into a trash bin. "It saves a lot of clean up."

Sienna made to reply, but she was prevented by the jingling of the bell as Bethel Bailey bustled in, drawing along another brunette in her wake. The woman shared Bethel's curving smile and bright eyes, but she was a good half-foot taller. She walked primly despite Bethel's urgent tugging on her arm.

"Sienna!" Bethel said, arriving with effort at the tea bar, "Please allow me to introduce my sister, Ava Stone. She's wanting to go into the tea business."

"How do you do?" Ava asked, extending her hand to Sienna. She was formal but warm, and though the smile on her lips was small, it started at her eyes. "I hope it's no trouble for me to burst in on a Sunday like this, but Bethel says you won't mind."

"I never mind meeting new friends," Sienna said, returning the smile. She gestured toward a table. "Please make yourselves comfortable, and I'll bring a tray." Sienna glanced toward Bethel and Ava. They reminded Sienna of nothing so much as a chicken and swan as they whispered to one another, the one fluttering and clucking, the other serenely replying in a staid manner. Yet their love for one another was clear. Sienna had no trouble following that love into an idea about the perfect tea for Ms. Ava Stone.

"Here you are. Your usual, Bethel, and for Ms. Ava, a fine golden Yunnan." Sienna set out the pots and mugs and placed a plate of cookies and mini scones on the table. "May I?" She poured the fine, fragrant tea into Ava's mug.

Tea & Crumples

Ava lifted the mug, allowed the steam to draw her attention, and sipped. "Wonderful," she said to Sienna, and to Bethel, "You were right. I owe you a paddleboat ride."

"A paddleboat ride?" Sienna asked, sitting back.

"Ava bet me you couldn't guess her favorite tea without knowing anything about her. So I said yes, you could, and I wanted her to give me a paddleboat ride when I was proved right."

"Bethel loves paddleboats, but they tire her quickly," Ava said delicately, cutting her eyes in a diagonal to emphasize the difference in their heights.

"Well, anyhow, I haven't had a place to ride them since we were girls." She scooped sugar and poured cream into her mug, then topped it up with dark tea. "That's why I brought Ava to see you. She's going to bring back the lake! And, well, I'll let her tell you about the rest."

"Mrs. Bannock," Ava began.

"Sienna. Please," Sienna nodded graciously.

"Sienna," Ava acknowledged. "What Bethel means is that our family used to own a lake. We still do, but we had to drain it in the 80's to keep college kids from using it as a midnight swimming hole. Safety hazard, you know, what with all the rocks." She paused and sipped her tea. "This is delightful, by the way." She smiled the small smile again. "It used to be a quarry, you see, but it was a lake for over a hundred years."

"And Ava is going to turn it back into one, only this time it will have a tearoom built with a patio right out over it, just like she saw in the Lake District in England!" Bethel gulped the remainder of her tea and started the process of refilling it.

"A tearoom?" Sienna asked. "How lovely. And is it going to have paddleboats?"

"For Bethel, yes." Ava nudged her sister lightly. "But for

293

customers, a few canoes. It's not a large lake, but there are beautiful old willows along the edge of the quarry where you can laze and hide away a bit."

"It's really romantic," Bethel said.

"Where is it?" Sienna asked. "I don't think I've heard of a quarry that used to be a lake—"

"That used to be a quarry," Bethel smiled.

"It's in the northern part of the county, not far from where the river splits," Ava said. "That's why I thought maybe you could help. We wouldn't really be competition, being a good half hour away."

"More like a compliment," Sienna said. "I mean the businesses *and* the fact that you asked me for advice. I mean, assuming you'd like my advice. Maybe you just wanted to share the good news?"

"Oh, I'd love advice!" Ava was suddenly much more animated. "Right now, I have a property, some funding, and a dream. But everything else I need to learn."

Sienna looked from Ava to Bethel, who was making her way through the plate of tea treats. She smiled. "Well, the first secret to a good teashop," Sienna leaned forward and lowered her voice, "is to invent a good recipe for scones."

"And cookies," Bethel added around a mouthful.

"And to have a good sense about tea, of course," Sienna finished.

"And a location you have," Bethel teased. "Well, at least you have a good pile of stones to get started with."

"Well, there you are," Sienna smiled. "Tea and scones and stones. That should about cover you."

"Tea and stones," Ava said, that small smile lighting her eyes again. "I like that."

Tea & Crumples

When she closed the door to the shop that afternoon, Sienna took her time before walking to her car. The afternoon sun shone golden pink against the front glass of the teashop. She raised her hand to trace the quill on the teacup logo, and her hand filled with light. It was a perfect pink cup, radiating gold, almost as though she were its source. Almost as though she were full of grace.

"And from his fullness have we all received, grace upon grace."
~John 1:16 RSV

Epilogue

"Oh, good. I was afraid I missed you." Peter kissed Sienna briefly on the lips. She stood back, and he walked through the door of Tea and Crumples. "The place looks fabulous." He pulled off his cognac leather messenger bag and set it on a chair near the end of the manuscript table. "I like the new tables." He grinned across the shop toward where Sienna stood by the tea counter. His smile widened as she came toward him with a tray. "Cozy."

"Let's sit." Sienna set the tray down at the nearest corner of the table Peter had chosen. "Oh. Just a moment. Let me go and get something I had made for you." She walked toward the stationery area and returned shortly with a single creamy envelope made from the finest thick cotton paper. She laid it upside down on the table and sat catty corner from Peter. "I'll pour." She handed him a cup of tea and looked on contentedly as he stirred honey and cream into it.

"Well," Peter said. He reached for Sienna's hand and held

Tea & Crumples

it gently. "Let's see how it turned out." He removed a book from his messenger bag. It was covered in plain white paper secured by a single piece of tape. He broke the seal and slid out the book of photographs. They looked through it slowly, their quiet broken only by sighs and small hums. Their fingers spoke for them, tracing favorite scenes that marked their faces with comfort as well as sadness. The last spread was the most beautiful. They held their joined hands into the sunlight on top of a high hill at their favorite state park. The rocks at their feet spelled, *Susan Was Here.*

Sienna smiled, and Peter cupped her face with his warm thumbs. "Thank you," she said. "For sharing this with me. For Susan. For our life together."

"For tea," Peter added. "For the joy of seeing you each day. For breath." Their conversation had become a prayer.

"For remembering."

"For hoping."

"For warm hands." Sienna raised Peter's hands and kissed his knuckles.

"And thoughts." Peter turned her hand in his and kissed the center of her palm.

"For this," Sienna smiled. Peter drew breath to speak, but stopped when he saw that she touched the envelope. She slid it across the table to him and waited.

Sienna followed Peter's hands with her eyes as he stroked the smooth paper, paused to smile appreciation at its quality, and picked it up. She found herself praying as he pried a corner and eased open a seam in the top. She prayed by lifting her teacup. She thanked God for remembering and seeing and for miracles that happened before she knew to ask. She asked now, that what she gave Peter would be true. She set down her cup and was certain that the gift had already been given.

Peter slid the card from the envelope and stared at it. He read out the letterpressed inscription. It was a date in the middle of the following summer. "What is this?" He ran his finger over the numbers, taking them in by touch.

Sienna smiled and flipped the card over. One word was printed on the other side. She read it aloud. "Due."

NOTES FROM SIENNA'S TEA FILES

Elizabeth Emily Bannock, 1.5, toddler, food critic: Decaffeinated Keemun with dried cherries, served warm with maple syrup and cream. Round, sweet, fragrant. Happy.

Recipes from Tea & Crumples

CRUMPLES QUICHE

For two quiches:

12-14 large brown eggs (pastured if available)

1 cup whole milk

2-4 cups shredded cheddar cheese OR 16-24 oz. crumbled goat cheese

Pie crusts (We use soy-free frozen shells. But you can use any type, including homemade. Or skip the crusts altogether and make a big pan of crustless quiche, which works best with a glass baking dish, 9" x 13".

2-4 cups other fillings (crumbled bacon, wilted spinach, red onions, caramelized onions, broccoli, wilted chard, corn, bell peppers, sausage, precooked potatoes, whatever goes well with eggs and cheese)

For our Artichoke Heart and Chevre quiche: To the egg and milk mixture, add two cans of artichoke hearts (rinsed, well drained, patted dry) and two 8 oz. logs of local chevre. If available, add another 4 oz. crumbled smoked Farmer's cheese.

If using crust, preheat oven to 400°F. Bake the empty pie shells for 5 minutes. Poke holes with a fork in the crust to prevent bubbles after you add the filling. Reduce heat to 375°F. (Or preheat to 375°F for crustless version.)

If using two pie crusts, place them on a lined baking sheet side

Tea & Crumples

by side to catch spills and to provide stability in transfer.

Add solid ingredients (cheese, meat, veg) to pie shells, evenly distributed between the two or evenly across the bake dish if making crustless version. If you want to add spices, put them in with the solids, or they will just float on top (they will float on top anyway). In a large bowl or very large measuring cup, combine about one cup of milk with a dozen eggs. With fork, beat together egg mixture and pour evenly over other ingredients. I like to use the mixing fork to lift the ingredients and stir them gently, to make sure the egg is distributed well around the other parts of the quiche. If you think the quiches need a bit more egg mixture, beat a little more milk together with an egg or two and add to the other ingredients, stirring gently to incorporate.

Bake quiche(s) for 45 minutes on center rack. Serves 12-16.

These are pretty good as leftovers and make great food for academic crunch times, early parenting meals, and parties. We serve about 6 quiches a day at Tea and Crumples.

SIENNA'S SOUTHERN DROP SCONES

2 cups all-purpose flour
3 teaspoons aluminum-free baking powder
½ - 1 teaspoon sea salt
½ cup brown sugar (or coconut sugar)
¼ - ½ cup granulated sugar
1 cup half and half, plus extra for coating
1 egg, slightly beaten
1 stick butter (or ½ cup coconut oil)
½ teaspoon vanilla

1 cup nuts, chocolate chips, or dried fruit (optional)

Preheat oven to 400°F. Sift together flour, baking powder, salt, and sugars. Cut butter into flour mixture until it is incorporated. It will resemble coarse bread crumbs. Add nuts/fruit/choc. chips. Add egg, vanilla, and cup of half and half. Stir with fork just until dough forms. It will probably take less than ten turns.

Drop onto ungreased baking stone or sheet by tablespoonfuls. Coat tops with half and half. (I add a tablespoon of H&H to the measuring cup that held the egg and use that mixture for the tops of the scones, so it's sort of like an egg wash). Bake for 12 minutes. Check and return to oven for additional time as needed, checking at 2 minute intervals. Done when light golden brown on top. Allow to cool for a few minutes before removing from bake sheet.

Serve warm or room temperature with clotted cream and fruit preserves.

Variations: for cinnamon pecan scones, add a teaspoon or so of cinnamon to dry ingredients. For cashew scones, remove granulated sugar and use an entire cup of brown sugar instead. For strawberry scones, add a little cardamom.

CHEDDAR-SUNFLOWER SEED DROP SCONES

This is our family's scone recipe adapted to the savory side. They are like the light, thick biscuits you might remember from your childhood, that nobody makes anymore.

2 cups flour

3 tsp. aluminum-free baking powder

1-1 ½ tsp sea salt

Tea & Crumples

Freshly ground black pepper to taste (~1/4 teaspoon)

2 tablespoons mustard powder

1 stick unsalted butter

1-2 cups shredded cheddar

¾ cup sunflower seeds (May substitute 2 Tablespoons minced fresh chives for another classic variation on savory scones.)

1 cup half and half

1 egg, slightly beaten

Preheat oven to 400°F. Sift or stir together first five ingredients, including mustard powder, if using. Cut in butter with pastry blender or with a butter knife and fingers until mixture looks like bread crumbs. Add in cheddar and seeds, stir to mix. In a measuring cup, mix together half and half and egg, then add to dry ingredients. Stir with a fork until just wet, around a dozen strokes (maybe a few more if you let the toddler measure the cheese and have more volume in the bowl).

Drop scones by handful-sized globs onto baking dish. Makes 8 big scones or 10-12 normal-sized ones. Bake for 14 minutes, then check. I added two minutes for my oven, but you should check at 14 mins. When light golden brown, remove from oven. Let rest a few minutes, then eat.

SIENNA'S RASPBERRY THUMBPRINT COOKIES

1 cup unsalted pastured butter, softened

⅔ cup sugar

½ teaspoon vanilla bean paste

2 cups all-purpose flour

½ teaspoon sea salt

1 tablespoon fresh thyme leaves, finely chopped

½ cup seedless raspberry jam

Mix together flour, salt, and thyme in a bowl and set aside. To the bowl of a stand mixer, add softened butter, sugar and 1/2 teaspoon vanilla paste in bowl. Beat at medium speed, scraping the bowl often, until creamy. Add flour mixture and beat at low speed, scraping the bowl often, until well mixed. Cover and refrigerate at least 1 hour.

Preheat oven to 350°F.

Shape dough into 1-inch balls. Place 2 inches apart onto ungreased cookie sheets covered in parchment. Make indentation in center of each cookie with thumb. Fill each thumbprint with jam. Bake 14-18 minutes or until edges are lightly browned. Let stand 1-2 minutes on cookie sheets, then remove to cooling racks. Cool completely, then serve or store in airtight containers for up to a week (if they make it that long). These freeze well, too. Makes about 3 dozen cookies.

Acknowledgements

My first taste of hot tea was brought to me by the man who would become my husband. He returned from a semester abroad in the United Kingdom smelling of cold winds and warm leaves. We toasted our engagement a few years later with tea poured in cobalt blue Depression glass cups. I still have the battered red Twinings tea tin from those first days exploring tea lore and life together. It's spackled with stickers from the varieties of leaves it's held in the nearly twenty years since. That tin still resonates with the first time I thought of Tea & Crumples and spoke its name across the tea table to the man I love. Thank you, Andrew, for tea together through our sorrows and many, many joys. I pray that God will grant us many more years of seeing each other's faces above our cups.

Andrew introduced me to tea, but my friend Cathy Smallwood taught me most of what I know about it. A tea master, Cathy drew me into a pocket of community from the first moment I walked into her teashop to rest from the rigors of graduate school. If I say something wrong about tea, blame me, but credit dear Cathy for any good tea sense you find here. Credit her also with the sense of intimacy that permeates the shop. Her warm hospitality and spiritual grace made me see it was possible.

My children patiently bore their mother's muttering to herself, scribbling book notes on their refrigerator art, and forgetting to pour their tea on occasion while I wrote this book. Thank you, children.

And thanks to Elizabeth Turnbull, my editor, for believing in me and loving this book as much as I do. You are the best book midwife ever.

Tea & Stones

A preview of Book 2 in the faith, tea, love collection.

308

Chapter One

"The Farmer's Almanac says this will be the hottest July on record." It was May, but Ava liked to plan ahead.

"Even more reason for us to do the mudslide, don't you think?" Sage's voice came across the speakerphone with a crackle. Ava couldn't hear the next part of Sage's speech, but she'd heard it often enough to guess. *The environment, Ava! Water conservation, Ava! Vacation Bible School shouldn't waste so much water, Ava!* The line crackled again. "And it behooves us as Christians to set an example. I mean, what's a little mud, when the Israelites had to slave in mud pits for generations?"

"Sage, honey," Ava said smoothly as she slowed to turn down a wooded gravel lane, "you know I always support your creative teaching plans, and you're right. It makes more sense to let the kids play in the mud for the lesson on asking God for a redeemer. But why are you telling me? Go present the idea to your pastor."

"You know how he is. They've done water balloon fights on the first night of Vacation Bible School for ten years, no matter the lesson. He doesn't want to hear a new idea."

"Maybe you can present it as an old idea. Oh, I know! Put the mud in kiddie pools and have them make bricks!"

"Huh. That might work." The sound of shuffling papers and scribbling came over the line. "Thanks, Ava. I wrote it down."

"Got the bee out of your bonnet?"

"Well, one of them. I still have a blog post to publish before Jonathan wakes up from nap. Did I tell you I found the stainless steel straws?"

"Found them? I thought that's all you used."

"It was, and then Jon-o hid them all. He toddled off with them every day, and I had no idea where they were going. Turns out, it was the air vent. I got them out with a magnet."

Sage waited for a response. Ava was distracted by the curve of the road. She had to go slowly over the gravel, and it looked as though there was a runner up ahead.

"Ava?"

"Yes. Good thinking on the magnet. What did you do in the meantime?"

"That's today's post. It's about how sometimes it's okay to use paper or even-" Her voice dropped to a stage whisper. "*Plastic* straws in a pinch."

"You're going to get mail from that. Hang on a minute, Sage. I have to pass a runner. Oh, glory! He's not wearing a shirt. Just a sec while I avert my eyes."

Ava had rules about propriety. She might not be able to get the world around her to behave appropriately, but that wouldn't stop her from staying modest. She slowed even more as she approached the runner. The man was running along the right side of the road, his bright blue headphones contrasting a

Tea & Crumples

thick, dark head of hair. The dappled sun made his bare golden shoulders glow. Ava drew a deep breath and turned her head to watch the left side of the road as she passed.

"I heard that breath! That nice looki--?" Sage began.

A thump interrupted her. Ava screamed. She slammed the brakes, set the engine brake, and jumped out of the car.

The running man was curled up on the gravel in front of her. His eyes were closed. Ava made the sign of the cross and knelt beside him. "Oh, Lord have mercy!" she said, touching his face. "I ran over you!"

"Only a little bit," the man drew a shuddering breath and opened green brown eyes. Ava sat back on her heels and watched as he lifted himself on his elbows. The man blinked slowly. Ava prayed under her breath. The man prayed under his breath. It was the same prayer. He smiled. "Well, if I'm going to get struck on my way to work, I'm glad it's by a fellow Orthodox." She started to return his smile, but the gravity of the situation hit her stomach in a cold wave.

"I'm so sorry for hitting you. It's just..." She bit her lip. It wouldn't do to tell him she was avoiding looking at his bare chest. Especially since she was looking at it quite thoroughly now. "So sorry. I just lost track of you, I'm afraid." She watched as he sat up and brushed gravel off his side. "You missed a spot," she said, reaching out automatically to remove a few pieces of grey stone from his arm. It was a well-muscled arm. Maybe he needed help with his other one. His skin was warmer than the stone. She squeezed the rock in her hand and blushed. "Oh, dear!" Ava said, snapping to. "Can I give you a ride somewhere? I was just heading in to meet someone, but I'm a bit early. I can detour."

The man stood and shifted his weight slowly. He raised his hands and smiled. "It's okay." He made steadying motions toward her with his hands. Ava stood up and looked him over for injuries. A few small cuts, but nothing serious. She scanned his shoulders and neck and looked into his eyes. "I'm okay," he said. "Just a little stricken." His small smile brought warmth back into her.

From the car behind them, Sage hollered, "Ava!? Ava! Is he okay? Give him some of the calendula gel I gave you!"

"Would you like some, um, calendula?" Ava asked. "Or a ride or," she looked at the piece of rock in her hand, "some basaltic quartz mixed gravel?"

"I think I'd better walk back to my work now. It will keep soreness at bay."

"You're sure?" Ava asked.

"I'm sure."

"Well, if anything goes wrong later, my name is Ava Stone. Here." She handed him the gravel and dug in her blazer pocket for a business card. She found one and set it in his open palm on top of the rock. "I would be glad to help in any way I can. Insurance. Calendula. Tea. Hot tea, I mean. Proper tea. It's the least I could do after hitting you."

He glanced at the card and smiled. "I might take you up on it."

"Which?"

"Tea. I've never had tea. Coffee, yes. Tea, no."

"Good. I'll introduce you the right way." She walked to the side of the car and stood between the open door and her seat. The man stood to the side. "I'll be going, then, if you're sure you don't need a ride."

He gestured for her to go ahead. She buckled in and released the brake. He stood back by the spring green trees, waiting for her to pass. *Well, of course he's letting me go first!* she thought. *If I ran over him once, who's to say I wouldn't do it again?*

"I said, 'Is he okay?'" Sage repeated.

"Hmm? Yes, he's fine."

"I bet he is." Sage chuckled. "Did you give him the calendula? It's magical."

Ava drove until the man was no longer in her rearview mirror. The construction company was just visible through the trees ahead. She took a deep breath and prayed on the exhale.

"Ava? You there? I just said calendula is magic." Sage prompted.

"Sage," Ava smiled, falling into their routine, "don't be irresponsible. The magical content of foods is not regulated by the FDA."

AVA'S STORIED TABLE COLLECTION: COIN SILVER SERVING SPOON

When Granny was little, she used to go up with Great Granddaddy to the quarry. He let her pick around in the gravel, looking for quartz. She loved rose quartz the best. One time Granny showed me the pieces she found there. Just a dozen or so pink pebbles laid out on her soft, wrinkled palm, but they were her girlhood's treasure. One day after a week of rains, she had to stay on the road to keep safe. She was poking the gravel with the toe of her boots when the ground shone under her foot. That's how she told it. "The ground shone up at me, Ava!" Granny knelt and dug up the shine. It was a coin silver spoon, flattened and pocked a bit from living its life in a wheel rut, but perfectly preserved by the layered mud. Granny gave me the spoon when I turned twelve, to start my collection. "Girlhood treasures are for your heart, Ava. But you're a woman now, and you'll treasure others more as you get older. This spoon will help you serve those you love." Granny kept the rose quartz.

About the Author

Summer Kinard is the mother of five, a tea lover, soprano, and author of inspiring novels and curricula for active learners. She writes about faithful people overcoming trials with the help of tea, friendships, and love. Summer's first novel, *Can't Buy Me Love*, was a USA Today Happy Ever After pick for Women's Fiction. Her paranormal Orthodox Christian romance, *The Salvation of Jeffrey Lapin*, has received glowing reviews from readers. Summer writes about faith, tea, and love in journeys of healing. Follow her family's journey with tea at TeaAndCrumples.com. You will find up to date posts on her writing life at her site: WritingLikeAMother.com, or follow her on Instagram for up to the moment updates: http://instagram.com/somemyrrh/

IF YOU LIKED THIS BOOK...

Check out Summer Kinard's debut novel, **Can't Buy Me Love***, a USA Today Happy Ever After pick.*

Look for the next books coming soon in the **Faith, Tea, Love** *series:*

> **Tea and Stones** *by Summer Kinard*
> **Tea and Symphony** *by Summer Kinard*

OTHER WOMEN'S FICTION TITLES
FROM LIGHT MESSAGES PUBLISHING

The Particular Appeal of Gillian Pugsley*
by Susan Örnbratt*
"memorable—feisty, unexpected" –*Kirkus Reviews*

A Theory of Expanded Love *by Caitlin Hicks*
"...enough charm to fill the corridors of Vatican City twice over" –*Foreword Reviews*

How to Climb the Eiffel Tower *by Elizabeth Hein*
"An empowering, redemptive novel filled with wisdom and kindness." –Summer Kinard

A Sinner in Paradise *by Deborah Hining*
INDIEFAB Bronze Medal Winner for Romance

A Saint in Graceland *by Deborah Hining*
coming Spring 2016

CPSIA information can be obtained at www.ICGtesting.com
Printed in the USA
BVOW08s0826121115

426847BV00004B/33/P